The year is 1917 . . .

In a small Indiana town, the Model T Ford, the first affordable car, is changing the way people travel—and revolutionizing courtship. The syncopated rhythm of ragtime has feet tapping. The antics of the Keystone Kops have people laughing. And Mary Pickford and Douglas Fairbanks reign on the silent screen.

But a darker time is coming. . . .

The three-year conflict that has ravaged Europe reaches American homes. President Wilson declares war against Germany.

At home, wives and sweethearts knit socks and scarves for the doughboys, buy Victory bonds and cheerfully endure "wheatless Mondays" and "meatless Tuesdays." An ocean away, America's sons are fighting.

It is a time of long, bittersweet goodbyes.

It is a time of lost innocence and extraordinary valor.

It is the time of Christine Brick and James Warren.

Dear Reader,

Have you ever looked forward to those visits with older relatives when they pulled out faded photographs and told you the stories of their youth? Of the days when motorcars vied with buggies and "talkies" became the greatest form of entertainment. When the Depression pulled families together. When soldiers danced at the USO and women wore seamed stockings. When TV was a novelty. When they fell in love with handsome John Kennedy and the miniskirt was revealed. When they marched and sang political ballads. When Armstrong took that historic step for mankind and Nixon lost eighteen minutes of tape. When *glasnost* came into our vocabulary and President Bush promised a kinder, gentler nation.

If you enjoyed those times, you'll love the Century of American Romance, a nostalgic look back at the 20th century—at the lives and loves of American men and women from 1899 to the dawn of the year 2000.

In this book—the third of the series—and in one of the four American Romances per month over the next nine months, you can relive the memories of a time gone by and sneak a peek at romance in an exciting future.

We hope you enjoy these special stories of nostalgia and romance, written by some of your favorite novelists. As always we welcome your comments.

Here's hoping that Century of American Romance will become a part of your most cherished memories....

Sincerely,
Debra Matteucci
Senior Editor &
Editorial Coordinator

SUZANNE SIMMONS GUNTRUM

1910s
THE
GOLDEN
RAINTREE

Harlequin Books

TORONTO • NEW YORK • LONDON
AMSTERDAM • PARIS • SYDNEY • HAMBURG
STOCKHOLM • ATHENS • TOKYO • MILAN

Published August 1990

ISBN 0-373-16353-3

Printed in U.S.A.

Chapter One

The Old Swimming Hole

"CAN!"

"CAIN-NOT!"

Christine Brick stood her ground. "I can, too, Billy Bathgate!"

The towheaded boy sneered at her. "Cain't! You're jest a girl. A Molly like all the rest of your kind."

Christine knew what *that* meant: Quakers were cowards because they refused to fight.

The color rose sharply in her small, pinched face; her hands tightened into fists at her sides. She wanted to punch the boy. Wanted to make him take it back. Every word of it. But she should not—indeed, she could not— box Billy's ears, whatever the provocation. Violence, in any form, was not the way of her people. There were times when she devoutly wished she wasn't a Quaker. Then she'd show the likes of Billy Bathgate who was a Molly and who was not.

"Dare ya! Double-dare ya!" Billy crowed, standing there dripping wet, his breeches plastered to his skinny legs.

"You daren't, Christine," whispered her best friend, Louise, as she tugged anxiously on her sleeve.

Christine turned to the pretty, dark-haired girl beside her. "Why not? Charlie and Jamie are going swimming. It looks like fun. And it's awful hot."

Louise Warren turned up her dainty nine-year-old nose and parroted the words she had no doubt heard her mother, or her grandmother, say: "It isn't seemly for a lady to get herself wet all over."

"She ain't no lady," the boy hooted. "She's jest a skeered little girl."

"I am not!" Christine stubbornly proclaimed, her face flaming with color.

"Are, too!"

"Am not!"

Again, there was a tug on her sleeve. "You don't know how to swim, do you?" whispered Louise.

"Hush!" But it was too late. The boy had heard.

Billy Bathgate began to chant in a singsong voice, "Christine cain't swim. Christine cain't swim."

"I can, too," she declared with more bravado than sense.

The boy leaned over and stuck his face down by hers. "Show me."

She put her chin up a notch. "All right, I will."

"Christine, you mustn't—"

Choosing to ignore Louise's warning, she plunked herself down on a patch of dry grass and began to undo her high-topped button shoes.

Her friend said persuasively, "Old Abe, the iceman, delivers to our house today, Christine. Why don't we ask Beulah to make us a pitcher of fresh lemonade? We can fill our glasses with ice chips from Old Abe's wagon and sit on the front porch and watch all the fine ladies and gentlemen stroll by." She added for good measure, "Cold lemonade would sure go fine with the honey cakes Beulah baked this morning. Honey cake is your favorite, isn't it?"

Christine stopped and thought about it for a minute. It was true, honey cake was her favorite. It was also true that she did not know how to swim. Sometimes she let her temper get the best of her. This was going to be one of those times unless she put her nose in the air like Louise and ignored Billy Bathgate and his stupid double-dares.

Still, it riled her being called a little girl, especially by someone like Billy, who was all bluster and show, and small for his age, besides. As the fourth of Ann and Benjamin Brick's surviving children she was always being told:

"You're too young to walk to the general store by yourself, Christine."

"Christine, you know you aren't old enough to tag along with your brothers when they go into town."

"You're too small to saddle up old Sal by yourself. Wait until your sister gets home."

Too young. Not old enough. Too small. That was all she ever heard. Just because she was the youngest and only eight years old. Well, she would be eight on her next birthday, anyway. Come September.

Christine Brick wiped the back of her hand across her upper lip. It was a real scorcher, as the farmers in these parts were wont to say. The sun rode high in a cloudless summer sky. The heat was relentless. Merciless. The air fairly rippled with it. The only sounds to be heard were a swarm of bumblebees buzzing about in a nearby patch of clover, the occasional chatter of a gray squirrel high overhead in a tree and the playful noises made by the boys who were swimming and frolicking on the other side of the country pond.

Their shouts of delight made her all the more aware of the properly starched and ironed dress and the cotton stockings that were sticking to her skin and, under the brim of her straw hat, the long braid of blond hair damp with sweat. The water sure looked dark and cool, she decided, like the inside of the storm cellar Papa and her eldest brother, Thomas Ezekiel, had dug last spring to withstand even the strongest thunderstorms and tornadoes that swept across the Hoosier farmlands.

Suddenly a sense of foreboding washed over Christine. There was a momentary chill in the air, as if the sun had dipped behind a bank of clouds, except there were no clouds today. She shivered; gooseflesh covered her arms and legs. She could hear the sound of her own heart beating frantically in her chest like a wild thing caught in a lightning storm.

The moment passed, as well as the strange sense of foreboding. Warmth returned. Why should boys be the only ones to have fun? Christine wanted to ask. She would never admit to being a little girl, but she certainly wasn't a full-grown lady yet, either.

She quickly removed her brown stockings and reached behind her. A button popped off as she struggled out of her gingham dress, but she didn't want her clothes wet through, and swimwear for females was almost unheard of in New Castle, Indiana, in the year 1907.

Then she was standing there in her cotton shift, barefooted, staring out at the cool, clear water of the old swimming hole. It did look inviting....

It wasn't long before Billy Bathgate started in again. "Betcha cain't do what I'm doin'." He scrambled over a boulder and grabbed hold of a thick vine that hung down from one of the huge oak trees beside the pond.

He turned and grinned at the two girls, wrapped his scrawny arms around the ropelike vine and pushed himself off. He swung back and forth over the pond several times, then gave a triumphant whoop and let go. There was a splash and the boy's thin, brown body disappeared beneath the surface of the water. Christine and Louise held their breaths until they saw his head bob up again.

He called to Christine, "It's your turn, *Friend*. 'Less'n you're too skeered to try it."

The girl swallowed hard. "I—I'm not scared."

"I am," confessed Louise. "Let's go, Christine. I want to go home."

"You go along, then. I got something to do here," she said in a determined and surprisingly adult tone of voice.

Christine Brick climbed up on the boulder and reached for the thick vine. Her hands were scarcely large enough to fit around it, and they were shaking. The twisted vine was rough to the touch and scraped the skin on her palms, but she held on the best she could. Taking a deep breath, she gave herself a good shove and swung out over the dark water....

"HE LOVES ME. HE LOVES me not. He loves me. He loves me not." One by one Hannah Brick plucked the soft, yellow petals from the wild daisy. She watched as the last one fluttered to the ground. "He loves me not." She sighed and tossed the stem away.

Every girl in their class at school had a crush on James Warren, better known to his friends as Jamie. Why should she be any different? But she knew that the handsome Jamie would never be hers. There were far too many pretty girls for him to choose from, and she was just plain Hannah. Hardworking, dependable, plain Hannah.

But sometimes, late at night, Hannah Marie would open her bedroom window and gaze out at the stars and the moon on the rise, and she would weave grand tales of romance and adventure with herself as the heroine. One night she had even fantasized of running off to Paris, France, and becoming an artist like Mary Cassatt, or that scandalous young Spaniard, Pablo Picasso. Or perhaps she would become a famous suffragette in the tradition of Susan B. Anthony, who had died only last year. Or maybe she would travel to Egypt to see the great pyramids.

After all, she had read dozens of stories about "traveling Friends," those special Quaker men and women who answered the "call," and often ended up circumnavigating the globe. Why, only last year there had been a young woman visiting their Meeting who had come all the way from Australia. Imagine that!

Hannah gave herself a firm shake and a firm scolding to match. It was time to stop woolgathering. It wasn't likely she would ever travel beyond the boundaries of Henry County, let alone across the ocean. And if she didn't finish picking the huckleberries she had promised Mama, there would be no huckleberry pie for dinner tonight.

She went about her business, reaching expertly into the thicket of huckleberry bushes and filling her basket as quickly as she could, paying no mind to the stains on the tips of her fingers. She supposed her lips were the same telltale blue color. Truth was, she had popped a huckleberry or two into her mouth as she'd worked. They had been warm and juicy and delicious.

Every now and then she would stop to wipe her brow and glance down the hill toward the old swimming hole. How pleasant it would be to cool off in the water!

Hannah's basket was soon overflowing with luscious dark blue berries. She was ready to start for home when a movement caught her eye. There was a child swinging by a long vine back and forth over the pond. From her vantage point on the hill she couldn't quite make out whether the child intended to jump into the water, or was about to fall.

Then the sunlight caught the blond hair that reached halfway down the child's back and turned it to pure gold. Hannah Brick's heart seemed to skip a beat. There was only one person she knew with hair that color.

Dropping the basket of huckleberries, Hannah raced down the hill toward the old swimming hole, for she suddenly realized that the child about to fall into the water was her younger sister, Christine. And Christine did not know how to swim!

EVEN AT THE AGE OF TWELVE James Wilson Warren was taller than the boys two and three years ahead of him in school. He was also handsome, intelligent and the only son of the richest man in New Castle. He might well have been stuck-up, but he wasn't. He was an all-American boy, folks said. And they were right. Several years later he was to become one of the first Boy Scouts in the state of Indiana.

On that particular hot summer afternoon James Warren was doing what all the boys were doing: cooling off at the old swimming hole just outside of town. Earlier that day a gang of them had followed the tar man as he worked on the road. As the tar had become firm, the boys had broken off small chunks and chewed it like gum. Even though he could afford the nickel it took to buy a package of five sticks of Juicy Fruit, Jamie knew most of the other boys couldn't. Besides, Black Jack was their favorite flavor and fresh tar tasted just like it.

After they'd chewed until their jaws were tired, the boys had pedaled their bicycles the half mile to the pond, changing into their bathing suits behind a cover of thick bushes. A few of the boys who didn't own special bathing suits were simply swimming in their knickers. The older boys, like Jamie and Charlie Brick, who was fifteen, watched out for the younger ones.

They'd been swimming and horsing around for nearly an hour when something caught Jamie's attention. He looked up and saw Billy Bathgate on the opposite bank. The farm boy was talking to two small girls he recognized as Christine Brick and his sister, Louise.

His gaze came to rest on the younger girl. Funny little thing, Christine Brick. She wasn't like his sister and the girls he sat beside at school, or sang with in the church choir on Sundays. They were always giggling behind their hands, or making cow eyes at the boys.

But not Christine. She was different. She had been, Jamie realized, right from the start. His first memory of her was the September day on which she had been born. Charlie Brick had come bicycling into town to tell him the exciting news: He had a new sister!

Jamie remembered clinging to the handlebars while his friend pedaled his bicycle the mile or so back to the Brick farmhouse on the outskirts of town. Before they were permitted to enter the large bedroom on the first floor of the house, the boys had been given strict orders to mind their manners and not speak unless they were spoken to.

They had quietly entered the room. Mrs. Brick was sitting propped up in bed with a mound of pillows at her back. A circle of neighbor women surrounded her. They were chatting and sipping tea.

The boys had been allowed to peer for a moment into the crib in the corner. There the baby was, all golden hair and soft, pink skin. Jamie didn't think he had ever seen anything quite so beautiful.

"What's her name?" he'd whispered to his friend.

Charlie had answered proudly, "Christine Elizabeth Brick."

Sticking out his forefinger, Jamie Warren had watched, utterly enthralled, as the baby grasped it blindly in her tiny hand. The miracle of touching a human life just as it was beginning created a funny feeling inside of him that Jamie couldn't explain. He only knew that as he bent over her, the baby had opened her eyes and stared straight up at him.

"Welcome to the world, Christine Elizabeth," Jamie had said reverently.

From that day forward, he had kept an eye out for her. He couldn't have said why. He never complained when she begged him to push her on the swing that hung from an old apple tree in the orchard adjoining the farmyard. He never minded when she tagged along with him and Charlie. Christine had been all blue eyes and blond hair from day one and she still was.

For a moment Jamie wondered who had accompanied his sister and Christine to the pond this afternoon. They must be with Hannah, or one of the Huckelby girls who worked off and on in the kitchen for Mrs. Brick. He turned his attention away from the younger children and rejoined the game of tag the boys were playing.

Several minutes later Jamie stuck his head out of the water. Something was wrong. It was the doggoned strangest sensation, like prickles along the back of his neck. He wondered if he'd been bitten by a bug, or a water snake, or maybe even a snapping turtle. He rubbed his neck once or twice, but the sensation would not go away.

"Hey, Jamie, it's your turn!" one of the boys shouted.

But Jamie ignored him. Trusting his instincts, he climbed out of the water and stood on the shore, looking around. In an instant he saw the scene played out before him: Hannah Brick racing down the hillside; his younger sister, Louise, standing by the edge of the pond, a horrified expression on her face; and Billy Bathgate beside her, white as a ghost.

There was no sign of little Christine.

It was like getting kicked in the belly by a horse: he couldn't seem to catch his breath. It was almost as though his head were underwater and he was drowning. He began to run. In seconds Jamie reached the other side of the pond. He dived in headfirst. He knew the exact spot where he would find her. Christine was there, where an old log stuck out of the water. He was sure of it. He could *feel* it.

SHE'D LET GO OF THE VINE just as she had seen Billy Bathgate do, but nothing had prepared Christine Brick for the shock of hitting the cold water. Even without the weight of her dress and shoes she could feel her body being pulled down, down, down into the murky depths of the old swimming hole.

She sank lower and lower. Then the instinct to survive took over. She began to flail her small arms and legs, trying to propel herself to the surface, gasping for air, wanting to see the bright sunlight again, to feel it on her face.

She had almost reached the surface of the water when something grabbed hold of her and would not let go. It was her hair. Her long braid was caught on a submerged log and she could not free herself. Panic set in, and she began to struggle with all her might.

Then she stopped struggling. Suddenly she knew it would be all right. Someone was coming for her. She was sure of it. She could *feel* it. Jamie. Yes, it was Jamie who was coming for her.

Just as she began to sink for the second time, she was set free. Strong arms reached out for her and she was pulled to the surface. She grabbed hold of Jamie and would not let go. She knew as long as she held on to him she would be safe.

First, there was sunlight.

Then voices all around her.

Shouting.

Crying.

Yet she couldn't seem to open her eyes.

She heard somebody weeping; it sounded like Louise.

Billy Bathgate blurted out, "Is she—dead?"

"Dear God, no," came her sister Hannah's fervent prayer.

"Why? Why would she jump into the pond when she didn't even know how to swim?" someone demanded to know.

"'Cause I dared her. I double-dared her," wailed Billy.

"She looks like an angel," said one of the other boys.

"Don't say that!" she heard Jamie bark. "It was her hair, you see. Her beautiful golden hair was caught on an old log." Then she felt his hand gently smoothing the wet strands away from her face.

"I better go fetch Papa," volunteered Charlie, in a voice that cracked with emotion.

She wanted to tell Charlie that she was all right, that he didn't need to go for Papa, but somehow she couldn't get the words out.

"Christine. Wake up, Christine." It was Jamie calling to her.

She was turned over onto her stomach and she began to retch pond water. She wanted to die of embarrassment, being sick in front of everyone like that, but somehow she knew she was lucky to be alive.

Then the air, the blessed air, flowed back into her lungs and she cried out his name, "Jamie!" She grabbed hold of him again and would not let go. He was real. He was solid. He was her anchor.

The boy held her as if he knew well enough how close it had been between life and death. When Ann and Benjamin Brick reached the pond it was with joyous hearts that they found their precious younger daughter sitting beside Jamie Warren. And no one thought it odd when little Christine refused to be parted from her rescuer until she was promised that he would come to the Brick home the next day to see her.

Nor did her parents think twice when she told them later that night she hadn't really been afraid. She had known that Jamie would come for her....

Chapter Two

A Country Picnic

He had never forgotten the day Christine almost drowned. It was one of the most dramatic days of his life, James Warren recollected as he studied his face in the mirror. The events of that long ago summer afternoon were permanently etched on his mind; they were as familiar to him, as much a part of him, as his own face.

He gazed into the mirror again. What he saw there neither pleased nor displeased him; it simply was. He had accepted himself—his looks, his intelligence, his natural athletic abilities—a long time ago. Contrary to what folks thought, it wasn't easy being the all-American boy; it was bound to prove even harder being the all-American man.

Yet, the hazel eyes with their flecks of green and yellow were the same eyes he had always seen staring back at him in the mirror. He liked to think they were older and wiser now that he was a man and a college graduate, instead of just another small-town boy, even if New Castle was considered the fastest-growing town in the state of Indiana.

His reflection told him it was the same nose, more or less, that had always dominated the middle of his face; it had been accidentally broken during his freshman year at Notre Dame when he'd teamed up with Gus Dorais and

Knute Rockne and had begun to make college football history. There were the same dark brown eyebrows, although they were slightly furrowed in thought at the moment; the same mouth; the same ears tucked close to his head; the same chin "chiseled from stone," or so his sister, Louise, claimed anyway.

James rubbed his hand back and forth along his jawline. It was rough and scratchy with a day's growth of beard. He needed a shave. He turned his head. His hair was long in the back; it would hang down over the top of his starched collar. He needed a shave *and* a haircut. He couldn't do much about the haircut until he got around to visiting the local barbershop, but the first problem could be rectified easily enough.

He reached for his razor and the leather strop on which to sharpen it. While he went through the motions of shaving, his thoughts returned to Christine Brick.

The very next summer, after her accident at the old swimming hole, she had come to him, begging, "Please, Jamie, you gotta teach me how to swim. I don't want to be afraid anymore."

He'd known she was still having nightmares about the accident. He would have known even if she hadn't told him about waking up in a cold sweat, her nightclothes drenched, unable to catch her breath, visions of drowning fresh in her almost-nine-year-old's head. But, of course, she had told him. Christine told him everything . . . in those days.

So, when none of the other boys and girls were around—she had been a proud little thing even then—he had taken Christine to the pond and shown her how to hold her breath and put her face in the water, the way to move her arms and legs to keep from sinking to the bottom, all the things that come naturally to some and only with great difficulty to others.

At first she had been frozen with fear. But he'd soon discovered that she was as brave as anyone he had ever met. In fact, he'd found himself admiring her courage, even though she was a girl and nearly five years younger than he was.

Once Christine Brick set her mind to something, nothing could keep her from it, James ruminated as he reached for a fresh towel and wiped the remnants of shaving soap from his jaw.

He remembered another incident, as well. This time his hazel eyes went all smoky when he thought about it. He had been nineteen and home from college for the summer....

IT WAS A STILL AUGUST NIGHT, not even the merest hint of a breeze stirred the air. It was the kind of night when the farmers claimed they could actually hear the corn growing in the fields. The crickets and the cicadas sent up a loud nocturnal chorus, then fell silent. James hadn't been sleeping well for a week. No one had. It was too damned hot. The heat and humidity made the air thick, heavy, hard to breathe.

He finally gave up on the prospect of getting any rest. Well before daybreak he arose from his bed and quickly dressed in a shirt, without bothering to add a collar, and a pair of lightweight trousers. Before he thought much about where he wanted to go or what he intended to do once he got there, James found himself by the old swimming hole. The moon was full; it hung suspended in the sky, a huge white sphere against the gray light of dawn. The birds were chattering and singing in the treetops as if the whole world were just awakening.

He heard a rustling in the nearby bushes and almost called out, but something stopped him. Then he watched, transfixed, as a lovely young creature stepped into the clearing. Part girl, part woman, she unself-consciously slipped out of her cotton dress and stood on the huge boulder at one end of the pond. Her hair was a golden cloud about her shoulders, a mantle of fine silk. Her face was intent, her teeth were sunk into her bottom lip in concentration.

It was Christine, of course. Christine poised on the brink of womanhood. James didn't think he had ever seen anything so beautiful: she was slender, ethereal, high-breasted, perfect in every way.

At the sight of her the heat flowed through his body, the blood pounded in his temples. There had always been a special understanding between the two of them, but this was different. This was something he hadn't expected to feel, something he wasn't sure he *wanted* to feel. In that moment he became aware of Christine in the way a man was aware of a woman. She was no longer a child, no longer the little girl who shadowed his every step, listened to his every word. The knowledge coursed through James Warren, from the top of his head to the bottom of his toes—indeed, through all six feet two inches of him.

He forced the air in and out of his lungs. He raised a hand to his face and it came away damp with sweat and shaking slightly. Without his knowledge, and certainly without his consent, the little girl he'd known was changing, had changed. It made him . . . uncomfortable.

But the last thing he wanted to do was embarrass Christine, or make her feel uncomfortable. She would be mortified if she knew that he had seen her without her clothes.

James quietly made his way back through the bushes. This time when he approached the old swimming hole he whistled loudly and made no attempt to hide his presence. He wanted Christine to know he was coming, to give her fair warning. And when he saw her for the second time that morning she was hastily buttoning the dress he had watched her only recently discard.

"Oh, it's you," she said, smiling, losing her nervousness. "You're up mighty early."

His hands were still shaky; he stuffed them into the pockets of his trouser. "I couldn't sleep."

"Me, either. It's so hot." She put both hands behind her head and raised the swath of silky hair off her neck.

The action caused the cotton dress to stretch taut across her damp body in ways he was sure she was totally unaware of. He was almost ashamed to admit that his hands itched to reach out and touch her, to cup her softness in his palms.

"As hot as I ever remember it being," James finally agreed. He nearly laughed aloud. What a silly, inane thing for him to say to Christine. Christine, whom he had known nearly all of his life, certainly all of *her* life. He even remembered the day she was born. And not once in all those years had they ever felt uncomfortable with each other, ever had trouble talking to each other. But things had changed. At least as far as he was concerned. He managed, "Are you going swimming?"

She nodded. "I thought it would feel good to cool off. Are you?"

He shrugged and reminded himself to breathe. "I haven't decided. It was unbearable inside so I started walking and here I am."

She reached out, grabbed hold of his hand and began to urge him toward the pond. For a moment it was like old times. "Let's jump into the water like we used to when you were teaching me how to swim," she said with some of her former childish enthusiasm. "Just the two of us."

Just the two of them. James was suddenly very aware that they were alone.

He hesitated and drew his hand back. "Maybe we shouldn't."

Christine stopped and looked up at him with eyes the color of the morning sky. "Why ever not?"

"Because..." He wasn't sure he could, or should, put it into words for her. "Just because."

"Don't tell me you turned into an old fogy this year at college," she teased, laughing at him.

"It's not that."

She wouldn't leave it alone. "Then what?"

"I guess I was just wondering if the two of us should be out here by ourselves."

Christine had always been bright, quick, even precocious for her years. That's what came of being the youngest child in a big family. She understood more than he had intended. Her face became suffused with color. "But we've always been like brother and sister to each other."

His eyes went a shade darker. "Have we?"

She wrapped her arms around herself as if she'd felt a sudden chill. "Special friends, then."

"Yes. We've always been special friends," he said thoughtfully. "You used to follow me everywhere, tell me everything."

"I still do."

"No. I don't think so. You're growing up, Christine. You always were a pretty child—" he reached out with one hand and lightly touched her cheek "—now you've become a lovely young woman."

Instinctively she turned her face into his palm. He could feel the warmth of her breath on his skin. He could smell that distinctive sweet scent that was hers alone, that he would always identify with her. One day, crouched in a hellhole, cannon shells exploding all around, he would close his eyes for a moment and bring her scent to mind and tell himself there was a reason to go on living.

"James—"

Jamie no longer. Jamie never again. Now and forevermore he would be James. It made him a little sad to see that change, too, he realized.

Christine continued, "I believe I would like you to kiss me."

"Christine!" he sputtered. "You shouldn't talk like that."

Her gaze did not falter. "Why not? I've always told you exactly what I was thinking. And just now I was thinking how nice it would be if you were to kiss me."

"Proper young ladies don't go around asking gentlemen to kiss them."

"I don't go around asking gentlemen to kiss me. I'm asking you."

There was that stubborn set to her chin, that determined tone to her voice. He may as well kiss her and be done with it, James Warren told himself. He bent over and placed a quick buss on Christine's cheek.

Two blue eyes stared intently into his. "Not like that. That's the way Papa and Mama kiss me. I want a real kiss from you."

He tried to instill a certain propriety in his manner. "A young lady shouldn't kiss a young man unless they're going to be married."

"Ask me to marry you."

"You're too young."

"Then promise you'll wait for me to grow up." With that, she threw her arms around his neck and pressed her mouth to his. He held her just for an instant. Savored the sweetness of her just for a moment. Then he unwound her arms from around his neck and took a step or two back.

Christine's eyes were shining with newfound knowledge and a hint of shyness. "Promise you'll wait for me, James." But she didn't wait for an answer. She turned and took off through the underbrush. The last he saw of her was the hem of her cotton dress as it snagged on the branch of a huckleberry bush.

JAMES REALIZED he was finished shaving and had been standing there for some time staring, unseeing, into the mirror above the basin. His eyes were dark and introspective.

Could it possibly be?

Was it the reason thoughts of Christine, memories of Christine, were always there just beneath the surface of his consciousness?

Had he spent the past few years waiting for her to grow up?

She was still half child, he reminded himself. Not even eighteen yet. Of course she had graduated from high school last spring and her birthday was in the fall. There were young men and women of his acquaintance who had married at that age.

But the world was fast becoming a different world, a less secure world, since Congress had overwhelmingly approved President Wilson's declaration of war against Germany last April. These days the talk was either about the Bolsheviks in Russia, or the ongoing conflict on the Western Front. Now that the United States was in on the action, however, everyone was confident that quick work would be made of defeating the Central Powers. This was, after all, the Great War, the "war to end war."

James recalled a newspaper article he'd recently read in the *New Castle Daily Times*. It was reported that the French commander in chief and hero of Verdun, Henri Philippe Pétain, had declared to his demoralized troops, "Wait for the Americans and the tanks."

Of course, there had been American volunteers fighting for Pétain's country for several years, serving with the French Foreign Legion—the lack of an oath of allegiance making it possible for the men not to forfeit their American citizenship. There were even rumors about town that Billy Bathgate had gone and joined up!

Staring at the face in the mirror, the words of a recruiting poster ran through James Warren's mind: Are You Half the Man Your Mother Brought You up to Be?

He hoped so. He liked to think so. He was definitely going to have the opportunity to find out. And soon. But the future would have to take care of itself. Today was all he had; all any of them had. He glanced out the window of his bedroom. The weather was sunny and mild. It was going to be the perfect day for a picnic.

CHRISTINE BRICK CLOSED the book she had been reading and gazed out her bedroom window at the far stretch of green fields and beyond to the Golden Raintree and the small cemetery atop the hill.

How many brave men and women were buried there in the family plot: her ancestors, pioneers all! What strength of character it must have taken for them to surmount the hardships they'd had to endure to reach the "promised land"—long, uncomfortable journeys by ship and in covered wagons; dangerous animals and wild, swollen rivers; separation from family and friends; loneliness, disease, even death. These were the extraordinary Bricks and Truebloods, Bankses and Sutters, who had settled this region of the Hoosier state nearly a century before.

Christine placed the well-worn volume neatly on the shelf above her bed. *A Girl of the Limberlost* had always been her favorite story. She supposed partly because it was one of the few novels her parents approved of. The author, Gene Stratton Porter, was from Geneva, Indiana, and most often chose to write about her beloved Limberlost swamp and its natural wonders. Like many Quakers, Christine's mother and father were very keen on natural history. Natural history was acceptable because it wasn't frivolous.

She could still hear her grandmother admonishing her in the language used by several generations of earlier Quakers: "Thee must try not to be so frivolous in thy thinking, Christine. The Friends have always lived simple, honest, somber lives. Thee would do well to spend more time seeking the Inward Light, like thy sister Hannah, and less time fussing with thy hair."

But her hair was her crowning glory, Christine had wanted to cry out. Everyone said so. Even strangers on the street stopped to pet her and tell her what a pretty little thing she was.

That had been years and years ago, naturally, when she was a mere child, Christine consoled herself as she reached for her hairbrush and pins. Now that she was grown-up she scarcely thought about frivolous matters at all anymore. Still, she couldn't help but wonder if this afternoon at the picnic James would admire her new dress, or remark on the long blond hair he had once adored.

THERE WERE FOUR HUCKELBY sisters in all: Rose, Violet, Lily and Marygold, otherwise known as Goldie.

Their mother had been an avid gardening enthusiast, even by the horticultural standards of the "Rose City," as some residents referred to New Castle. Mrs. Huckelby had also been a rather silly sort of woman of whom it was frequently said: "Thank the Lord she wasn't blessed with sons!" Little, if anything, was ever said of Mr. Huckelby.

When Mrs. Huckelby took the typhoid fever back in '05 and passed away, the eldest girl, Goldie, came to help out at the Bricks for a small salary and all the fresh eggs and vegetables her family could use.

When Mr. Huckelby was fatally injured in the devastating tornado that swept through New Castle on March 11, 1917—it killed twenty-one citizens and destroyed more than one million dollars' worth of property—the Bricks were the first to offer the protection of their home to the poor orphans, even though the Huckelbys were Methodists and Mr. Huckelby, himself, had never been a churchgoing man. That was the way of the Friends.

The youngest girls slept three to a feather bed and thought the large Brick family farmhouse was the finest house they had ever seen. Goldie, as the eldest, had her own room and her own opinions. She was expressing some of those opinions that morning when, unbeknownst to her, Christine came downstairs to check on the packing of the picnic basket.

"People in these parts say she takes after her great-grandma," Goldie was gossiping. "Right pretty thing, but in-de-pen-dent. Stubborn's what some might call it. Mark my words, it will take a mighty strong man to round off the sharp edges, if you get my drift." She winked at her sister. "Course the other one has taken to calling herself an old maid—" Goldie shook her head at this and made a disapproving clicking sound with her tongue "—and her being only two and twenty. Ask me, Hannah calls herself an old maid before anyone else can.''

''Why, you're three and twenty yourself, Goldie,'' the younger girl pointed out.

''That's what I'm saying. Two and twenty don't make a woman an old maid even if she is plain-looking. Some men prefer a plain wife.'' It was obvious that Goldie was exasperated. ''Know what Hannah says to me this morning?'' She didn't wait for an answer. ''She looks me right in the eye and quotes from one of them books she's always reading.''

''What'd she say?''

''She up and declares—let me get this straight—'Thee knows it takes a mighty good husband to be better than none at all.' Them was her exact words. Now, what do you make of that?''

Lily Huckelby shrugged her thin shoulders.

There was an old adage about eavesdroppers that said they rarely heard good of themselves. Christine had certainly heard enough. She cleared her throat and walked into the kitchen. Only the slightly heightened color in her cheeks revealed that she had listened to what the Huckelby girls were saying about Hannah and her.

''Something smells wonderful,'' she said, sniffing the air.

''We got some of your favorites packed for the picnic,'' Goldie volunteered, not the least bit embarrassed. ''Fried chicken and fresh baked bread. Cherry pie and peach pie made from preserves we put up last summer. Some of your Mama's prize pickles and my special corn relish.''

''I made a jug of lemonade and another of ice tea,'' piped up the younger Huckelby girl.

"Thank you. I'm sure everyone will be delighted. Are you sure you girls won't come with us?" Christine asked.

A slightly smug smile settled on Goldie's face. "My young gentleman friend is calling on me this afternoon, and Lily here is going to the moving picture show in town. All the same, it's right nice of you to invite us."

"There's the Warrens in their big fancy automobile now," Lily called out excitedly.

"I hope Hannah and Charlie are ready to go," Christine said, the anticipation rising in her throat. She went to the stairs and called up to her brother and sister, "James and Louise are here for us."

"I believe I have enough old quilts for us to sit on," Hannah announced with her usual common sense as she entered the big, sunny kitchen several minutes later. Her arms were filled with hand-stitched coverlets of every color and pattern.

Charlie informed his sisters, as he swung his knapsack over his shoulder and picked up the wicker basket filled with food, "And I've packed my binoculars and my Audubon, of course."

Christine sighed and echoed, "Of course." She knew as well as anyone that her brother's instruction in bird-watching was the justification for their outing.

"Papa would never have approved otherwise," Hannah remarked unnecessarily as they prepared to leave. "I think Mama must have cajoled him into letting us go in the first place."

"Papa is so stern." Christine voiced the complaint aloud.

"Papa is a serious man," corrected Hannah.

She sighed again. "Yes, and Thomas Ezekiel is just like him. We'll never be allowed to know the words to the popular songs of the day, or wear the latest fashions that are all the rage in Paris and New York, or read any best-selling novels.''

"It's best not to wish for things you can't have," Hannah said succinctly, plunking an old straw hat down on her head and pulling on her gloves.

"I suppose you're right."

"Of course I'm right." She paused in the front hall to help Christine secure her plain white hat to her hair. "I know Papa's rules are harder for you than they are for me. I'm older. I understand these things better than you do. Besides, I was never a pretty girl, anyway. I'm plain as porridge to look at. That's not likely to change now that I'm a full-grown woman."

On an impulse Christine threw her arms around her sister and hugged her tightly. "Hush, Hannah Marie Brick. I won't have you talking about yourself that way." Her eyes shone bright with unshed tears. "You're beautiful! Far more beautiful than I could ever hope to be."

"You say the silliest things sometimes," Hannah retorted. But her features softened and they both recognized that her gruff manner was mere pretense.

Each of the Brick girls was wearing a slightly watery smile when she joined her brother and her friends that afternoon, but the drive through the countryside to a favored picnic spot along No Name Creek quickly turned into a time of carefree joy and laughter. It was a perfect summer day. There was a touch of warmth in the air, and the sky was so brilliantly blue that it hurt the eyes.

The local farmers had been hard at work. The planted fields of corn were more than "knee-high by the Fourth of July." By summer's end driving along this stretch of road would be like traveling through a tunnel of lush, green foliage higher than a man's head. That's how tall the stalks of corn would grow between now and the onset of autumn.

For this was country that came to life again in the spring after lying dormant the winter long. By high summer the once fallow fields were plowed, seeded and ripe with crops. The giant maples and oaks were flush with new growth. Trumpet lilies grew wild alongside the fences, cow parsnip flourished in the unplowed pastures, small patches of brilliant blue chickory sprouted up by the side of the gravel road.

"I believe summer is my favorite time of year," Christine said to James with a delighted laugh as they unloaded the wicker hamper and selected a site for their luncheon under the shade of a sprawling tree. She stood and gazed off toward the horizon. "Sometimes I almost imagine I can see the Happy Valley from here."

"I don't think so, Christine. We must be at least several miles from your family's farm," he pointed out.

"I don't know why you persist in calling it the Happy Valley, anyway," Hannah spoke up as she spread a faded quilt on the ground. "I've never heard anyone else use that name."

A smile touched Christine's lips. "One of our great-grandmothers did. I read it in her diary."

Louise had joined them, with Charlie in tow. "Truly? Your great-grandmother?"

Christine knew they all thought her a bit fanciful, but she didn't care. "Yes. I found her diary in the attic one day and I've been reading it a little bit at a time ever since. Her name was Elizabeth Banks and she came to Henry County as a bride. She wrote of the 'blue mist on a summer's eve as it drifts across our happy valley.' "

Louise sighed. "How romantic."

Charlie piped up, "More than likely she and her husband had to keep the home fires burning every night just to keep the wolves from their doorstep."

The pretty dark-haired girl at his side shivered. "Wolves?"

"Yes. There was a one-dollar bounty on wolf scalps back when this region was being settled," he said enthusiastically, sounding like a member of the Henry County Historical Society—which he was. "One dollar was a fair amount of money in the days when a hot meal at the local tavern cost 18½ cents."

Christine knew from experience not to encourage her elder brother in that direction. Charlie Brick had been known to expound at great length on any subject from the early history of Indiana to the best method of cultivating roses. It was a perfect day for an outing and she was going to enjoy herself with as little edification on history—natural or otherwise—as possible. "I hope you brought your croquet game," she said, linking arms with James and Louise.

"Mallets, wickets and all," James Warren assured her. "And the badminton equipage." He grinned at her, the very devil in his eye. "Perhaps you'll beat me this time."

She grinned back at him. "I have every intention of doing just that."

"When it comes to athletics, men have an unfair advantage, of course," Hannah declared as she sat down unceremoniously on the grassy bank of the creek. "We women are hampered by the type of apparel society dictates we must wear in order to be considered properly attired. Long skirts and high-button shoes do not lend themselves to facile movement."

Louise Warren smoothed the fashionably straight skirt of her silk dress and lifted a dainty pink shoe as she set tled herself on a quilt. "Surely you wouldn't want to wear *bloomers* like some females." The word was uttered in an appropriately distasteful tone of voice.

"I expect that one day women will adopt some form of pantaloons," Hannah said, perfectly serious, as she opened the nearest picnic hamper and began to dispense china plates and cups.

"I see you've been reading about those suffragettes again, Hannah," her brother chimed in.

"Mark my words, Charlie Brick—" a butter knife was waved at him "—one day women, like men, will have the vote."

Louise looked from one to the other as she bit a smile from the corners of her mouth. "Do you really think so?"

"Equality for all men, and between men and women has been a tradition among us Quakers from our founding nearly three centuries ago. Some of the early suffragettes, like Lucretia Mott, were members of the Society of Friends," Hannah informed her. "As you know, women already have the vote in states like Arizona, Kansas and Oregon. I expect we'll see the same right here in Indiana in the next few years."

James had been listening to their conversation with amused interest when he suddenly realized that Christine had wandered off from the rest of them. She was some distance from the shady spot they had selected for their picnic. He left the others to their discussion of women's rights and followed the figure of the young woman in white.

Stooping to pluck a handful of small blossoms from the wild myrtle growing at his feet, he came up to stand behind her. "I assume your sister with her newfangled notions speaks to your very heart and soul?"

Christine turned, blinked several times in quick succession and said, "What? I'm sorry, James. I didn't hear what you said."

He knew she was telling him the truth. There was a faraway look in her eyes, a slightly bemused expression on her face, that said she'd been somewhere else altogether. He wondered where and what in the dickens she'd been thinking about.

"I suppose it doesn't matter," he mumbled, knowing full well that his annoyance with her stuck out all over him like prickles on a cactus.

After all, Christine didn't have to tell him everything. She wasn't a child. She had a right to her own counsel. That's what he tried to convince himself of, anyway.

"I was thinking," she began tentatively.

"Yes?" he prompted.

"I was wondering what I should do with my life now that I've graduated from high school."

So that was it. That was what she'd been contemplating: her future. James let out a sigh of relief. "What do you want to do with your life?"

The color rose in her face as she confessed, "My dreams may sound rather foolish—"

He spoke softly, "We all have our dreams, Christine."

She was silent for a moment, then declared passionately, "I want to *see* the world, James, not just read about it in books. I want to smell the spring tulips growing in Holland. I want to walk along the golden halls of Versailles. I want to stand before the Taj Mahal and marvel at its beauty. I want to learn about life for myself, not simply be expected to believe what others tell me. I want to be part of something worthwhile, something important." She gave her head a little shake. "I'm sure my dreams sound like the prattle of a schoolgirl to you. You've already seen so much, done so much.''

"Not so very much," he assured her.

She disagreed. "You've graduated from college. You've traveled to New York and to Boston and to our nation's capital. And now you will take your rightful place in your family's furniture business."

"That's what everyone expects me to do," he said, without confirming or denying that was his intention.

She sighed wistfully. "Sometimes I wonder what the future will bring. It must be comforting in a way to know what it holds for you."

A frown creased his brow. "No one knows what the future holds for them, Christine." Then James pressed the bouquet of hastily gathered posies into her hands. "I almost forgot. These are for you."

She smiled. "How lovely. Periwinkle."

"Periwinkle blue to match your eyes," he said, his voice a little husky.

Her cheeks colored prettily.

"I suppose any number of young bounders have tried to give you flowers and tell you what beautiful eyes you have, and that your hair is like golden silk." He reached out to touch her. She did not draw back from him.

"A few." She wasn't being coy.

James was stunned by his reaction. He was . . . angry. No, he was jealous. How dare any man—*cad* was, no doubt, the better term—approach his Christine!

But was she *his* Christine? Wasn't *his* Christine still half a child, not even eighteen yet? A girl, not a woman? Hadn't he told himself that just this morning?

James Warren opened his eyes and looked at Christine Brick. Yes, she was young. But she was no child. She was a lovely young woman. The loveliest young woman he had ever seen.

"Why are you staring at me like that, James? Is anything the matter?"

"No. Nothing's the matter," he said in a brisk tone as he took her arm and resumed walking.

Christine asked a little breathlessly, "Where are we going?"

"Somewhere, Miss Brick, where the two of us can be alone." And this time he wasn't going to be accused of being an old fogy, James promised himself.

Several minutes later they stopped beneath an aging weeping willow. Its branches created a natural shelter, bending to touch the ground here, dipping into the trickling waters of No Name Creek there.

Christine squeezed his arm and exclaimed, "Oh, James, what a wonderful place!"

He could not take his eyes from her. Even with the rich scents of summer all around them he could still make out that distinctive sweet scent that was hers alone.

She laughed; the sound was musical.

She took hold of his arms and twirled around in a circle until they were both dizzy.

It reminded James of another time and another place....

They were children. It was a warm summer evening. Their parents were sitting on the front porch of the Warren house, talking and laughing quietly among themselves while the five youngsters—Charlie, Hannah, Louise, Christine and he—played a game of "statue" in the yard. One by one they twirled around and around, and finally struck a pose. Then they took turns guessing what each of them was supposed to be. Christine had chosen the Statue of Liberty. She was quite put out with him when he correctly guessed as much on his first try.

An innocent enough memory, James recalled now. Although not all of his memories of Christine were quite so innocent or childlike.

It was as if she'd read his mind. Standing there, gazing out toward the creek, Christine murmured, "Do you remember that dawn we met by the old swimming hole?"

He returned a guarded "Yes." How could he ever forget?

She continued, "I asked you to kiss me and you said I was too young."

"You were too young."

"Then I asked you to make me a promise."

James moved closer, her voice, her scent beckoning to him. "You said, 'Promise you'll wait for me to grow up.'"

She turned to him, her eyes filled with questions she didn't know how to put into words. "I'm all grown up now, James. Did you wait for me?"

He brought his hand to her face, gently cupping her chin. "Yes, Christine. I waited for you. Only you."

Then he bent his head and touched his lips to hers, tasting her, savoring the sweetness of her, the promise of her. She was everything he had ever dreamed of and more, his Christine. She was the breath of life in his lungs. She was nourishment for his hungry soul. She was the love that filled his heart, that stirred his body. Somewhere deep within her he felt the passion she was capable of.

Slowly, reluctantly, James released her.

Her eyes were the color of the midnight sky as she gazed up at him and voiced her doubts. "You aren't disappointed, are you?"

His throat constricted with emotion. "Oh, my darling girl, my dearest Christine, I could never be disappointed with you. We were meant for each other. Don't you know that?''

She looked straight at him, never flinching for an instant, as she confessed, "I've known for a long, long time, James Wilson Warren. For as long as I can remember. I wasn't certain *you* knew."

"I do. Maybe I always did." He reached for her hand. "We should rejoin the others now. They'll be wondering where we are."

With complete trust Christine placed her hand in his. They had nearly reached Charlie and their sisters when she said, "That day I almost drowned—you knew where to find me, didn't you?"

James kept his eyes straight ahead. "Yes, I did." Then, "And you knew I was coming for you."

"I knew."

He looked at her. "I will always come for you, Christine."

"And I will always be there, James."

It was not something they took lightly. It was a solemn vow they gave to each other on that fine summer day, one of the last carefree days of summer and sun, July 1917.

Chapter Three

The Silent Meeting

Silence.

There was only silence in the white frame meeting-house. Silence stretching out to fill minute after minute. Rows of silent men and women, sitting, waiting.

One man finally stood and said simply, "It takes a strong man not to fight." He sat down.

Silence.

Then an old woman spoke. "On this First Day I would like to share with you from the Gospel of Matthew." Her hands were wrinkled with age; they shook as she held the thick, leather volume in front of her. There was no need for her to see the words, however, she knew them by heart. "'Blessed are the meek, for they shall inherit the earth. Blessed are the peacemakers, for they shall be called the children of God.'"

There was silence once again.

A child squirmed in his seat. A page rustled as it was turned. Someone coughed. Through an open window, a soft summer breeze entered the small church. The sound of buzzing insects could be discerned in the bushes outside, the faraway lowing of a herd of cattle.

But in this place there was only a sense of simplicity, of peace, of serenity.

Christine Brick sat quietly.

Simplicity. Peace. Serenity. These were, indeed, the principles upon which the Society of Friends had been founded. She knew her ancestors had come from a time when the majority of men ascribed to either the pomp and ceremony of the Church of England, or the strict, repressive beliefs of the Puritans.

The Quakers had done neither. They had adopted no formal religious beliefs, no rituals, no sacraments. There were no pastors in their meetinghouses, no set service of worship, no hymns. They simply sat and waited for God to speak through one of their members.

From England the Bricks and Bankses had sailed to the shores of North Carolina. The year had been 1672. Eventually, when the issue of slavery could no longer be tolerated, they had migrated west along the Cumberland Road to eastern Indiana. They were among the first settlers arriving in Henry County in 1821. The first organized religious body in the county was a Friends Meeting. In nearly every small town and village in the area, there was now a meetinghouse like the one in which Christine and her family sat on this glorious summer morning.

A young man cleared his throat and awkwardly struggled to his feet. He stared down at the floor. "I was in town last week. There was a gang of local bullies across the street. They called out to me, sneered, said I was a regular Molly, a coward. They were carrying a placard with lettering on it. They tried to force it into my hands. I was ashamed as I read the words: 'I am the latest war baby. I always stay at home safe with Ma. I let the other fellow do it. I am the man who is afraid.'" His voice cracked on the last word.

Christine felt hot, sympathetic tears sting her eyes. She remembered a summer day long ago—sometimes it seemed like only yesterday—when she, too, had been taunted, had been called a coward and a Molly.

When he was finally able to go on, the young man's words tumbled over each other in the heat of his confession. "I *was* afraid, too. Afraid and angry. I wanted to strike out at them, but I knew it was wrong. I threw the sign down and ran away." He slumped to the wooden bench and buried his head in his fists. An older man sitting next to the boy reached out and placed a comforting hand on his shoulder.

It was some time before a firm, clear voice from the back of the room offered: "'Love your enemies. Bless them that curse you. Do good to them that hate you, and pray for them which persecute you.'"

"Amen," said another.

Five minutes passed.

Ten.

Fifteen.

Charlie Brick, tall and lanky even at the age of twenty-five, rose to his feet. He deliberated for a moment, his brows drawn together. Then he expressed his thoughts aloud. "Everybody here knows me. I work on my father's farm. I grow roses. I'm an avid bird-watcher. I'm not a violent man."

Christine watched her brother intently, her heart slamming against her chest.

He took a deep breath. "But it also says in the Bible that there is 'a time to kill and a time to heal; a time to keep silence and a time to speak; a time to love and a time to hate; a time of war and a time of peace.'"

Ecclesiastes, chapter three. Christine recognized it as one of Charlie's favorite verses.

Her brother continued, "This is a time of war whether we like it or not. I won't go against all I've been taught, or what I believe in as a Quaker. I don't think I could kill anyone. Like a good many young men gathered in this meetinghouse, I have registered as a conscientious objector. That's not a popular stance to take in these times, as young Jacob here has found out." He nodded to the boy who had spoken earlier. "But we don't have to just sit here and recite scripture to each other, either. We can do something."

There was an expectant silence in the hall.

Charlie rubbed the scruff of his neck. "We believe that each man and woman of us must look within and try to find the truth of what we should do. That's what I hope I've done." He paused and looked around at the familiar faces. "So I want to share with you—my family, my friends, my neighbors—the news that I have joined the Friends' Ambulance Unit. I sail for England in two weeks and from there I will be assigned to the front lines in France." Without further ado, Charles Jordan Brick sat down.

The silence in the meetinghouse was deafening.

Christine realized she had been holding her breath all the while her brother was speaking. She exhaled tremulously. Charlie? Dear, sweet, ineffectual Charlie had volunteered for an ambulance unit overseas?

She must have heard wrong, Christine told herself. But in her heart she knew she hadn't. It was true. Charlie had volunteered in his own way for the war effort. In the same instant she was both proud of him and afraid for him.

The world was changing, *her* world was changing, whether she liked it or not, whether she was ready or not. That's the way the world was these days. The war could no longer be kept at arm's length. The war had come home.

"YOU HAVE TO UNDERSTAND," she heard Charlie explaining to their parents as Ann and Benjamin Brick gathered around the large kitchen table with their younger son, "I'm no longer a boy."

Christine hovered at the top of the stairs and listened a moment longer.

"I didn't mean to hurt you. But I'll never be like Thomas Ezekiel. I wasn't born to be a farmer. I've thought about this for a long time. I know volunteering as an ambulance driver is the right thing for me to do. I'm a man now. I make my own decisions."

She heard Mama's voice. "But, son, have you considered exactly what it is that you will be asked to do?"

"Of course I have."

"It's coming on to harvest time," pointed out their father. "We need you here on the farm."

There was the sound of a chair leg scraping along the kitchen floor, then Charlie's softly spoken but firm reply. "I will be needed more where I'm going, Papa."

There was silence in the room below. The grandfather clock in the front parlor sounded the quarter hour. Christine made her way quietly down the hall toward her bedroom at the back of the house.

Charlie had a right to his privacy. Especially now.

The afternoon sun slanted in her bedroom window, bathing the room in its brilliant light: the bed with its pretty coverlet, the starkly plain yet beautiful furniture she had always associated with her great-grandmother—it had been handed down from mother to daughter, from generation to generation until it had become hers on her tenth birthday—the sheer curtains at the windows, gently billowing now as a soft summer breeze slipped in between the frame and the sill.

Christine stretched out on her bed and pulled a light-weight quilt over her.

The quilt was her favorite: a family heirloom sewn by her grandmother. The date, 1868, was embroidered in the center, along with a replica of the Brick farmhouse, much as it was to be found then and now. The remainder of the family album quilt consisted of colorful fruits and flowers, an elegant teapot, a horse and rider, two small handprints, gaily beribboned baskets and several majestic trees. It was a work of art.

She could still hear her grandmother's instructions. "Thee must take smaller stitches with thy needle, Christine, if thee ever hopes to become a true quilter."

"But, Grandmother," she had protested as a child of six, "I keep pricking myself with the needle. My finger is bleeding."

"Does thy finger hurt, my child?"

"No, Grandmother."

"Then wash the blood from thy hand, Christine, and begin again."

Wash the blood from thy hand and begin again. It was the last thought Christine Brick remembered having before drifting into sleep.

WAS SHE DREAMING?

Christine found herself standing in the doorway of the old general store. The wooden floorboards creaked and groaned underfoot with each step she took. The air smelled of sawdust and linseed oil, dried herbs and small cakes of imported lavender-scented soap. Sometimes on a rainy day in the late autumn there was the enticing aroma of fresh popcorn in the air, and the scent of tart apples and gunpowder and tobacco.

A bushel barrel of walnuts stood in one corner by the potbellied stove, and an empty bird cage in the other. There were dusty postcards on a wire rack over by dry goods, and a glass display case filled with pretty trinkets and topped with jars of penny candy.

She could hear voices nearby.

"What in the tarnation happened?"

"She's fainted. Do you have any smelling salts?"

"Sure do. Back in potions and medicinals," said the man as he shuffled off, the floorboards creaking and groaning under his weight.

"I'll go fetch a cool cloth for the young lady's head," a woman kindly offered.

Christine tried to open her eyes and couldn't. She wanted to move her arms and found that she had no control over her body. Then someone took her hand and held it gently. It was a man. She could tell from the size and strength of the fingers and the calluses on the palm.

She opened her eyes.

A young man was leaning over her. He was dressed in a drab brown uniform with jodhpur-style pants and his legs were wrapped with strips of cloth from ankle to knee. He wore a metal helmet on his head and there was a canteen slung over one shoulder. She spotted a gas mask and a rifle and a cartridge belt on the floor beside him.

Then she recognized the uniform. She'd seen it on recruiting posters and in the newspapers. The young man was dressed in the standard uniform of an American doughboy.

She opened her mouth and whispered, "Is that you?"

The soldier did not answer. He didn't seem to hear her.

She had something to say to him if only she could remember what it was. She struggled to remember, knowing that it was important. Then it came to her. Her voice grew frantic as she pleaded with him, "Don't forget to come for me. You promised. You promised to always come for me."

The soldier did not reply.

Her eyes would stay open no longer. No matter how hard she fought against it, they closed again.

CHRISTINE AWOKE WITH A START. She was bathed in a light film of perspiration. Her mouth and throat were parched. The quilt was tangled around her body.

She threw the coverlet aside and stood. Her legs were wobbly, but she managed to reach the washbasin. She poured tepid water over her hands and raised them to her feverish face. She filled a glass and drank deeply.

She'd had another nightmare. It wasn't the first of her life, and she suspected it wouldn't be the last. This time she hadn't been drowning—as she had in so many nightmares when she was a child—yet there had been the same sense of urgency about the awful dream, the same struggle between life and death. She was certain of it.

Christine raised a hand to smooth her rumpled hair and glanced up at her reflection in the mirror. She looked dreadful. Her skin had a pasty appearance to it, her lips were unnaturally white, even her hair seemed the color of hoarfrost in the afternoon light.

She wetted her lips and took another drink of lukewarm water, deliberately avoiding her reflection.

She wondered if she'd eaten something for dinner that hadn't agreed with her. Or perhaps she was coming down with a case of "summer disease." Mama always said that sour milk or improper food could bring it on.

But her eyes told the truth. There was no denying the haunted expression that stared back at her in the mirror. The truth was there if she cared to see it.

A quiet knock came on her door.

"Yes," she said, and did not recognize her own voice.

"It's Hannah," came the announcement as her sister entered the bedroom. When the elder Brick girl saw the deathly white face on the younger, she came rushing up and took her by the arm. "Christine, are you ill?"

"No, I'm not ill."

Apparently Hannah did not believe her. She reached out and placed a hand on her forehead. "You seem feverish to me."

Christine tried to brush her sister's concerns aside. "I don't have a fever."

Hannah was not entirely convinced. "Maybe I should go fetch Mama. She'll know if something's wrong with you."

"I told you. There's nothing wrong with me. I fell asleep with Grandmother's quilt covering me and it was too warm for the afternoon. That's all."

"Are you certain you're all right?"

Christine attempted a smile. "I'm fine. I think a breath of fresh air would be in order, however."

Her ever-practical sister marched across the bedroom and proceeded to open the windows wide. "There. That should help. It really is warm as an oven in here."

"Yes, it is."

Christine's gaze went to the open window and the hillside beyond. There was a flash of color in the afternoon sunlight. How odd. She hadn't realized the Golden Raintree was in bloom. She wanted suddenly to walk beneath its cooling shade and feel its shower of brilliant golden-yellow blossoms on her face.

Without turning her head, she said to Hannah, "James will be coming soon. Would you please tell him that I will be up at the Golden Raintree?"

"But—"

Christine never gave her the chance to say more, but dashed from her room and the house. She climbed the hill, the wind, the glorious wind, in her hair and face.

Later she watched as the young soldier came up her hill. And she knew in her heart it was James.

Chapter Four

When Johnny Comes Marching...

Raising a hand to shield her eyes from the glare of the afternoon sun, Christine watched as James climbed up the hill.

The uniform was wrong.

No, not wrong, she concluded as he covered the distance between them, just different.

In her dream the soldier had worn a metal helmet and there had been strips of cloth wound about his legs from ankle to knee in a style known as puttees. A gas mask, a rifle and a canteen had lain at his side, she recalled.

James, on the other hand, was wearing an officer's cap of the same olive drab material as his dress uniform and a pair of knee-high leather boots polished to a sheen. There was no gas mask or rifle in evidence, but hanging from his cartridge belt was a revolver; cold, black and deadly looking.

A chill ran down Christine's spine.

She should have been surprised to see James dressed in the uniform of an army officer, but she wasn't. Somehow she'd known he had enlisted. It was all mixed up with the frightening dream she'd had earlier that afternoon and with the special bond that had existed between the two of them since childhood. Sometimes they could almost *sense* what the other was thinking and feeling.

Since returning home from college last spring, James had often mentioned his admiration for those who were volunteering to serve in the Great War. Now that she thought about it, bits and pieces of conversations she had overheard came back to her. There had been times in the past few months when the conflict in Europe seemed to be the single topic of discussion among their friends and acquaintances.

Only this morning, of course, her brother had announced at Meeting that he was going to France to serve as an ambulance driver. Charlie was determined, it seemed, to do his part for the war effort. It should come as no surprise to her that James was equally determined to do his. If only he had chosen a less violent way to participate...

The wind decided to play havoc with Christine's golden locks, tossing them to and fro like the silky tassels atop the stalks of corn growing in the Happy Valley below. Brushing aside a strand of hair, she stepped into the cooling shade of the Golden Raintree and waited for James.

He came to a halt several feet from her and politely removed his hat. Glancing over her shoulder for a moment, he mentioned, almost as an aside, "I hadn't realized the Golden Raintree was in bloom."

"Neither had I," said Christine, her mouth tasting oddly of sawdust.

"Remember when we were children—" the expression on the handsome features was one of wistfulness "—we used to stand beneath this tree and shake the bottom branches until the blossoms fell down into our outstretched hands."

"We called it golden rain."

His eyes came to rest on her. "You remember."

"I remember."

After that, there was a strained silence between them.

Christine took a deep breath and broached the subject uppermost in both their minds. "You've joined the army," she stated with forced calmness.

"Yes, I have." There was a lengthy pause while James stared off into the distance, hazel eyes squinting against the bright summer sunlight. At last his attention swung back to her. "You don't seem surprised."

"I'm not." But in a softly accusatory tone she said, "Why didn't you tell me you were going to enlist?"

James fingered the brim of the military cap he held in his hands. "I didn't think you would approve."

Her voice was low and fervent. "I don't approve."

He blew his breath out expressively. "And I figured you wouldn't understand, either."

"You're right." Her throat constricted painfully. "I don't."

He shrugged his broad shoulders. "I guess I couldn't expect you to understand how a man feels about defending his country, about doing his patriotic duty. After all, you're a girl—and a Quaker to boot."

The hurtful words were a reminder of the cruel taunts she'd had to endure in her childhood. They echoed in Christine's ears: *"You're just a girl, a Molly, a coward like all the rest of your kind."*

She bit back the tears. Well, she wasn't *just* a girl, and Quakers weren't cowards!

Blue eyes flashed with anger; heated words spilled forth in a torrent of emotion. "For your information, James Warren, the early Quakers were persecuted in England, even thrown into prison, for believing in equality and democracy, for professing that no man was better than another simply by an accident of birth.'' She watched his eyes grow wide with surprise at her outburst. "In our own country there were three Quaker men *and* a woman hanged in the Massachusetts colony for standing up for what they believed was right. How can you say those valiant souls knew nothing of their patriotic duty, nothing of personal sacrifice?''

James was utterly taken aback. "I—I didn't say anything of the kind.''

"But that's what you meant.'' Christine was determined to set him straight on the subject, once and for all. "I'll have you know that many brave Friends dedicated themselves to helping the antislavery movement and the Underground Railroad during the Civil War. The Quakers have worked long and hard for prison reform and improved care for the mentally ill, education for the poor and peace with the Indians. Yes, we believe that violence is wrong. Yes, our men often refuse to serve in the military. But we are courageous and we are loyal to our country. It is both unfair and untrue to imply otherwise.''

James obviously wished he'd never mentioned the subject. "I think you misunderstood what I said,'' he claimed in his own defense.

Christine met his claim with a challenging lift of her chin. "Perhaps it's life and death you believe I know nothing about.''

He heaved a great sigh and stuffed his hands into his pockets. "We both know better than that. Your family cared for the living and the dead when the tornado hit New Castle last spring.''

She could feel herself trembling with righteous indignation. "I can only think it must be killing you find me ignorant of, then. 'Tis true. I know nothing about killing another human being. I hope I never do.''

"I hope you never do, either." James drew in a long, slow breath and let it out. "War is a terrible business, Christine. Fighting in a war is, at best, a necessary evil. But it's something a man has to do—something *I* have to do."

She shuddered and blurted out, "Why? Because you're afraid people in town will say that a rich man's son doesn't have to go to war? That he can *buy* his way out? Do you care so very much for other people's opinions?"

His entire body stiffened. "I don't give a damn for other people's opinions!" he declared without a trace of gentleness.

Unshed tears burned her eyes. "Then why did you volunteer for the army?"

"The army came to me. They offered to make me an officer."

It was the first she'd heard of it. "When?"

"They approached me last spring while I was still a student at Notre Dame." James ran his hands through his hair, resulting in a slightly disheveled appearance. "Apparently the army thought I would be a natural for the job."

She was horrified. "Of killing?"

His lips compressed into a thin line; his voice snapped with authority. "Of leading men, of inspiring them on the battlefield the way I'd been doing for the past four years on the football field."

A frenzied whisper was directed toward him. "But war isn't a game!"

"Isn't it?" A faint cynical smile appeared on his handsome face. "There are offensive and defensive maneuvers in battle as there are in the game of football. Each side tries to outwit the other to gain valuable ground. Sometimes people get hurt in the process. The stakes are higher in a war, but in the end you do whatever it takes to win. Victory is, after all, the ultimate goal."

Christine stood there and stared at James, her heart drumming violently in her chest. Surely he didn't believe that a life-and-death struggle in which millions had already lost their lives was some kind of awful game. He couldn't believe that! It was inhuman. Of course, war was inhuman.

James went on. "Uncle Sam needs every able-bodied man he can get, Christine. The draft lottery went into operation at the end of July. Sooner or later, there's a good chance I'd have to go anyway. At least this way I'll be commanding my own troops."

She bit down hard on her bottom lip. "But you'll be leading other men to their deaths."

He stared at her fixedly and added a grim indictment. "That goes with the territory when a man serves as an officer during wartime."

Christine took a handkerchief from the pocket of her dress and dabbed at her lip. When she took it away there was a spot of bright red blood on the white material. She quickly stuffed the hankie back into her pocket and concentrated on her hands. They were visibly shaking. She clasped them together in front of her and closed her eyes for a moment. She tried to think. She had to do something to stop James before it was too late.

She opened her eyes and looked straight into his soul. "I know you are a good man, James Wilson Warren, a man of strong convictions. I could not love you if you were otherwise. You have always done what you believed was right. But this—" there was an undertone of abhorrence "—we both know that it's wrong to kill another human being."

"The enemy should have thought of that before they started killing innocent people, before they declared themselves the enemy," he staunchly defended.

She took a deep, steadying breath and tried again. "Just because the other side kills doesn't make it right for us to kill in return. Have you forgotten the commandment 'Thou shalt not kill'?"

A rash of hot color crept up James's neck and into his tanned cheeks. "I haven't forgotten. But the Bible also says an eye for an eye and a tooth for a tooth."

"Even if that means a life for a life?"

His lips tightened. "Yes, even if it means one life in exchange for another."

Christine reached out and placed her hand on James's arm. She could feel the tension radiating from him. She wanted to do something, anything, to lessen the awful feeling inside of her that she knew must be inside him as well.

"There was a boy in Meeting this morning. He talked about being called a coward and a war baby by a gang of local bullies. He spoke of being afraid. It takes a strong man to fight, but we believe it takes an even stronger man *not* to."

James's voice was soft and cold when he said to her, "That may be the way of the Friends, Christine, but it's not my way. It's easy to say it takes a strong man *not* to fight, if you refuse to put your life on the line for what you believe in."

She drew a breath of distress. "It's not just putting your own life on the line. It's taking someone else's life," she pointed out. "Are you willing to kill for what you believe in? Because that's what you will be asked to do."

"Dammit, don't you think I haven't thought of that?" James looked at her a long, hard while. "I've been lying awake night after night asking myself the same question: Can I kill another human being? I don't know the answer. Maybe I won't know until I get into the heat of battle.''

A painful silence fell between them.

Christine studied the stern, uncompromising outline of his profile against the soft, yellow blossoms of the Golden Raintree. Where was the boy she'd grown up with? Where was the young man he had become? Talking to James was suddenly like talking to a stranger.

She waited as the pain inside her increased to anguish. Her voice became a forlorn whisper. ''Why must you fight in a war that's halfway around the world from us?''

James straightened briskly. ''Because if we don't fight the enemy in Europe, we may well have to face them right here at home. Have you forgotten the Zimmermann Telegram?''

She shook her head. ''No, I haven't forgotten.''

Nevertheless, he reiterated the facts. ''The German government announced its plans for unlimited submarine warfare knowing full well that the United States would no longer be able to remain neutral. Behind our very backs they were proposing an alliance with Mexico, urging our neighbor to the south to 'reconquer' part of this country and make Texas, New Mexico and Arizona their own.''

What did she care for secret telegrams and decoded messages? What were governments and military alliances and submarine warfare to her? All she cared about in this world was the man standing before her now!

For all the high-minded ideals she professed, Christine knew what she really wanted was to keep James with her, to keep him safe at home. Was that so very wrong of her?

Shorn of her defenses, she blurted out, "I'm afraid for you, James, and for your safety."

"My dear Christine, don't—"

On a near sob, "I'm afraid of what this war may do to you, to both of us."

"I'm afraid of what it may do to all of us," he admitted grimly.

She shivered and moved closer to him. "Every minute you're away I will worry that something may happen to you."

There was an underlying invincibility to his whole manner as he reassured her, "Nothing is going to happen to me. They predict the Central Powers will surrender by Christmas. The war will probably be over before I'm even shipped to France."

Despite his optimism, she was still trembling with fear. What was she so afraid of?

The answer came to her: she was afraid of all the ways she could lose him. Disease. Death. The horrors of war. They could all take him from her. Love had *not* made her brave; it had made a coward of her.

"You are—" The declaration faltered and died on her lips. She began again. "You are the other half of myself, James Warren. Without you I can never be whole. What if you are hurt? Or wounded? Or perhaps even…killed?"

James took her small hands in his larger, stronger ones and gazed down into her face. He could shield her from many things, it seemed, but not the truth. "We both know that there are worse things than dying, Christine."

She understood that on some rational level, but she wasn't feeling particularly rational at the moment. Her emotions were on the surface, raw and exposed. Hot, salty tears pricked the corners of her eyes and threatened to slide down her cheeks.

His gentle voice made her look up. "A man has to be able to live with himself."

The breath shuddered in her lungs. "A woman, too," she said, blinking away the tears.

"A woman, too," James repeated with the first hint of a smile she'd seen from him all afternoon. "I will stay alive for both our sakes, I promise."

Suddenly she wanted to feel his arms around her. She needed to draw from his strength. "James, hold me. Please."

His cap forgotten, he pulled her into his arms and stepped back beneath the thick, concealing foliage of the Golden Raintree. It was a private moment.

Christine pressed her face into the front of his uniform. The tunic was new and crisp and freshly laundered. She went up on her tiptoes, her arms slipping tentatively around his neck. The hair at his nape was surprisingly soft and lush. She threaded her fingers through it, taking liberties that would never have occurred to her until this afternoon. She'd thought they would have all the time in the world to love each other. Now that was not to be. Time was suddenly very precious. James was leaving her.

They stood, in silence, underneath the golden canopy of the sprawling tree. Christine felt surrounded by James's presence, by the scent that clung to him: it was a subtle mixture of shaving soap, something akin to the crisp, tart apples in the big barrel at the general store and a natural maleness that emanated from his skin. His breath was even warmer than the summer breeze that stirred the tendrils about her face.

All of her senses were heightened: the sky was bluer, the sun brighter, the song of the meadow bird more melodious, the joy of loving this man both bitter and sweet to her. Unsteadily, Christine's heart began to pick up speed.

Her pulse beat double. "James—"

"Shh—" He touched the tip of his finger to her mouth; a whisper of a caress that lingered only for a moment or two.

Then he propped his other hand against the tree trunk and she was caught between the rough, cool bark and the smooth warmth of his body, a warmth that seemed to beckon to her. She was intensely aware of his vibrant form, the long line of his thighs an inch away from hers, the heat penetrating through the material of his shirt. She sensed rather than felt an imperceptible movement; then his lips skimmed her forehead in a feathery light kiss. She heard a sharp little intake of air and knew it was her own.

Christine put her head back and looked up at James, suddenly reminded of the sheer size, of the sheer magnitude of him. He towered over her. The top of her head barely reached his chin. His shoulders were broad. His arms were long and muscular. His chest was granite hard. His legs were strong and sure as they pressed against hers.

His eyes appeared to be closed, but she could *feel* him watching her. His face was so near that she could make out the tiny lines at the corners of his mouth and the slight protrusion of his Adam's apple above his collar. Her hands were splayed across the front of his military tunic. She could feel the rhythmic pulsing of his life's blood beneath her fingertips. She placed one hand above her own breast—her heart was racing like some wild thing.

James's voice came to her softly. "We are two hearts that will always beat as one." He bent his head, his hand curling around her shoulder.

Then he kissed her, and she forgot to breathe.

She had not known it could be like this. Once, as a girl, she had chastised him for kissing her the same way Mama and Papa did. She'd informed him that she wanted a real kiss from him. The one he gave her on that long ago summer morn had left her as skittish as a colt. She'd bolted and run away.

But not this time. The kiss James gave her now inflamed her. It created a wild song that echoed through her veins. It left her aching for another and yet another. It revealed an emptiness, a loneliness inside her that she hadn't known existed. She was fascinated. Enthralled. Bemused and a little saddened. She was surprised to find there was so very much left to learn about him, about herself. She was stunned to discover that she was capable of feeling a woman's passion.

When the kiss ended, she opened her eyes and looked deeply into his. "I love you, James."

He held her gaze. "And I love you, Christine. You are my first and only love."

She caught the tip of her tongue between her teeth. "I am sorry we quarreled."

"So am I."

"We will not always agree," she said, sighing.

His mouth turned up at the corners. "That's true."

She might as well tell him everything. After all, he had a right to know. "I'm a woman with her own opinions."

He laughed lightly under his breath. "So I noticed."

Christine gave her head a little shake, dislodging a wisp of blond hair. She swallowed hard and confessed, "I will miss you."

He tightened his arms around her; his voice had a rough edge to it. "I will miss you more than I can say."

She finally brought herself to ask, "When do you have to leave for the army?"

James seemed reluctant to answer the question. It was some time before he replied, "I leave in two days' time."

Her head flew up. "In two days!"

He fought to sound neutral as he said, "I have to report to my commanding officer at Camp Taylor, Kentucky, by the end of the week."

She clutched at his sleeves. "Two days. Even Charlie doesn't have to leave for a fortnight."

"I know."

Her brows rose quizzically. "He told you, then?"

"Charlie and I have discussed our plans," he said, measuring out his words.

"Mama and Papa are nearly beside themselves with worry," she admitted. "I heard them talking in the kitchen this afternoon. Charlie was trying to explain why he felt he had to volunteer as an ambulance driver." She wetted her lips and ventured, "How did your family take the news about you becoming a soldier?"

For a moment James hesitated, then he came right out and told her, "I left my mother in hysterics and Louise dissolved in tears. They were both going to lie down in their rooms. Beulah was digging out the smelling salts and my father, the brandy." He shook his head all the while he was speaking. "I think Father approves of my decision, or, at least, understands."

"I wish I could understand," Christine said hollowly.

Dark eyes engaged hers. "So do I."

"I will try," she said at length.

"I know you will." James brushed a wisp of blond hair from her cheek. He spoke softly, reasonably, as to a child. "You always were a brave little soul, Christine Brick."

She wasn't feeling very brave at the moment, but she kept any doubts she had to herself. The Good Book said there was "a time to keep silence and a time to speak." This was, perhaps, a time for silence.

"Charlie has agreed to drive me to the train station on Tuesday. Will you come to see me off?" James inquired, retrieving his cap from where it had fallen at their feet.

Her voice came out small but firm. "If you wish."

Wary eyes engaged hers. "Mother and Louise are afraid to say goodbye to me. My father will doubtlessly be needed at home to comfort them."

Christine raised her chin a fraction of an inch higher in the air. She was no shrinking violet, unlike Mrs. Warren and Louise. "Of course I will come to the train station to see you off. I'm not afraid to say goodbye, for I know in my heart you'll come back to me."

He seemed relieved and even tried to make light of it. "I did promise to always come for you, didn't I?"

"Yes, you did. And I'm holding you to that promise."

"Just remember, Miss Brick, *you* made a promise, too."

For a moment her heart was laid bare. "I will always be there waiting for you, James. Always."

IT WAS TUESDAY MORNING. The three of them were in the Brick family's Maxwell Tourabout, a fourteen-horse-power motor car that Benjamin Brick had purchased locally nearly a decade before for $825, and had declared time and time again was still "plenty good enough to get us wherever we're goin'."

Charlie Brick was driving. James rode in the front passenger seat and Christine sat quietly behind the two young men. There was a small hamper beside her filled with food: a cold meat pie, green tomatoes taken before the first frost, peaches conserved in sweet cider, two slices of Beulah's special honey cake wrapped in waxed paper and enough various and sundry foodstuffs "to feed an army," according to James. Beulah had not shed a solitary tear when he'd gone to the kitchen to bid her farewell, but she was the only one who had thought to pack him a picnic lunch for the first leg of his journey.

It was a bright, clear morning now that the sun had come up and burned off the blue haze. Christine had arisen well before dawn, dressing in the dark while the rest of the household still slept. Truth to tell, it was no bother getting up at that hour. She hadn't been able to sleep the night before, anyway.

She sat in the back seat of the roomy Maxwell, hands folded demurely in her lap. James was sitting tall and straight-backed, his profile to her. Charlie was doing most of the talking.

"I heard in town yesterday that Billy Bathgate was one of the first soldiers to arrive in France this summer with General Pershing and the American Expeditionary Force."

Christine repeated incredulously, "Billy Bathgate? Surely you don't mean the same Billy Bathgate we knew as children?"

"The scrawny little hooligan who nearly got Christine drowned?" James piped up.

Charlie nodded his head. "That's the one. They were saying at the barbershop that Billy could shoot the eyes off a potato from fifty paces while he was still in short pants."

"The way I heard the story, it was more likely to be wild turkeys from the back of a horse as he got a little older," James said. "Billy always was a wild one—gambling, drinking moonshine and, in general, raising hell." He caught Christine's eye. "My apologies. I meant no offense."

"None taken," she reassured him.

He went on, directing his conversation to her brother. "They say that 'Black Jack' Pershing is of the old faith—he prefers his troops to be highly trained marksmen. We both know that some of the best marksmen serving in the army are country boys like Billy."

"I never could learn to handle a rifle well myself," Charlie admitted.

James Warren placed a hand on his friend's shoulder and said affectionately, "It's just as well, then, that you won't be asked to."

As he parked his father's automobile alongside the depot, Charlie volunteered, "I'll find a porter to load your trunk onto the train."

Christine watched as her brother opened the door on the driver's side of the touring car and took off at a lope across the station platform. "He's going to miss you."

"I'll miss Charlie, too," James said thoughtfully. "He's been a good friend to me, perhaps a better friend than I realized."

None of them were quite sure how to say goodbye to each other on that splendid summer morning toward the end of August; they'd had no practice at goodbyes yet. The three friends stood in a small circle on the platform, having already stowed James's personal belongings aboard the train, and talked about the harvest to come, the weather, the bales of hay in the fields and how they would miss the molasses-making this year.

They spoke of small, insignificant things, knowing that to speak aloud of what was truly in their hearts would only serve to make them inconsolably sad. They knew well enough that this might be the last time the three of them were together.

"All aboard!" came the call.

The two young men shook hands, then clasped each other by the shoulders.

"Take care of yourself over there, Charlie."

"You do the same, James." Then Charles Brick quickly turned to his sister and said, "I'll wait for you in the car."

Christine found herself alone with James. He grasped both of her hands in his. "We won't say goodbye."

There was a great heartthrob in her throat. She swallowed and shook her head, "No, we won't say goodbye."

"I'll be home on leave for Thanksgiving."

She bowed her head as she whispered, "I will be counting the days."

Holding her chin in his hand, James looked into her eyes and said softly, "Write to me."

"Every day," she promised.

He bent his head and kissed her. It was like a whisper of wind against her lips.

In the next moment, James was gone.

Christine bravely stood there, waving and smiling, until the train was out of sight. Then she realized she was all alone on the platform. Turning, she slowly walked back toward her brother.

Chapter Five

Letters from Home

New Castle, Indiana
September 3, 1917

Second Lieutenant James W. Warren
Second Division, Company H
Camp Taylor
Louisville, Kentucky

Dear James,

I have a secret to tell you. You must promise not to let on to your family or mine. If Papa or Thomas Ezekiel found out, they would be terribly upset with me. And your mother and father would be simply furious with Louise. Yesterday Louise and I sneaked out to the moving pictures at the Strand! That's the new theater those men from Anderson opened up on North Main Street. We thought it quite a lark, although a guilty conscience almost did us in, for your dear sister and I had told everyone we were going to the weekly band concert at the Court House Square. We were shaking in our high-lace shoes for we were certain that someone would see us who shouldn't!

But James, oh, James, it was so exciting! The newsreel was all about the derring-do of the Canadian flying ace,

Billy Bishop. Of course I had to cover my eyes when they showed the German, Richthofen, and his "Flying Circus" shooting down the flimsy canvas aeroplanes of "our dear brave boys," as Louise is wont to call the French and British fliers.

Louise talks about volunteering to sell war bonds, and Hannah spends every evening knitting socks and scarves and all varieties of woolens. "Knit your bit" is the slogan of the American Red Cross, and my sister seems determined to knit enough for our entire army by herself.

The War is what everybody in New Castle is talking about these days, even at our house. Papa says we must never forget that war is a test of strength, not a search for truth and justice. I know you believe you must fight in this awful Battle, but I am still torn between my belief that war is fundamentally wrong and your belief that we must sometimes fight for and perhaps even kill for what we believe in. That has always been the dilemma of the Quakers, for there are those who would call us cowards and not even bother to do so behind our backs.

But I must not go on so, James, when I started out to tell you what is happening in our fair city. The town is all atwitter with talk that a woman may serve on the School Board. "What an outrageous scandal!" I overheard old Mr. Popplewell declare at the general store. I'm sure I don't understand what the fuss is about. There are any number of intelligent women who are permitted to teach in our schools.

I must say goodbye for now and help Mama prepare supper. I almost forgot to tell you. Papa is talking about getting a telephone!

God be with you,
Your Christine

Camp Taylor
Louisville, Kentucky
September 10, 1917

Miss Christine Brick
Rural Route #1
New Castle, Indiana

Dear Christine.
I will try to answer as many questions from your last letter as I can.

I share my quarters with a splendid fellow named Robert Hershel Cooper, who also volunteered this past summer and was commissioned by the army as a second lieutenant. "Coop," as we chaps call him, hails from Ohio and was graduated from Oberlin College last spring where he took his degree in literature. We often sit in our room in the evenings, smoking our pipes and speaking of our favorite writers. He, too, favors The Good Gray Poet—Walt Whitman—as well as Lord Tennyson.

The food here is passable but the army cooks serve too much of a dish they have named "Hopping John," which seems to consist primarily of cowpeas, rice and salt pork. I am already dreaming of Beulah's traditional roast turkey and pumpkin pie for Thanksgiving dinner.

You asked what we junior officers do with our days. Mostly we attend lectures given by the senior officers and drill the men who serve under us. It has been raining a great deal so that some days the mud is up to our ankles. An unpleasant business!

I must confess that I agree with your parents on the subject of higher education. You should pursue your studies at Earlham College and become a teacher. I know it is difficult to think of these things when everyone around you is involved in the war effort, but you have always admitted to being a disaster at knitting and other forms of stitchery, and I can't see you, dear girl, working in a factory.

I have written to Charlie to wish him "Godspeed." I know your family, and especially you, Christine, will miss him. Try not to worry.

Tomorrow is your eighteenth birthday. You wrote in your letter of the gift you know you will receive from your parents. How extraordinary to think that you look so much like the miniature that has survived of your great-grandmother. She must have been a beautiful woman.

I think of you every day, Christine, and read your letters two and three times apiece.

Yours, James

New Castle, Indiana
October 6, 1917

Dear James,

Our entire household is in an uproar. Goldie has decided to leave us to marry her young gentleman friend, and Lily Huckelby has gone off to work in a steel mill. Can you imagine such a thing? Mama says we cannot do without their help, but Papa insists that we can and will. So many young men from Henry County have gone to war that the young women must necessarily take their places in the factories. Besides, as Papa has pointed out, the steel being made is for a Friends Church on South Main Street, as well as the new city hall and several other important buildings in town.

Mama and Papa have agreed that I need not start at Earlham College until the spring. We are all feeling a bit melancholy now that Charlie has set sail for England. I am not idle, however. Part of each day is spent helping Hannah cultivate the last of her vegetables. The plot of land at the edge of town has been designated for the use of war gardeners.

No doubt Louise has written you about the splendid teas and poetry readings she and your mother are giving in your family's home. After the "entertainment," of course, the mayor, or someone of equal importance, stands up and speaks on the virtues of supporting the war effort. The patriotic spirit of our community is apparent in the vigorous buying of Liberty Bond issues, and Red Cross subscriptions, according to your dear sister.

I am hurriedly but always your
Christine

P.S. The gossips are saying that Goldie's young gentleman friend proposed marriage to her so that he could avoid being drafted into the war. Naturally we try not to listen to the "wagging tongues."

P.P.S. Every night I write in the beautiful leather-bound diary you gave me for my birthday, and I think of you.

C.

Camp Taylor
October 13, 1917

My dear Christine,

You have my abject apologies. I realize that I have not written in a week. Or is it two? Time seems not to have the same meaning here at Camp Taylor; one day fades into the next with little to distinguish it. It has rained all month long and we are up to our knees in muck and mud.

The men I must train are a sorry lot in many ways. Unless they are country boys and used to physical labor, they are poor specimens of manhood, indeed. They are not even capable of walking five miles without great fatigue and numerous foot problems that cause half of them to fall by the wayside. I cannot imagine that we will have these men ready for combat in less than two months' time.

Since the draft law went into effect, there have been rumors of thousands of men who have changed their names, run away or simply failed to show up after receiving the fateful letter, "Greetings, Your neighbors have selected you..." Most communities have been closely guided by the army when making their selections, although some boards have not been able to resist the temptation to get rid of their town's misfits and half-wits.

Still, the military men are relieved that the waiting is over and we are about to do our part in the war. Many of them were embarrassed or angered by President Wilson's assertion several years ago that the United States was "too proud to fight."

I have gone on too long about military matters. They are much on my mind these days. Perhaps you would find it of greater interest to know that for all the high standards supposedly taken in the drafting of men, there are over 100,000 illiterates in the American forces. There are also reported to be more than 50,000 former teachers. General Pershing, himself a teacher at West Point in earlier days, has set up schools all over France.

Coop has just come in to tell me we're having a staff meeting in five minutes. Therefore, I must quickly put this letter in the mail to you.

Please know that you are in my thoughts and dreams always.

> I love you,
> James

Would you please tell Hannah that I have received the knitted socks and they are most welcome as the nights are turning cooler?

> New Castle, Indiana
> October 18, 1917

My dear James,

I have just returned home from one of your mother and sister's Liberty Bond teas. They are always hailed as a great success and are becoming a weekly fixture in the social fabric of New Castle. Louise is kind enough to say that they could not do without my help, but the truth is I am of little use to them as a hostess. I have not Louise's gift of small talk, nor your mother's ability to organize refreshments for a large gathering.

Hannah's war garden has produced its last harvest of pumpkins and squash, so we have asked Thomas Ezekiel to plow under the few remaining stragglers damaged by the frost and will begin again in the spring.

Last week I decided it was time to do something about the melancholia this autumn seems to have brought upon me. So I marched into Dr. Smith's clinic and volunteered to be of whatever assistance he deemed useful. I have gone twice this week to tend to the sick. Sometimes a kind word or a gentle touch do much to make the ill person feel better. Dr. Smith is an esteemed physician and an exemplary Friend, as you may remember. He claims I have the makings of a "healer," but I do it as much for myself as for the patients. It has partly eased the terrible restlessness I have been experiencing.

Sometimes I wonder, James, in what ways this war will change each one of us. For change us it surely will. Of that I am certain. I ask myself what will be my own small part in this great challenge we must all face. I do not yet have the answer.

> But I am always
> Your Christine

Camp Taylor
October 27, 1917

My own dear Christine,

I have often asked myself the same question: What will be my own small part in this great challenge we must face as individuals and as a nation? This week the answer seems to be the supervision of my men as they dig holes in the ground.

Several French officers have arrived here at Camp Taylor from the Western Front with the explicit purpose of teaching us the proper method of digging and building a trench. Unfortunately none of the officers speaks our language, but the translator tells us that they have said the trenches stretch along the French and Belgian border for hundreds of miles. We are finding this difficult to believe.

I, too, wonder what changes this war will bring. I know that I grow weary of all this training and I am ready for action. I have had enough of mud and rain and the endless sameness of each day to last me a lifetime.

Coop sends his regards to you. Although the two of you have never been introduced, he feels he has met you. Perhaps because I have talked about you so much.

I am afraid this letter is not as cheerful as I had hoped it would be. Blame it on the rain and, dear heart, forgive my foul mood.

Always,
James

New Castle, Indiana
November 3, 1917

Dearest James,

I was standing at the window in my bedroom tonight and there was a pale orange moon hanging low in the sky just above the treetops. I opened the window and the smell of autumn was on the night air: the familiar tang of crisp, brown leaves and burning firewood, of ripening pumpkins on the vine and the promise of morning frost.

The days are warm and sunny still, the nights turn chill and damp. Summer has come and gone, I fear, and in its place are the golden fields of corn ready to be harvested, and the deep, dark trees turning to vivid reds and oranges and golds. I am sad to see the summer go this year.

Last night you were in my dreams again, and I awoke at an hour long past midnight to find my heart pounding wildly in my breast and the tears streaming down my face. I took your letters from the table beside my bed and read them over and over until I knew every word by heart. I do miss you so, James.

I try to think of happier times for my heart's sake and my soul's sake. Remember when we were children and on the day the ice wagon made its deliveries, we never planned any other activities? We loved to follow Old Abe because he would let us pick up small chips he shaved off the larger cakes of ice. We would take these to Beulah and she would make lemonade for us. Sometimes she would cut us a small piece of fresh honey cake, too. I think upon these things and they lighten my heart for a while.

Then the night comes again and the curtains are drawn, the household is still, and in the firelit dark I think of your touch, your kiss.

> Your loving
> Christine

> Camp Taylor
> November 12, 1917

My dearest one,

You have been much on my mind, and I realize that in the past several months I have written at great length of the rain and the mud and the ill-prepared state of the men I am to lead, but I have not written what was in my heart.

I want you to know, Christine, that it is your own sweet face that I see when I close my eyes each night. When I tire of hearing the sound of male voices by the hundreds, indeed, by the thousands, I think of the sweet music of your voice: it is sunlight on the pond in summer, the song of a bird soaring high above the trees, the whisper of the wind in the sycamores.

I will never forget the beautiful September morn when you were born, and I thank God for putting you on this earth to be my own sweet love. I remember the day you nearly drowned in the old swimming hole and how I knew where to find you. We have always been meant for each other. The day of our summer picnic you told me you'd known that for a long, long time. For as long as you could remember. These are the thoughts I hold close to my heart when I despair to see you and all the other dear ones at home.

You are now eighteen and a woman, a fact you have reminded me of several times. I will soon be home on leave and I have an important question to ask you.

I count the moments until we meet again.

All my love,
James

New Castle, Indiana
November 19, 1917

My dearest James,

I am writing this letter in the beautiful diary you gave me for my eighteenth birthday. I will always remember the day Louise delivered your package along with her own thoughtful gift of lavender sachets for my bureau drawers. I know it sounds silly, but at first I'd thought you had forgotten my birthday. I should have known better.

I am feeling particularly melancholy this evening. I have been dreaming about Charlie almost every night: dark dreams, terrifying dreams that I try not to remember upon awakening. Then only today we have had a letter from him that is most distressing, and somehow I know it is a letter that I cannot share with you. You may well be sailing for France and the Western Front yourself, for all your brave talk to the contrary. And as I keep reminding myself, "...there is a time to keep silence and a time to speak...."

I know the words of my brother's letter by heart and I will write them down here, but you shall never see them, my love.

Charlie writes, "...I hear the soldiers talking at night, especially the wounded and the dying. Many are no more than boys. They are tired and disheartened and sore afraid they will never see home again. Who can promise them that they will? Surely not the commanders, who are invariably old. Some even wear the uniforms of the last war, and favor its weapons and battle techniques. They still believe it is the only way to win this War. The young men of many nations will die—have died, I fear—to prove them wrong.

"Trenches are necessary on a miserably grand scale. Flares light up the sky at night to stop marauders on both sides. Of course, the barbed wire makes crossing No-Man's-Land treacherous.

"I drove an engine-powered ambulance when I first arrived in London. Now that we are out in France, I sometimes drive a horse-drawn vehicle as well. There is a confusion of men and machines and animals on all the roads. And mud. There is mud everywhere. We're up to our knees in the damnable stuff.

"They say there are worse things than dying, and dear God, I have seen too many of them...."

Even as I write my brother's words in my diary, James, the tears sting my eyes and my heart begins to pound. I can only imagine the horrors Charlie has seen and heard, and it makes me sick at heart. I wish we were all children again and the world was still innocent. And yet I know that is the one wish that cannot be.

Thomas Paine once wrote that "these are the times that try men's souls." I believe this time, our time, is another to try the heart and soul of each man and woman of us. I also believe that you and I can survive anything as long as we remember to love each other. In your darkest hour, please remember that I love you now and always.

Forever,
Christine

Chapter Six

Keep the Home Fires Burning

When Charlie left for England in September, Ann and Benjamin Brick presented their youngest son with a Bible and a measurable dose of good advice. Hannah gave her brother several pairs of warm, woolen socks and a scarf she'd knitted herself. And Christine—an affectionate smile tugged at the corners of Hannah's mouth—Christine sent Charlie off with a tearful kiss and a slim volume of poetry.

It was typical of each of them, Hannah Marie decided as she stood at the front parlor window, lace curtains discreetly parted an inch or two in the middle. Their parents had thought first of Charlie's religious soul, she, being the practical sort, of his creature comforts and Christine of his heart. Through the years she'd been able to accept her younger sister's physical beauty without jealousy, but there were still times when she envied Christine her tender, if impulsive, nature.

Hannah sighed and continued to gaze out at the unseasonably warm November day. Last month there had been a record-breaking snow on the ground. Only the previous week she clearly remembered seeing her breath in the cold morning air as she'd hiked out to the chicken coop to collect fresh eggs for breakfast. Now it was the day after Thanksgiving, and Indian summer—with all its accompanying warmth and splendor—had arrived, better late than never. A light cover-up would suffice for the walk she and Christine had been taking together every afternoon.

A familiar black automobile drove up in front of the Brick residence. Hannah watched as the tall, long-legged man inside got out. He was dressed in military finery, and there was no denying that the tailored cut of the uniform flattered him. Pausing for a moment, he simply stood there and looked around as if the sight of the farmhouse, the cluster of red barns and the golden fields beyond gave him immense pleasure.

When had she fallen out of love with James Warren?

The question popped unbidden into Hannah's head. She imagined that one fell *out* of love much in the same manner as one fell *in* love: day by day in what seemed like little, insignificant ways at the time. Perhaps she'd fallen out of love with James years ago, and simply hadn't noticed.

Or perhaps it had been this past summer when she'd come to realize, as everyone had, that Christine and James were truly in love with each other. She'd always known, of course, that the handsome Jamie would never be hers. There had always been too many pretty girls for him to choose from. And Christine was one of the prettiest girls in the county.

Her younger sister was utterly and completely in love, and she was afraid for her, Hannah admitted to herself. Not because she had any doubts about the depth of James's affections. It was as plain as the nose on her face that he loved Christine. But this was wartime, and war could do terrible things to a man. She didn't want to see her sister's heart broken.

The front door opened and the sound of an excited, girlish voice rang out. "James! James, you're here!"

Hannah meant to look away as Christine flew down the steps and into the waiting man's outstretched arms.

She meant to look away as James effortlessly picked her sister up and twirled her around once, twice, three times, before letting her feet touch the ground again.

"Christine!" The sound of his voice, the look in his eyes, left no doubt as to James Warren's sentiments.

Hannah closed the lace curtains, and then went along to the kitchen to see if there was any pumpkin or mincemeat pie to offer to their guest.

"WE USUALLY TAKE A VIGOROUS walk every day, Christine and I," Hannah was telling James as he finished the last bite of his mincemeat pie and pushed the plate away. "Why don't you come with us this afternoon?"

Christine piped up eagerly, "Yes, why don't you?" Then, she had second thoughts. "Unless, of course, you've had enough of walking in the army."

"Believe me, it's one thing to hike for miles through the mud and the rain with a platoon of disgruntled recruits. It's quite another to enjoy a leisurely outing with two of my favorite ladies," said James, looking from one to the other with an appreciative smile. "You still make the best piecrust in Henry County." He directed the compliment to Hannah. "But don't tell Beulah I said so."

She blushed with pleasure as she cleared away his plate and fork. "I'll just go along and get a jacket for Christine and myself."

Once they were alone in the kitchen, Christine found herself tongue-tied. She hadn't expected that.

"You don't have to say anything," James assured her as if he had read her mind. "Just let me sit here and look at you." She could feel his eyes on her. After a moment he murmured intensely, "Lord, you're lovely, Christine. Even lovelier than I remembered."

She wanted to say something, anything, but the words simply would not come. Her tongue was thick in her mouth. The breath was caught in her throat. She could feel the heat rising in her cheeks.

He stated softly, "Now I've embarrassed you. I didn't mean to."

"It's not that I'm embarrassed exactly," Christine finally managed, unsure of what she was feeling. Then she confessed, "You've been gone less than three months, James, but sometimes it seems like a hundred years since I've seen you."

"I know. It seems like forever to me as well." He reached out for her hand and pulled it toward him across the kitchen table. "I've thought about this moment, dreamt about it. . . ."

"I have, too," Christine blurted out. Her eyes darted about the kitchen and finally came to rest on the man sitting across from her.

She had envisioned it in her mind a hundred times: the way it would be when she and James were together again. Now that he was here, they seemed almost like strangers. Even James's appearance had changed. His face was leaner and he moved with a quick, silent skill that she imagined was not unlike that of the native Delaware Indians who had roamed Henry County nearly a century before. He seemed older. And a little tired, now that she took a good look at him. There were faint lines at the edges of his eyes and mouth that she knew had not been there three months ago. There was no boy left in James, she realized. He was hard and muscular, and he was a man.

"You haven't changed," he said as if reassuring himself that, indeed, she hadn't.

A quiet "You have."

He didn't deny it. "Maybe a little." He exerted pressure on her hand, pulling it closer still. With the tip of his finger he began to trace the pattern of pale blue veins just beneath the surface of her skin. His touch made her tingle from head to toe. She marveled at the fact. "One thing hasn't changed, Christine, and that's the way I feel about you. I love you as much as I ever did. More."

Her voice shook a little. "And I love you, James."

"I've missed you more than I ever thought possible," he declared, gripping her fingers so tightly she winced.

She found herself listening to him as if she craved every word he spoke. "It was no more than I missed you."

"I need to talk to you—"

He broke off. They both turned when they heard footsteps in the hallway outside the kitchen door. It was Hannah. She was wearing a plain, brown, lightweight jacket and there was another draped over her arm.

"Shall we go for that walk now?" she inquired.

"Of course," said James, who was already rising from his chair.

"Thank you, Hannah," murmured Christine as she was handed the extra jacket.

Once they were outside, James said to them, "I didn't know how much my hometown meant to me until I went away." He stopped on the bottom step and looked around at the prosperous farm. "Or how I would miss this place."

"With college and traveling and all, you've been away a great deal the past few years," Hannah pointed out.

"That's true, but it's not the same when you *can't* come home," he told her.

"We've never really been away from home, either one of us," Christine said. Then she added, letting out a sigh, "Except for the times when we visited our aunt and uncle in Richmond, and that's only thirty-five miles from here."

"Lots of folks don't go any farther than thirty-five miles from home in their whole lives. Not everybody's got the wanderlust like you, sister." Hannah seemed about to say more on the subject and then apparently changed her mind. Instead, "Why don't we skirt around the big barns and head along that path beside the sycamore trees? It should be reasonably dry."

With that, she took off across the farmyard, expecting James and Christine to follow her.

"Your sister reminds me of someone," James observed with a wry smile.

"Really? Who?" Christine asked guilelessly.

"My commanding officer," James answered as he fell into step beside her.

She suppressed the urge to laugh. "Hannah is the practical sort, that's all. She sees what has to be done and does it."

He didn't quibble with her logic. "Hannah likes to be the boss," he said, his tone bordering on exasperation. "Someday she will meet a man who'll set her back on her heels. Then we'll see who's in charge and who isn't."

Christine bit back a retort. It was true that her sister liked to have her own way about things. But she doubted if there was a man within a fifty-mile radius who was willing, or able, to take on Hannah Brick and her "ways."

They caught up with her on the outer side of the barnyard. The three of them walked abreast along the leaf-strewn path, James between the two sisters. Sometimes they talked; sometimes they simply enjoyed the beauty of the day and their surroundings. It was rare weather for this late in November and they were determined to appreciate it.

Later James remarked, "Neither of you has said anything about Charlie. How is he?"

The minute the words were out of his mouth, he undoubtedly wished he could have them back. Cheerful, lighthearted smiles became guarded, unhappy expressions on the faces of both young women.

"Charlie was very foolish to go running off as he did," Hannah said emphatically. "He never was a strong boy when it came to chores like choosing a chicken or a turkey from the flock for table. He even fainted once at the sight of his own blood. I don't know how he thought he could handle the job of dealing with wounded men."

James frowned and suggested thoughtfully, "I don't know if any man can be prepared for that kind of experience."

"I think Charlie is a hero," Christine blurted out, her hands gripped together till the knuckles were white. "He's doing what he believes he must in all good conscience, despite his own fears and misgivings. Isn't that what it means to be brave—to do what you fear most?"

Hannah opened her mouth as if to reply, but no words came. She turned her head away, but not before two huge tears appeared on her cheeks.

Christine quickly stepped around James and slipped an arm through her elder sister's. She patted Hannah's hand and looked up at James. "We're all worried about Charlie."

His dark eyes were sober. "I know you are. I am, too."

"It doesn't seem right somehow that he should be so far from home and conceivably in grave danger, while our lives go on much as they did before."

"It isn't right," Hannah murmured as softly as either of her companions had ever heard her speak.

Christine tried to keep the quiver out of her voice. "You are doing everything you can to help, sister. I've never seen anyone work as tirelessly as you have the past few months on behalf of the Red Cross and the war effort."

The elder Brick daughter expressed a rare moment of cynicism. "Knitting socks and scarves?"

Christine was suddenly the practical one. "It's a job that needs to be done and you're doing it. Our men can't go barefoot in the snow and ice this winter. Warm socks on their feet and woolen scarves around their faces will do more for the health and morale of our soldiers than anything the generals do."

James concurred. "She's right, you know."

Hannah studied the horizon. "I suppose so."

"I know so," he stated firmly. "The War Department has revealed that the startling sum of $156.30 is needed to provide each infantryman with the basic clothes, eating utensils and arms that he requires. We must have all the help from civilians that we can get. We must have the help of people like you, Hannah."

That seemed to settle the issue. They walked on, following a natural path through the trees and up one of several rolling hills. The sky was blue on blue, and the sun surprisingly warm at their backs. Their spirits began to rise again as they spoke of other things.

"Mama has said that I may go see the new Mary Pickford film next month with Louise," Christine spoke up.

James smiled. "Has she now?"

She nodded. "And I read in the newspaper that Charlie Chaplin is going to get a yearly contract for one million dollars. Can you imagine that?"

"No, I can't."

"If you two are going to talk about the moving pictures and such, I believe I will sit here for a while and read." Hannah plunked herself down on a tree stump and took a small book from the pocket of her jacket. "Why don't you go on a bit farther by yourselves?"

"All right." Christine gave Hannah's shoulder an affectionate squeeze before she and James continued on their way.

"I like your sister—" he reached out and laced his fingers through hers "—but I'm glad we're finally alone."

She smiled at him. "So am I."

He glanced up and spotted an old red barn just off the beaten path. "I recall an autumn day much like today— it must have been eight or nine years ago. We sneaked into one of your father's storage barns."

"I remember!" she exclaimed. "We grabbed handfuls of wheat and ate until we nearly burst."

His eyes shone. "The raw wheat tasted like nuts."

They looked meaningfully at each other.

"Come on!" urged James as he pulled her in the direction of the barn.

The door was standing ajar. They stepped inside. The air smelled faintly of horses and old leather, dusty cobwebs and sweet hay. A shaft of sunlight poured in from an opening in the roof above, giving a kind of yellowish hue to the barn and its contents. There was an old buggy with a broken wheel in one stall; the rest were empty. A rusty bucket had been discarded in a nearby corner, a cloth feed sack in another. An ancient harness and tackle hung from a threepenny nail pounded into the wall.

Christine walked about, kicking at the loose straw on the floor with the toe of her sensible walking shoe. "I don't think I've been inside this barn in years."

"From the looks of it, no one has," said James, as he surveyed their surroundings. His eyes lit up. "I love old barns like this one. At Camp Taylor whenever I was homesick, or tired, or cold, I would close my eyes and conjure up an image of your family's farm. I suppose it sounds a bit silly now, but I always felt better afterward. Maybe because those memories brought back a piece of my childhood."

She laughed for the sheer joy of it. "I could never understand why a boy from town would want to spend so much time on a farm."

James Warren shook his handsome head. "For a long time I didn't understand it myself. Then, one day, I realized that it wasn't the sight of the ocean stretching before me in an endless expanse of blue that made my heart beat faster. It wasn't the purple mountains' majesty, either. It was a field of golden grain as far as the eye could see that touched some part of me that must surely be the soul."

In a breathy whisper she said, "Why, that's beautiful, James. As beautiful as a poem."

Self-consciously he cleared his throat. He took a pressed handkerchief from his pocket and wiped his upper lip. "Boy, it's warm in here."

"Why don't you take your coat off?" she suggested shyly.

"I believe I will," he said.

A shaft of sunlight highlighted James's head and shoulders as he unbuckled his Sam Browne and slipped out of both the traditional officer's belt and his military tunic.

Christine found her eyes riveted to his masculine form. She was tempted to take the hankie from her own pocket and wipe the beads of perspiration from his brow: the brow of a soldier and a poet, she told herself. It pleasured her simply to watch the smooth play of his arm and chest muscles straining against the fabric of his shirt.

Her gaze moved lower. The khaki jodhpurs emphasized the well-formed length of his legs. The material clung to his flat, lean belly before flaring just above the hips. An overwhelming curiosity caught her up in its grip: how would James look without the remainder of his uniform? The forbidden thought sent a heated stain up her neck and spreading across her cheeks.

Christine looked up and found James watching her.

"You appear a mite warm yourself." It was impossible to tell whether or not he spoke ironically.

"I am. A little," she admitted.

"Would you like me to help you off with your jacket?"

She wet her lips with her tongue. "Yes, I would."

They were excruciatingly polite with each other as he did what any gentleman would and came to her assistance.

Dark eyes encountered hers. "Shall I hang it over the horse stall with my things?"

She was suddenly nervous; she couldn't have said why. "Yes, thank you."

James dispensed with her jacket and then came to stand directly in front of her, his fists thrust into his pockets. "You received my last letter?"

"I did."

His expression was utterly serious. "You may recall I said that I had something important to ask you."

Christine knew every word of every letter he'd ever written to her, but she had no intention of reminding James of that fact. She still had her feminine pride. "I seem to recall your mentioning something of the sort."

He took one hand from his pocket and drove it through his hair. "I would like to ask you that question now."

"If you wish." Her heart began to pick up speed.

All of a sudden the tension in the air was thick enough to cut with a knife. James took a shaky breath and blew it out. He reached for her hand. His skin was surprisingly cold and a little damp, she noticed.

He stared down into her eyes. "Christine Elizabeth Brick—" how solemn he sounded when he recited her entire name "—knowing that I love you as I could never love another woman, knowing that we were meant for each other from the time we were children, knowing that I cherish you above any other being on this earth, knowing all of this, will you consent to become my wife?"

The breath was knocked out of her. She suddenly found that she existed in a universe occupied only by her own heartbeat.

James seemed slightly stunned himself. When she failed to respond, he stammered, "S-surely my proposal of marriage doesn't come as a complete surprise to you."

Christine managed to shake her head. It didn't come as a *complete* surprise. She'd thought about James proposing to her, even dreamed of it once or twice. But thinking and dreaming about a proposal and actually having it happen weren't the same thing. Not at all, as she'd just discovered.

He went on, his words tumbling over each other in his nervous state. "I realize you're young, Christine—barely eighteen—and you're planning to attend college. I can wait."

"I don't know if *I* can," she finally said in a beautiful voice.

He reached out and brought her up against him. "Your parents are bound to have reservations about an engagement between their daughter and a soldier."

"They're bound to," she echoed.

He tightened his arms around her. "I will speak to them while I'm on leave. We won't make an official announcement until they give us their blessing."

She flung her head back and looked up at him. "I'd like that. But I will be yours, James Wilson Warren, with or without my parents' blessing."

He pulled her closer still. "Are you certain?"

"Yes, I'm certain," she said in a low, earnest voice. "I have loved you for as long as I can remember. I will go on loving you for this life and for whatever comes after."

"Christine, my dearest Christine..."

She could feel James threading his fingers through the mass of hair at her nape, using a fistful as a silken cord to bring her to him. There was no hesitation as their lips met in a kiss that bonded them together for all time.

He seemed embedded in her heart and her soul and her flesh. The smell, the feel, the taste of him were now a part of her as well. Where did he end and she begin? Christine was no longer sure.

James ended the kiss and took half a step back. "Will you come with me and be my love?"

She felt slightly demented. "Now?"

"Now."

"Where?"

"Up there." He indicated the loft above them. "I just want to hold you in my arms with the sweet-smelling hay beneath us."

She couldn't say no.

James started up the ladder first, turning back to give her his hand in assistance. They climbed to the top and stood there for a moment. In front of them the floor of the loft was covered with soft, fragrant hay. Without a word, he sat down and held out his arms to her.

Christine went to him. She curled up beside him and put her head on his shoulder. It was good to be there in his embrace. It felt right.

A few minutes later she blinked and thought to sit back. She was suddenly warm all over. It was as if the sun were hot on her skin. But there was no sun in this part of the barn. The heat was generated from the inside out. It poured forth from her, leaving her skin aglisten like early morning dew on the grass.

A strange little struggle seemed to be taking place within her, Christine realized. She wanted something—more. She wanted to bury her face against James's chest, to wrap her arms around his lean waist, to seek out his strength and make it her own.

But she sensed there was impending danger here, as well. The danger of allowing James to kiss her, to touch her, as she wanted to be kissed and touched. Once she had a taste of the excitement he could offer, she knew she would never be the same again.

She failed to heed her own warning. She turned toward him and murmured, "James . . ."

Long, strong fingers gently but firmly held her face up to his, covering the pulse at the base of her throat. His hand slid inside her collar to find the enticing warmth of a bare shoulder, the defined outline of a delicate bone. His touch was hot and slightly rough as it grazed the softness of her skin. She shivered in spite of herself.

"I would never do anything to hurt you," whispered James. "You must know that."

"I know that." Was that low, husky voice really hers?

He moved closer. She was aware of no sound, but the sound of her heart beating wildly against his hand. She saw nothing but his face before her eyes. His was the scent she smelled, the taste on her lips. Her eyes and hands and mouth seemed filled with him.

She clutched at his shirt. "James—"

"I love the way you smell, the way you feel," he groaned, his fingers encircling her throat.

She found herself responding to him beyond anything she had ever dreamed herself capable of. It shattered every silly schoolgirl notion she had of what passion was between a man and a woman. This was no polite, genteel, lukewarm emotion. This was a white-hot flame that threatened to burn out of control. This took over the mind and body and even the soul.

JAMES WATCHED INTENTLY AS Christine's hair fell across his arm like a golden cloud. There were a thousand secrets he would know, he told himself, beginning with the taste and the touch of that mouth of honey. He bent his head, his hand curling around her shoulder to urge her closer. It was good to feel her there in his arms.

She rained little kisses over his face and neck, kisses that teased and provoked, kisses that promised far more than they delivered. It nearly drove him to the brink of madness. Yet he knew that Christine was only vaguely aware of his physical reaction to her.

When he could stand it no longer James turned her gently in his arms. In one fluid motion she was stretched out on the floor of the loft. He eased himself down beside her. Her back was pressed into the warm hay. Her hands were trapped between her own quivering form and the unyielding hardness of his.

Christine gazed up into his face. He knew she couldn't be blind to the need that drove him, to the desire that burned brightly in his dark eyes. He had no wish to hide it from her. He was a man. He loved her. Sometimes a man's love for a woman took on a real and tangible form.

"Am I frightening you?" he whispered, burying his lips in her hair.

"No." She trembled. "A little." But she did not draw back from him nor try to stop him when he traced an imaginary line from her throat to the swell of her breast.

He thought of that long ago summer morn by the old swimming hole. He remembered it as if it were yesterday. From the bushes he had watched, transfixed, as Christine stepped into the clearing. She had been part girl, part woman. Her hair had fallen about her white shoulders like a mantle of finely spun silk. He had never seen anything so beautiful: even as a girl she had been slender, ethereal, high-breasted, perfect in every way.

She was even lovelier and more desirable now. But she was still very young, he reminded himself.

"James?" His name encompassed all the questions she could not articulate.

"I want you!" he muttered in a voice that was strangely hoarse even to his own ears.

"And I want you!" she cried out.

He knew she wasn't thinking clearly, if at all. Her eyes were soft and dreamy one minute, then glazed over with passion the next. He was the man and he was nearly five years older than Christine He must do the thinking for both of them. He must do what he knew was right.

But first he would hold her a moment longer. He would kiss her lips one more time. Then he would release her, put her away from him before it went too far, before it was too late.

She whimpered softly as he drew back from her. "Don't go. Don't leave me," she pleaded.

"I must." James tenderly engulfed her in his arms, his embrace a shield to protect her from the world, his kiss a promise of all that still awaited them. "One day," he vowed, getting to his feet and holding his hand out to her, "I will not leave you." He brushed at the bits and pieces of straw caught in her skirt. "We'd better start back. Hannah will be wondering where we are."

The color was riding high on her cheeks. She patted at her hair, all unbound and kissed by sun reflections as it lay in a tangle about her shoulders. "I must look a frightful mess."

"You are more lovely than I have ever seen you look," he told her feelingly.

They descended from the hayloft and retrieved his military tunic and Sam Browne belt from the empty horse stall. He helped her on with her jacket. When they stepped outside the barn they found the sun lower in the sky and the air cooler.

"I wish it could stay Indian summer forever," Christine said aloud.

His smile was indulgent. "For your sake, so do I."

A little sadly, "Winter is on its way."

There was resignation in his voice. "I'm afraid it's going to be a very long, cold winter."

They spoke little after that.

Hannah was sitting where they had left her an hour before. Or had it been two hours? Neither of them had any idea how long they'd tarried in the old barn.

The three of them began the walk back to the Brick family farmhouse. Once or twice, without a word, Hannah reached out and plucked a particle of hay from her sister's clothing.

Chapter Seven

A Soldier and a Dreamer

Minnie Mae DuBois was in dry goods, inspecting a new shipment of cotton corduroy, when she turned to the woman standing beside her. Lowering her voice to a theatrical whisper, she said, "I hear tell some girl from the country has gone and gotten herself engaged to James Warren."

Miss Julianna Scully, local spinster and sometime pianoforte teacher, was literally agog. She looked down her narrow, pinched nose at the other woman. "A gold digger, no doubt, seeing how James Warren's father is the wealthiest man in town."

Minnie DuBois decided against the corduroy and picked up a bolt of winter flannel. She ran the material through her hands. "They say she's uncommonly pretty."

A third voice chimed in. "That's true enough. She's one of the prettiest girls in Henry County. Maybe in the entire state of Indiana. But in-de-pen-dent. Stubborn's what some might call it. They say she takes after her great-grandma. Jamie Warren will have his hands full with that one, I'll tell you."

The two women twittered and drew nearer. One of them said to the newcomer, "You seem to know a great deal about it. Who is the lucky girl?"

Lily Huckelby drew herself up to a self-important height of five feet two inches. "Christine Brick's her name."

A collective "Ah—"

"That would be the elder of Ann and Benjamin Brick's girls, I take it," the first gossip speculated.

"No, indeed," Lily corrected her. "*That* would be Hannah Brick. She's the one who calls herself an old maid even though she's only two and twenty." She became momentarily flustered. "Begging your pardon, Miss Scully."

The pinched nose went a notch higher in the air, as if to say that one couldn't expect good manners from an orphan *and* a common factory worker.

Impatient to learn more, the first woman prompted, "Tell us about the girl who's become engaged to the Warren boy."

It was a rare opportunity for her to be the center of attention. Lily Huckelby decided to make the most of it. "Well, Christine is the younger Brick daughter. Only eighteen this past September. Hair the color of pure gold." She sighed and continued with her tale. "Why, I remember one day last summer when Jamie Warren came to call in his big, beautiful automobile. He and Miss Louise Warren were collecting their friends for a gala picnic down by No Name Creek." She tacked on self-importantly, "*I* made the lemonade and ice tea, myself."

A censorious eyebrow was raised. "An unchaperoned outing?"

"No, ma'am," the Huckelby girl snapped, afraid she had gone too far. "Mister Charles Jordan Brick was escorting his sisters and instructing them in the habits of the natural wildlife of the area." Lily's explanation sounded like a lesson she'd memorized out of her McGuffey's

Reader. "Charlie Brick is a member of the Henry County Historical Society," she added, as if that alone would vouch for his having a sterling character.

"Charlie Brick. Charlie Brick." Miss Julianna Scully said his name as if it had some significance for her. "Tall, homely boy, I believe."

"That's the one," Lily interjected.

"A fine young man," the spinster declared with an emphatic nod. "From all accounts he has quite a green thumb when it comes to growing prizewinning American Beauty roses."

Minnie DuBois put in her two cents' worth. "Isn't Charlie Brick the young Quaker man who volunteered overseas as an ambulance driver?"

"That's Charlie," Lily Huckelby confirmed. "Anyway, his younger sister is the girl who recently became engaged to James Warren."

"I see," said Miss Julianna Scully.

Apparently Minnie DuBois did, too. She shook her head from side to side and muttered something that sounded remarkably like tsk-tsk. "Mark my words, ladies. There will be trouble in paradise yet."

Hers was a captive audience. "Why do you say that?" Lily was dying to know.

"The girl is from an old Quaker family. The boy wears the uniform of an army officer." She shrugged her ample shoulders. "It simply will not do."

The sometime piano teacher concurred. "It would be like trying to mix oil and water."

"That's the kind of trouble that comes from not marrying your own kind," pronounced Minnie DuBois, as if her words were the gospel truth.

Lily Huckelby's hand flew to her mouth. "Speaking of the devil!"

"Watch your tongue, missy." She was warned.

Craning her neck to see around the girl, Miss Julianna Scully inquired, "What is it?"

Lily was frantic. "I didn't mean nothin' by talking about her. I swear it."

"You'll do no such thing in my presence," sniffed Minnie DuBois. "I'm a churchgoing woman, I am. And I don't cotton to swearing or cussing under any circumstances."

"Hush, Minnie Mae," urged her companion. "What is it, Lily?"

The Huckelby girl slowly raised her hand and pointed at the front window of the general store. "There she is comin' across the road now."

Both women followed the direction of her forefinger.

The word *who* formed on Minnie DuBois's lips.

But Miss Julianna Scully thought she knew *who*. She made an educated guess. "Is the pretty young woman coming this way the Brick girl?"

Lily's eyes grew round as saucers. "Yes'm, that's her all right. That's Christine Brick."

CHRISTINE WAS HUMMING SOFTLY under her breath; it wasn't a real song, just some aimless ditty she made up as she went along. She strolled across the road and headed for the front door of the general store. As she entered she heard the familiar jingle of the bell overhead.

"Good afternoon, Mr. Popplewell," she called out cheerfully to the proprietor.

"Howdy there, Christine," he said pleasantly. "What can I do for you today?"

"My mother sent me for a bottle of syrup of ipecac and a tin of powdered arrowroot," she informed him.

He ambled out from behind the counter. "Somebody sick at your house?"

"No, sir. We're all as healthy as a horse. But you know Mama. With winter coming on she likes to have her medicine chest well stocked."

He nodded and went off to take care of Ann Brick's order.

Out of the corner of her eye, Christine spotted Lily Huckelby conversing with two of the town's biggest busybodies. All three women turned their heads and stared at her. Then they made a beeline in her direction. She groaned softly under her breath, for there was no escape.

"Why I do declare, if it isn't Christine Brick."

She fixed a pleasant enough expression on her face. "Hello, Lily. How have you been?"

"Tolerable. Just tolerable. And you?"

"I'm fine, thank you."

Lily was obviously on her best behavior. "I believe you know Mrs. DuBois and Miss Julianna Scully."

She nodded her head in acknowledgment. "Hello, ladies."

"Miss Brick," said the first one.

The woman with the narrow, pinched nose simply nodded her head in return.

"We understand congratulations are in order," Minnie DuBois announced boldly.

It may not have been very neighborly, but at that moment Christine would like to have wrung Lily Huckelby's neck. It was awkward enough being the subject of local gossip without being accosted right there in the general store, as well.

Lily giggled. "It's so romantic to think of you being engaged to the handsome Mr. Warren."

One of the busybodies spoke up. "Have you two love-birds set a date for your wedding yet?"

Christine cautioned herself to patience. "No, we haven't. My intended is an officer in the military, as you may know. With the war and all, it's difficult to know when we will be married." She attempted to change the subject by inquiring after Goldie. "How is your elder sister getting along?"

Lily sighed heavily and admitted, "Goldie is mighty unhappy since her mister done gone and signed up for the army. Mighty unhappy."

Christine tried again. "How do you like working in the steel mill?"

The girl's lower lip protruded in a pout. "It's mighty hard work. Mighty hard."

Thankfully their conversation was interrupted by the store's proprietor calling out to Christine, "What size tin of powdered arrowroot do you think your mama needs?"

She inclined her head slightly and said, "If you will excuse me, ladies..."

"I only carry the one size of powdered arrowroot," old Mr. Popplewell confessed to her rather sheepishly. "But I couldn't stand by and watch as them three gossips ganged up on you. You looked fit to be tied, girl."

"I was." She smiled gratefully at the man. "Thank you for coming to my rescue. I'm much obliged."

He gave her a well-meaning wink. "It weren't nothing. Now, you sure you got everything your mama wants?"

"I'm sure. How much do I owe you?"

He told her and Christine paid him the exact amount out of her coin purse. She was about to leave the store when a trinket in the glass-topped display case caught her eye. She stopped to take a better look.

That was when it began.

Christine put a hand to her face. She was surprised to find that her skin was hot to the touch, and she was suddenly feeling a little faint. She wanted to tell someone, to warn them, but she couldn't seem to breathe. The room was closing in on her. Then her feet went out from under he and she was falling....

WAS SHE DREAMING AGAIN?

She could hear two, perhaps three, distinct voices nearby. They were talking.

One of them demanded to know, "What happened?"

"She's fainted."

"Do you have any smelling salts?"

"Back in potions and medicinals," answered a man she now recognized to be old Mr. Popplewell. He shuffled off, the floorboards creaking and groaning under his weight.

"I'll go fetch a cool cloth for the young lady's head," a woman kindly offered.

Christine tried to open her eyes and couldn't. She wanted to move her arms and legs, and found that she had no control over them. Then someone took her hand and held it gently. It was a man. She could tell from the size and strength of the fingers and the calluses on the palm.

She opened her eyes.

He was bending over her. At first she thought he was dressed in the drab brown uniform of an American doughboy. She looked a second time and realized she'd been mistaken. He wasn't a soldier. There was a band encircling his upper arm. She could make out the insignia: it was a red cross against a background of pristine white.

She blinked several times in quick succession. This time when she opened her eyes she saw that the color had drained from the man's face, and there was a bloodied bandage wrapped around his chest. He grimaced, obviously in great pain.

She whispered, "Is that you?"

There was no answer. He didn't seem to hear her.

Her voice grew frantic as she pleaded with him. "Is that you? Are you hurt?"

Still, no answer.

"Please, speak to me," she begged. "Is that you, Charlie?"

But her eyes would stay open no longer. No matter how hard she fought against it, they closed.

CHRISTINE SLOWLY OPENED her eyes and looked up into the familiar, beloved features of James Warren.

It was a moment or two before she managed to ask him, "What happened?"

"You fainted," he said, speaking softly.

"Fainted?"

"Yes. Dead away."

She took two deep, shuddering breaths. "I was having the strangest dream."

A flicker of genuine concern crossed his face. "I thought as much. You called out."

"What did I say?"

He hesitated.

She repeated, "Tell me, James. What did I say to you?"

He gave in and told her. "You asked me if I was hurt."

She knew there was more. "And—"

James sighed. "And then you called me by your brother's name."

"I remember now. I said, 'Please, speak to me. Is that you, Charlie?'"

"I believe those were your exact words."

She was puzzled. "Don't you find it all very strange?"

He continued pressing the cool cloth to her forehead. "Yes, as a matter of fact, I do."

Her brow creased in several places. "I wonder if I was having a hallucination."

He seemed evasive. "I don't know."

She looked up and saw the store's proprietor peering down at her anxiously. "I'm fine now, Mr. Popplewell. Don't you worry." She pushed the cloth aside and sat up slowly. "I just felt lightheaded for a minute, that's all."

"That's not all. You fainted," insisted James.

Old Mr. Popplewell chuckled, the sound rattling around in his chest. He addressed the younger man. "Always did have a contrary streak in her, Christine did, from the time she was a little girl. Why, she'd come in here with her pennies all tied up in a clean, white hankie, and if I didn't have the kind of candy or treat she wanted, she'd march out of here again without buyin' nothin'. Always did have a mind of her own, that one."

Christine sat up straighter and rested her head against the counter behind her. "That's telling tales out of school," she reminded the storekeeper.

"People always did say she took after her great-grandmother." He went on, warming to his subject. "Don't rightly remember Mrs. Elizabeth Banks myself— I was only knee-high to a grasshopper when she passed away—but she had a reputation for being one difficult female."

"Mr. Popplewell—" Her tone warned him he was skating on thin ice.

The old man glanced down at her and started to back away. "Guess I'll be about my business since you seem all right."

"I appreciate your concern." Christine took the damp cloth, folded it into a perfect square and handed it to James. "Thank goodness Lily Huckelby and her companions left before this happened."

He agreed. "Minnie Mae DuBois and Miss Julianna Scully are known to be two of the biggest gossips in town."

"The fact that I'd fainted would be all over New Castle by suppertime if they were still here." She gazed up at him, choosing her words carefully. "It was the oddest thing, though. While I was unconscious I thought I saw a soldier bending over me."

"That doesn't seem so odd. I was here and I'm dressed in uniform," James pointed out.

She frowned. "I don't think it was you." She gave herself a careful shake. "It's all so confusing."

"You've taken a nasty bump on the head. Under the circumstances, it's natural to be a little confused."

She went on, measuring out her words. "At first I didn't know who the man was in my dream. Then the face seemed to change, and it became Charlie's." Unknowingly she dug her fingernails into the tender flesh of his palm. "Only he was badly hurt—there was a bandage wrapped around his chest." She swallowed hard. "What do you suppose it meant?"

The oddest expression appeared on James Warren's face.

In a mere whisper she asked, "What is it?"

"I didn't just happen to come by the general store. I was sent here on purpose. Your parents asked me to fetch you home. There's been a telegram."

Christine felt her color drain away. "A telegram?" Then she knew. Dear God, somehow she knew. "It's Charlie, isn't it?"

James didn't want to be the one to tell her, she could see. "Yes, it's Charlie."

She made herself ask. "Is he—dead?"

"No, but he's been wounded. Apparently in the chest."

Christine was stunned. "Just like in my dream?"

In a husky baritone, he answered, "Yes, just like in your dream."

She heard her voice come out small but firm. "I want to go home now." She couldn't feel her lips. "Will you take me home?"

"Of course," he said, helping her to her feet. "My car is right outside."

She turned to the shopkeeper. "Thank you again for gathering up Mama's purchase, Mr. Popplewell."

"It wasn't no bother, Christine." He followed the young couple to the front steps of his store. "I'm real sorry to hear about Charlie." Distressed, he shook his head. "A fine young man, your brother. They don't come any finer."

THEY WOULDN'T let her sleep. Concussion, that's what they said they feared most with any kind of blow to the head. So she was forced to sit upright in her bed, a large mound of pillows at her back.

Mama fussed and fretted and insisted on making her a light supper of cream toast as if she were an invalid.

Papa sat with her and read aloud from the Scriptures until she very nearly did fall asleep.

Like clockwork Hannah appeared every hour with a cup of hot chamomile tea, or a dish of boiled custard, or a warm towel to refresh her hands and face.

James sat downstairs on an uncomfortable horsehair sofa in the front parlor until she took pity on him and sent word that she was quite herself again. He should go along home.

After a late afternoon house call from the local doctor, she was pronounced surprisingly fit and healthy despite her recent fall. She was finally allowed to sleep.

What Christine *didn't* tell her family was that as soon as she closed her eyes, the image of her brother, white-faced and grimacing with pain, returned to haunt her. It would do so for years.

The next morning, she arose from her bed, bathed and dressed as she did every morning. She was giving her hair its daily brushing—taking particular care to avoid the painful lump on the back of her skull—when a knock came at her bedroom door. It was Hannah bearing a cup of medicinal tea in one hand and a bottle of St.-John's-wort ointment in the other.

"St.-John's-wort is considered a most effectual remedy for bruises, according to Mama," her elder sister informed Christine. "You may need it, yet."

"You're all taking such excellent care of me. I almost feel guilty." She couldn't help but wonder if poor Charlie, so far away from home, was half as fortunate.

Hannah sat down on the straight-backed chair beside the bureau drawers. She folded her hands in her lap and cleared her throat. "James has told us about your dream."

She took a sip of tea. "I see."

Her sister was plainspoken, always had been. "You're not crazy, if that's what you're thinking."

A slightly bitter laugh shook Christine. "That's of small consolation to me."

There was genuine solicitude in the elder girl's voice. "As you know, I have read a number of journals and letters penned by our fellow Quakers. These sensitive, intelligent Friends have written down their dreams and premonitions—some joyful, some tragical. You are not alone, Christine.'' When there was no response from her listener, she went on. ''You have always had the gift of understanding how other people feel, and you have a tender heart. Is it any wonder, then, that you should dream of Charlie at a time like this?''

Christine stood at the bedroom window and gazed up at the small hillside cemetery. ''It's not a gift—it's a curse.''

''It is whatever you make of it.''

Her voice was reed-thin. ''You don't understand what it's like. You just don't know....''

''You're right, of course,'' Hannah said, biting her lip. ''I don't know what it's like.'' She stood, straightened her shoulders and walked to the door. With her hand on the brass knob, she paused and turned back. ''I do know one thing, however. There is a young man who loves you very much. A young man who has received his orders and will be shipped overseas in a matter of weeks. And he doesn't know how to tell you. Especially now that we've had this news about Charlie.''

Christine shot a quick sideways glance at her elder sister. ''James?''

''Yes, James.''

She tried to ignore the pounding in her head. ''When?''

''I understand his unit sails for England and then on to France after the New Year.''

''He didn't tell me.''

''Perhaps he thought it best to wait. He apparently found out himself only yesterday.''

''I see.'' And she did see. With all that had happened the previous afternoon, how could James have told her of his own distressing news? ''This is the last day of his leave," Christine said aloud. "Tomorrow he returns to Camp Taylor."

"You will have to say goodbye to him."

She suddenly felt chilled to the bone. "I will have to say goodbye."

"You must be brave for both your sakes."

For a moment she looked wildly around her. "How can I be brave when I'm trembling with fear?"

Hannah marched over to her and clasped her by the shoulders. "Only last week you told me what it was to be truly brave. Do you remember what you said?"

Tears stung Christine's eyes. "I don't want to remember."

"You must." There was an intractable expression on Hannah's face. "You said to be brave meant doing what you feared most."

She choked on a sob. "I can't. I don't know *how* to say goodbye to James."

For the first time Hannah seemed to be on the verge of losing her composure. "Bravely. Without tears. With your pretty head held high. As you did when he left for Camp Taylor this past September."

Christine clutched her sister's arm. "But this time I may never see him again."

Hannah's voice was very gentle. "I know."

It was almost her undoing.

The silence between them stretched into minutes. Christine put a hand to her burning face. Hannah was right. She would have to be brave for both her sake and James's. She had no choice. He was leaving for the war and she could not change that if she cried a million tears.

She thought of that summer morning—it seemed so long ago now—when her brother had stood in Meeting and spoken his favorite verses from Ecclesiastes: *To every thing there is a season, and a time to every purpose under the heaven . . . a time to weep, and a time to laugh . . .*

This was not a time of laughter, but it was also *not* a time for tears.

Christine Brick dried her eyes and put away her self-indulgent fears. She wasn't like Mrs. Warren or Louise: a woman to be coddled. James needed her to be brave. And so she would be brave. Once she set her mind to it, she could do anything. Nothing was going to keep her from it.

"I KNEW YOU WOULD BE MY own sweet, brave girl!" exclaimed James, once they were left alone in the front parlor of the Brick farmhouse.

"Perhaps it's more a matter of vanity than bravery," Christine said, striking a light note. "I wouldn't care for you to see me all ugly with red splotchy eyes and a runny nose."

"You would be beautiful even then," he declared.

She teased him. "Perhaps that's why they say that love is blind."

"Not today it isn't," he said, seeming to drink in the sight of her. "I don't think I've ever seen you look lovelier."

She had taken great pains to make sure that was true. She'd even added a touch of color to her cheeks by pinching them when Hannah had remarked that she was too pale.

It was no accident that she was wearing his favorite dress: a woolen in a clear shade of blue that he always claimed matched her eyes. Her hair was unbound and fell below her shoulders in a mass of soft curls.

But it wasn't vanity that had driven her to take such pains with her appearance. Everything she'd done was for

James. This was her gift to him, her gift of love: to have him leave and carry with him a perfect memory of her.

It did not matter that inside, her own heart was breaking.

He tried to continue their conversation. "Hannah tells me that the doctor came by after I left yesterday."

She gave him a reassuring smile. "He declared me to be as fit as a fiddle. Just a small bump on the head. No more."

"Thank God. You gave me quite a scare in the general store, I don't mind admitting it."

"I'm feeling fine," she began, not entirely truthful. "So you needn't worry on my account."

His eyes went a shade darker. "And I don't want you, my dear, to worry needlessly about me while I'm overseas."

She managed a fairly optimistic "I'll try not to."

"Keep busy and as happy as you can."

She went on with forced enthusiasm. "I'll not have a moment to spare between filling my hope chest with linens and tea towels and crocheted doilies, and helping out at Dr. Smith's clinic, not to mention the Liberty Bond teas and Hannah's Red Cross work."

Christine glanced down at her hands and found that they were still. How odd, she thought, when she was shaking so on the inside.

James laughed. "I hope you'll find time to write to me."

Her head came up. "Of course, I will."

His voice changed. "Your letters mean more to me than you will ever know."

She tightened her throat against crying. "I will write you every day, I promise."

"I will try to answer as often as I can."

She knew the time was near. "Take care of yourself," she said, forcing the words out of suffocated lungs.

"Let's have no long drawn-out goodbyes, my dear Christine, my own dearest love. Kiss me and send me on my way."

Her heart was beating painfully in her breast. Her eyes began to fill with scalding tears. She bit the inside of her cheeks until the tears stopped. Going up on her tiptoes, she pressed her mouth to his, inhaled his life's breath for a moment, took it greedily into her lungs, into her very soul.

"I will love you always," she whispered.

James kissed her, deeply, passionately. "And I, you." A muscle in his face started to twitch. He quickly released her, turned and walked away.

It seemed an eternity later that Christine heard the front door slam shut behind him and then the sound of an automobile engine start up. For one insane moment she considered running after him.

In the end, she didn't. She simply let him go.

She stood white and silent where James had left her. She was still standing there long after he had gone and the darkness had come.

Chapter Eight

Voices from the Past

Christine waved to Louise one last time and backed out of the driveway that ran alongside the Warrens' large, stately home. She steered the Maxwell Tourabout down the main street of New Castle and headed out of town.

Once she was in the open countryside, she noticed there was a light dusting of snow on the ground: pristine white on the dark, earth-turned fields. The cold of winter had begun its embrace of the land. Christine sighed and turned the car in the direction of home.

With both Charlie and James gone, and Thomas Ezekiel needed more than ever on the farm, Papa had been surprisingly agreeable when Christine had suggested to him that she be taught to drive the family automobile. After all—as she had pointed out to him at the time—she had her fund-raising and her volunteer work at the clinic, Hannah had her Red Cross duties, and there were always errands in town that Mama needed done. Someone had to do the driving and available men were in short supply.

Her father had taken her out on a back road that very afternoon and started her driving lessons. In the past several months she had become quite adept at handling the

Maxwell. If the truth were told, she was a better driver than any of the Brick men.

Christine turned down the dirt lane that led to their farm. Pulling into the small barn behind the house, she turned off the automobile, grabbed the tin of cookies from the seat next to her and opened the car door.

She clasped her coat around her to ward off the winter chill and made her way across the farmyard. A welcome blast of warm air greeted her as she raced up the back steps and into the farmhouse. Her mother was standing at the kitchen sink peeling potatoes for supper.

"Is that you, Christine?" she called out.

"Yes, Mama." She dropped a kiss on Ann Brick's cheek and set the tin on the counter. "Mrs. Warren sent some of Beulah's special sugar cookies home with me."

"That was mighty nice of Abigail," she said, without looking up from her task. "How did the Liberty Bond tea go this afternoon?"

Christine shrugged her coat off and hung it on a hook by the back door before answering. "The tea and the fund-raising went without a hitch, as they always do at the Warrens'. Louise and her mother are the perfect hostesses."

Her mother nodded and remarked, "Abigail Warren was brought up to be a fine lady. I imagine she's raised her daughter much the same way."

Christine was in complete agreement. "And she's succeeded. Louise is just like her. She always knows the right thing to say and when to say it."

Ann Brick laid her paring knife on the side of the sink and proceeded to fill the teakettle with water. "I'm sure they appreciate your contribution to a good cause."

"Perhaps. Although I don't see that I'm really much help to the Warrens. There's nothing I do that couldn't be done by any number of willing young women."

With that, Christine plunked herself down on a kitchen chair and picked up a skein of wool yarn and a pair of knitting needles. She was attempting to make a sweater for Charlie. So far she'd had to pull out her knits and purls several times and start from the beginning. At this rate the war would be over and done with before she was finished.

Her mother took cups and saucers down from the cupboard above her head. "Did Abigail mention anything about the Endicotts?"

Christine furrowed her brows. "Yes, I believe she did."

Ann Brick lifted the kettle off the back burner of the stove and poured the steaming water into the teapot on the kitchen counter. "The Endicotts are the family who were burned out of house and home Saturday night. They lost everything." She clicked her tongue. "They've got seven little ones, too."

Christine's head came up. "Seven children?" She'd only been half listening to her mother's chatter.

"Seven children under the age of ten. They're like stair steps, one right after the other," Ann Brick explained, then went back to peeling potatoes for their supper.

"I remember now. Mrs. Warren said she was sending Louise over tomorrow to collect any clothing and blankets we can spare."

"We'll need to get some things together yet this afternoon, then."

"I'll see to it, Mama," Christine spoke up, gladly putting aside the rather miserable attempt she was making to knit a pullover. "You have enough to do as it is with the Huckelby girls all gone. And Hannah won't be up and about again for at least a week since she's taken fresh cold.''

"It would be mighty good of you, Christine. I know how busy you've been with helping both the Warrens and Dr. Smith, and filling in for Hannah down at the Red Cross headquarters, but I understand from Abigail that several of the Endicott children are still young enough to be in diapers." After a moment she said, "You'll find some infants' clothes in a trunk in the attic."

It was never spoken of, but Christine knew the clothes were those of a premature girl, who had died the year after she was born. Sadly, there had been no more babies in the Brick household after that.

"Are you certain you want to give *those* clothes away?" she asked, a little stunned.

Ann Brick stiffened her back, and, apparently, her resolve. "They've been packed away long enough. Too long, in fact. It's high time someone got some use out of them."

"I'll see to it right away, Mama."

The woman dried her hands on the dish towel wrapped around her slender waist, then glanced at the clock on the wall. "It's time I was taking your sister her tea."

"Here's the gingerroot for the tickling in Hannah's throat," said Christine, as she placed it on the tray alongside the china teacup.

"It wouldn't hurt if you were to chew a little yourself," her mother admonished. "You're much too thin as it is. And I wouldn't want both of my girls to take cold."

Christine obediently took a small piece of gingerroot and began to nibble on it. "Is there anything you'd like me to help with before supper?"

A shake of her gray head. "Everything's done that can be done. You run along and see to the clothing for the

Endicotts. Oh, and there are two woolen blankets in the chest in the hall that we can spare," she said, thinking aloud. "And mind the dust and cobwebs when you go up into the attic. I can't think when it was last aired out, or even swept. If you don't take care, you'll get your clothes dirty."

"Don't worry, Mama. I'll change first." Christine glanced down at the blue wool she was wearing. "This is one of my best dresses." And James's favorite.

Ann Brick picked up the tea tray and made her way toward her elder daughter's sickroom. But not before she announced, "Supper's at half-past five."

"I'll be down in plenty of time to set the table," Christine assured her.

"Gracious, I nearly forgot to tell you, my dear," her mother called back over her shoulder. "You have a letter from James. It was sent all the way from England, too. You'll find it on the table in the front hallway."

Christine dashed into the hall and found the letter exactly where she was told it would be. She recognized the familiar scrawl on the front. Her heart was pounding by the time she reached her bedroom and tore open the envelope.

It was a single page and obviously written in a great hurry; some of the words were run together. The message was straightforward, however. James had arrived safely in England and would soon be making the Channel crossing to France aboard a troop ship. He was well. He sent his love to her and his fond regards to her family. And he missed her terribly.

Christine quickly read through the letter and then read it again at a more leisurely pace, savoring every word, clasping the solitary sheet of paper to her heart, knowing that James had held it in his hands just a week or two before. She would read the letter a dozen times before carefully stowing it in the special box she kept in the bottom bureau drawer.

There were times when she was so lonely for James that she wasn't certain she could bear another day without him in it. It was those times that she took his letters out and read them all through again. At least for a little while he seemed closer to her and not so far away.

Christine read the letter posted from England one last time before tucking it beneath her pillow. She would read every word again after she was in bed for the night. For that was often the time when she missed James the most.

Then she changed into an old skirt and blouse, and headed toward the attic.

The entrance to the attic was tucked away between two smaller bedrooms at the end of a hallway. Christine opened the door and climbed the flight of stairs to the third floor of the farmhouse. She stopped at the top of the steps and looked around.

The light of the afternoon sun was flooding into the cavernous room through a row of windows on the west end of the house. The sunlight gave a warm glow, a kind of golden patina, to the large, dusty attic and its contents.

She'd always thought there was something rather wonderful, even peaceful, about this little-used room filled with trunks and dressmaker forms, discarded furniture and stacks of books, empty picture frames and a favorite white wicker chair, now colored with age.

There was a child's rocking horse on one side of the attic, and wooden pants stretchers leaning up against an unfinished beam on the other. In between was an old oil lamp, a black Underwood typewriter, a rocker with several spindles missing, a pair of ice skates hanging from a hook pounded into a post, a hand-cranked ice-cream maker that was only brought down for very special occasions and a ladies' vanity with a large crack down the middle of the mirror.

Christine stood there and, with a critical eye, studied her reflection in the broken looking glass. Her hair was an unruly mass of blond curls that seemed to escape from their pins and combs in spite of her efforts. Her skirt and blouse hung on her body, shapeless. Her face was too thin. Her cheekbones were too prominent. Her neck was as scrawny as a chicken's. Maybe Mama was right. Maybe she *was* too slender.

"*Skinny* is the word for you, Christine Brick," she said out loud.

She took a step closer and peered at herself in the mirror. At least her complexion was good. She was a bit pale, perhaps, but this was February and even a country girl lost her color in the dead of winter.

Her eyes—they'd always been her best feature. They still were, she supposed. Large and wide, an unusual blue in color, fringed by long, light brown lashes: they were the first thing people noticed about her.

She stared at herself, brooding. A fine thing it was for a Quaker to be so vain about her appearance! What a woman was on the inside counted for far more than anything she might be on the outside.

She could still recall her grandmother's words on the subject: "The Friends have always striven for plainness in speech, in dress, in behavior. Plain is better than fancy, Christine. Thee would do well to remember that."

"I'm trying to remember, Grandmother," she whispered as she turned away from the mirror.

She inhaled a deep breath. The air in the attic was cold and slightly stale, yet there was a faint, familiar odor to it. She frowned. It was camphor. Mama insisted on using it to keep the moths and other infestations away from their stored belongings. She only hoped that the Endicotts were not among those who found the smell disagreeable. There would be no time to properly air the clothing and bedding Mama intended to donate to them.

As she walked by the spindleless rocker, Christine gave it a push with her hand and watched as it teetered back and forth on the uneven floorboards. She could still clearly recall the first time she'd sat in this chair and rocked and rocked for what seemed like hours....

She couldn't have been more than four or five years old. It had been a Sunday afternoon in early autumn, and it was raining cats and dogs outside. Her parents had unexpected company—a family from a neighboring farm. While the women and older girls were busy chatting in the parlor, the men had dashed out to the barn to see Papa's prize milk cows. Unobserved, she'd found her way up to the third-floor attic.

It had been silent except for the sound of the rain on the gabled roof overhead. In the gray light filtering in from the outside, the dusty room with its castoffs had seemed a land of enchantment. Climbing up into the chair, she had rocked back and forth, imagining herself to be a fairy princess and the attic her magic kingdom.

It still was. Indeed, it was one of the places she loved best in the whole world.

"Not that you've seen much of the world, Christine Brick!" she exclaimed with mild reproof. "Enough of your daydreaming and dillydallying. You were sent up here for a purpose. Now get to work."

With that self-administered scolding, she began to search for the large brown trunk filled with baby clothes. She found it shoved behind a chest of drawers at the far end of the attic. Going down on her haunches, she brushed the cobwebs aside, undid the leather straps and pushed the lid of the trunk open.

The pungent odor of camphor and mothballs assailed her senses as she laid aside a protective covering made of soft flannel. She nearly cried out at her first sight of the tiny clothes underneath. She gingerly removed the top garment: it was Quaker plain but each stitch was perfectly and lovingly sewn by hand. There were dresses and gowns, drooling bibs and knitted caps, a stack of crib blankets and several pairs of booties small enough to fit in the palm of her hand.

How painful it had to have been for Mama and Papa to lose their last child, she thought sadly. It must have broken their hearts. It would surely break her heart if she were to lose a baby, hers and James's.

Would she and James ever marry and have children now? There was no answer to that question, of course. The war had made everyone's future too uncertain. Only a few short months ago she had wondered what to do with her life. The greatest question facing her then was when to attend Earlham College and begin her studies as a teacher. Now she wondered if the man she loved was tired, or hungry, or chilled to the bone as he crouched in some filthy trench. For James's unit must surely have crossed the English Channel and joined the British and French troops along the Western Front.

Perhaps he was fighting for his life even as she thought of him.

"Dear God, please keep him safe," Christine quickly intoned, as a familiar and awful ache began deep within her.

It wasn't fair for her to be safe if James wasn't safe, as well. How could she eat if he was, perhaps, going hungry? How could she sleep at night in her warm, comfortable bed if he was lying awake somewhere a thousand miles away? How could she be warm if there was a chance that he was cold? How could she be safe if he were in grave danger?

It wasn't until she noticed a damp spot here and there on the tiny gown she was holding in her hands that Christine realized she had started to cry. She sniffed and brushed her tears away. Mama and Papa had no use for her tears now, and James...

It was better if she didn't dwell on the future. The future wasn't promised to any of them.

She spread the piece of flannel on the attic floor and went about the business of emptying the brown trunk of its contents. Once the job was finished, and the baby clothes bundled up and waiting at the top of the staircase, Christine took a moment to explore.

Only last spring she had discovered an even older trunk in a dark, dank corner of the attic, and had dragged it out under the natural daylight of the windows. Inside, carefully wrapped in tissue paper and placed in the bottom of a small cedar chest, she had found a sampler stitched with the name Elizabeth and the year 1812.

As she'd held the delicate needlework in her hands, a distinct feeling of happiness and contentment had crept over her. Somehow she'd known that the young Elizabeth had been happy and content when she had held the piece of fabric in *her* hands over one hundred years before.

That was also the day she had first discovered the diary.

Christine opened the battered old trunk now and removed the leather-bound book filled with her great-grandmother's handwriting. She loved the adventurous story of Elizabeth and her husband, Joshua, as they traveled from North Carolina to their new home in Indiana. It was a journey into another time and another place for her.

She sat down in the rocking chair, turned to a page she had marked with a piece of lace and read in Elizabeth Banks's neat hand:

April 19, 1821

On this day we did reach Cincinnati and meet up with a man named John James Audubon, who offered to paint my portrait and a miniature for the sum of two dollars. I thought it unseemly, but Joshua insisted. "Thee knows it would make me happy, Elizabeth. Thy portrait will be the first thing we place in our new home." To please my husband, I agreed.

April 24, 1821

Joshua is pleased with the portrait done by Mr. Audubon. He paid the Gentleman three dollars and we bid him "Adieu" this very morning, since it is time we traveled upriver. We hear the Land is rich in Indiana and we grow anxious to reach our new Home.

July 10, 1821

The wolves do howl so at night. 'Tis a lonely and haunting sound. They do not dare to come too near our cabin door, for the dogs raise a mighty ruction.

I often lie awake and think of all the dear souls we have left behind. I know it is written "whither thou goest, I will go." I have always honored my husband's wishes. But I do feel like a Stranger in a Strange Land. Will this Indiana wilderness ever seem like Home?

CHRISTINE LOOKED UP FROM the diary and gazed out the row of windows in front of her. From where she sat she could see the family cemetery atop the hill. Elizabeth and Joshua Banks were among those who were buried there.

She treasured the miniature of her great-grandmother, given to her by Mama and Papa on her eighteenth birthday. Just as she truly treasured knowing the story of how the miniature came into being. The journey from North Carolina to Indiana had been long and treacherous at times, but Elizabeth and Joshua had faced its dangers together.

As she continued rocking back and forth, Christine's attention returned to the diary open on her lap. She casually turned the page, and it was then she made an exciting discovery. For there, wrapped in muslin and preserved between the next two pages, was a daguerreotype of Mary and Elijah Long.

She studied the face of the young Quaker girl who had been her grandmother. A bittersweet longing, like some distant memory, stole over Christine. To her, Mary had been an old woman known only as Grandmother. Yet, here she was pictured as a young wife going west with a wagon train.

Christine carefully put the copperplate aside and examined a small bundle of letters that were with it. She unfolded the top piece of paper. It was written by Mary in the spring of 1849 and addressed to her mother, Elizabeth Banks. Mary and her young husband were temporarily at an encampment where the settlers gathered before heading west to Oregon and California. She had concluded her letter with:

> ...It has started to rain, Mama, and I have moved inside our wagon. The wind blows so fiercely that everything and everyone gets wet through and it takes days to dry out.
>
> We have had our portrait taken by a photographer here in St. Joe. I will send it to thee, along with this letter in the hope that it will give some measure of comfort. I look at the miniature thee gave me every night and I pray that God will keep thee safe.
>
> Thy loving daughter,
> Mary

Christine refolded the first letter and placed it back where she had found it. She wished that she'd known Mary Long when she had been a girl much like herself, and not the old woman she had, in time, become.

"Oh, Grandmother, if only you were here now. What tales you could tell me," she whispered.

Still, she was beginning to understand something about the previous generations of pioneer women, women like her grandmother and her great-grandmother. They lived and worked and sometimes even died alongside their men. They didn't send them off to face the dangerous unknown alone. It was another kind of danger than the current war, perhaps, but it was a danger that men and women had faced together.

Driven by curiosity and a strong sense of anticipation, she took the next letter from the stack and held it in her hands. This was her family's history, its legacy, passed from generation to generation, from mother to daughter.

Christine opened the single sheet of paper and read about the hardships encountered by young couples like Mary and Elijah Long, and the loneliness.

> ... We have been on the trail nearly six months now and even Elijah is weary of the journey. I am not saying the guidebooks lied, but they did not allow for the drenching rains, nor the flooded rivers. There was no mention of the horrible heat we would face during the day and the miserable cold at night, nor the thousands of mosquitoes that have nearly eaten us alive.
>
> We made eight miles today, passing seven new-made graves, nine dead cattle and four dead horses. I had to wash the dust out of my eyes so I could see to cook supper and roast coffee. Now I have come into the wagon to write this letter and make our bed.
>
> I feel lonesome tonight, Mama. Sometimes I cannot bear the thought of never again seeing the blue mist on a summer's eve as it drifts across our happy valley. Oh how my heart yearns for the sight of thee....

"...THE BLUE MIST ON A summer's eve as it drifts across our happy valley." Christine read the words aloud to herself. They were words that had always had a special meaning for her, never knowing, never dreaming, of what they had meant for a young Mary Long. It seemed she was more like her grandmother than she had realized.

Growing impatient to learn more of Mary's story, she tore into the next letter and the next, learning of her grandmother's fear for their safety when so many good and innocent people began the journey and never saw its end. For death and disease were a part of daily life for pioneer women, yet until this moment Christine had never truly understood the painful losses women of that time had had to endure.

The first flush of Mary Long's girlhood was gone. Her hopes for the "promised land," and the people in it, had been shattered by month after month on the trail. She had watched her husband grow thin and pale and lose his dreams. It was a harsh existence. An existence in which youth and innocence were soon sacrificed to the reality of survival.

Christine sat up straighter in the rocking chair. Perhaps it was time she gave up her own romantic notions concerning the world. Her safe, secure existence was as much in jeopardy as her grandmother's had been. For the man she loved was not only in danger of losing his dreams, but his very life.

Yet she knew that adversity made some men and women strong. Through the letters, now yellowed with age, she had come to admire and love the strength, the courage, the character, of the woman she had called Grandmother.

Christine unfolded the last letter and read:

January 17, 1850

Dear Mama,
I have not had the heart to put pen to paper these past few weeks. I do not know if I can find the words to tell thee even now.

I wish I were a little girl again so I could climb up on thy lap and have thee hold me close and croon soothing words in my ear in thy own sweet voice.

I was just a babe when Papa and sister Louise died in the cholera epidemic that spread through New

Castle back in '33. Truth to tell I don't even remember what Papa looked like or the sound of his voice. But I always loved listening to thy stories about when he was a boy and lived down the road from thee in Carolina. Papa going fishing with thy brother. Papa and his dog. The first time Papa spoke out at Meeting on First Day morning. The journey Papa and thee made to thy new home in Indiana. They were thy memories, but they became mine, too.

O Mama, I feel old. And I despair that I have no child of my own to share my memories of Elijah with.

It seems I must finally tell thee. Elijah died the third of January. He came down with cholera in the morning and we buried him by the side of the road later that same afternoon. I did not like leaving him there under a pile of rocks and snow in that desolate, godforsaken place, but I had no choice. Sometimes I still cannot believe that I will see him no more in this life.

A family named Sutter have been most kind to me. I have not felt well enough to drive the team so their eldest son, John, has taken over the reins. I plan to go on to the settlement on the other side of the mountains. I will wait there for the next group going East.

I'm coming home, Mama. I will be home in the spring!

> Thy loving daughter,
> Mary

CHRISTINE WEPT. SHE WEPT for Mary and Elijah, for Elizabeth, for James and for herself.

What if James should die far from home and be buried beneath the rocks and soil of some distant land? Like Mary, she would have no child of her own to share her memories of him with. She could not bear the thought that she might never see James again. She had to! God could not be so cruel as to separate them now!

It was some time before Christine dried her eyes and placed the letters and the diary back in the old trunk. She took some comfort in knowing the rest of Grandmother's story. For Mary Long had, indeed, returned to Indiana and to her beloved mother with the next group of settlers and 'forty-niners' traveling east. One day John Sutter had journeyed back to the heartland, claimed her for his bride and settled in Henry County. Mary's story had had a happy ending. She wasn't so sure if her own would.

One thing was for certain, Christine realized. She was going to make some drastic changes in her life. For months she had been filling her days with volunteer work and fund-raising teas, knitting and housework. She had told herself that she was doing her part in the great challenge facing her country and the world. But now she knew that while it was something, it was *not* enough.

Her grandmother and great-grandmother had not stayed behind while their men faced the dangers of the unknown. They had been right there beside their husbands.

She had sent James off with tears in her eyes and fear for him in her heart, but she had not been willing to truly face the dangers of war alongside him.

Another of Grandmother's favorite sayings echoed in her ears: "Whenever thee does not have the answer, my dear Christine, look within thyself, and thee shall find it."

Christine looked within herself and she saw what she must do. The time had come for her to take action. Tomorrow she intended to visit the Red Cross office in town and put in a request for overseas duty. Then, once her application had been accepted and she was on her way to France, she would write and tell James.

As she left the attic that afternoon, Christine knew she had her answer at last. The war could no longer be kept at arm's length. For her, the war had, indeed, come home.

JAMES RIPPED OPEN the envelope and eagerly ran his eyes over the letter from Christine; the first to arrive in nearly two weeks. Mail delivery to the little town in France where he was billeted had been sporadic at best.

He read the letter all the way through once and then a second time before softly swearing under his breath, "What in the bloody hell can she be thinking of?"

Robert Hershel Cooper glanced up from the week-old Paris newspaper in his lap and grinned at the man sitting across from him. "I take it you've finally heard from your dear Christine."

James sprang to his feet and began to pace the floor in front of the tiny inn's only fireplace. "You're never going to believe what she's gone and done."

An amused brow was arched in his direction. "I wouldn't be so sure about that, James. From what you've told me about your intended, I would believe almost anything."

James went on as if he hadn't heard the other officer. He held the letter in front of him and occasionally quoted directly from its pages. "Christine decided that staying home and doing volunteer work in New Castle wasn't enough. So she put in an application with the Red Cross for overseas duty. Lo and behold, it seems that she has been accepted. She sets sail for England next month and from there will be assigned to a location somewhere right here in France."

"Good Lord!" exclaimed Coop.

"Exactly." James repeated the sentiment. "Good Lord!"

"What a brave young woman your Christine must be," declared his companion.

An agitated hand was driven through his short-cropped hair. "I've got to write her immediately, Coop, and tell her not to come."

Lieutenant Robert Cooper stood and rummaged around in his pocket for the pouch of tobacco he always carried with him. He methodically filled his pipe, held a match to the bowl and puffed on it several times before replying, "Isn't it a little late for that?"

"Christine doesn't understand what she's letting herself in for," James said insistently.

"Maybe not. But I don't see how you can stop her."

"I've got to," he claimed in a hard, dry voice. "I can't let her do this."

"It would appear that she's already done it," his friend remarked.

James threw him a withering glance. "Dammit, Coop, I've got enough to worry about without having Christine here in France. She'll be too close to the war."

A thoughtful "I know."

"Why didn't she give me some warning of what she intended to do? Maybe I could have stopped her if I'd known," agonized James.

Apparently the other man felt compelled to point out, "Did she have any advance warning when you joined the army?"

His face suddenly went hard. "That was different."

Coop eyed him. "Why? Because you're a man?"

"Yes, because I'm a man and I can take care of myself."

"Doesn't Christine worry about you, anyway?"

"Of course, she worries about me," James said, on the verge of losing his patience.

"But you don't want to have to worry about her. Is that it?" After a moment the man went on, "If someone had written to you and said don't enlist in the army, don't come to France, would you have listened to them?"

There was a tense moment between the two young officers before James expelled a breath and admitted, "Christine always did have a mind of her own."

Coop added with a flash of perception, "Would you really want her to be any other way?"

He shook his head and said quietly, "No."

"Maybe she's only doing what she sees as her patriotic duty."

Remembering a conversation he'd once had with her on the subject of Quakers and patriotism, James cleared his throat awkwardly and said, "If Christine has decided it's her patriotic duty, believe me, nothing will keep her from it."

Coop puffed on his pipe for a minute, then ventured, "I guess you won't be writing that letter telling her not to come."

James shrugged his shoulders. "How can I?" He glanced down at the letter still clasped in his hand. "She says that this way she'll be able to see her brother in London before making the trip across the Channel. Under the circumstances, I could hardly begrudge her—or Charlie—a reunion."

"Maybe you'll have your own reunion with Christine," Coop suggested.

James grew thoughtful as he stood and stared into the glowing embers of the fire. "Maybe I will if I'm very lucky. If I'm very lucky, indeed."

Chapter Nine

A Brother and Sister Are Reunited

"Charles came to us in February of this year, 1918," the matron said in a crisp, no-nonsense British accent. "His medical records indicate that he was first treated in a field facility somewhere near Passchendaele and later transferred to a *hôpital* in Paris."

"Passchendaele?" The word was awkward and foreign on Christine's tongue, as so many words were these days.

One stern eyebrow arched into an inverted V. "The Third Battle of Ypres. The men here usually call it Passchendaele, for a small village in the region." The head nursing sister seemed disapproving of her visitor's ignorance. "Haven't you heard of the killing fields of Passchendaele on your side of the Atlantic, Miss Brick?"

"Yes, of course. The Third Battle of Ypres. It was last summer and autumn. The weather was awful from the start." Christine felt like a schoolgirl reciting her lessons. "A great number of men died."

"We British lost more than a quarter of a million men." The matron's face went painfully blank. Her hands were clasped together on the desk in front of her; her knuckles were quite white. "Many of them had been badly wounded, but they managed to crawl into shell holes for safety. There, they slowly drowned in the mud and the rain, and there was no one to help them.''

Christine was thankful she was sitting down. Her legs were wobbly enough as it was after the long voyage across the Atlantic, not to mention the train trip from Glasgow. She'd only been in London since yesterday, and she was still trying to recover her "land legs."

Not knowing what she was supposed to say to the matron, she tried a simple "I'm sorry."

The glazed-over eyes cleared and focused on her once again. "I beg your pardon..."

"I said I was sorry."

A succinct "I don't understand."

She swallowed and tried not to appear a fool. "While you were speaking of Passchendaele, I had the impression that you'd lost someone there who was dear to you."

The Englishwoman looked at Christine with a steady gaze. "As a matter of fact, I did. My younger brother, who was also named Charles. He was nineteen at the time."

Christine forced herself to speak. "I am so sorry."

The woman waved the expression of sympathy aside with her hand, and even attempted a tentative smile. "Our Charles was a bit like your Charles, actually. A gentle boy without a mean bone in him. We were all very proud of him. He was at university. He loved gardening—he grew roses.''

"So does my brother." She felt a stab of anguish. "At least, he did."

The matron's voice softened momentarily. "Charles has told me something of this 'Rose City' of yours. I believe it is situated somewhere in the middle of the United States, isn't it? He makes his hometown sound like the Garden of Eden when he speaks of it." She cleared her throat and resumed reading the official records lying open on the desk. "As to your brother's physical condition—" she shuffled the papers in front of her "—he received a bullet wound to the chest from nearly point-blank range. The bullet punctured the lung, just missing the heart" She glanced up. "That was most fortunate, of course."

Christine paled, but agreed. "Of course."

"Unfortunately, the lung became infected and lobar pneumonia set in, as well as several subsequent medical complications."

She tried to steel herself for whatever might come next. "Exactly what does it mean for Charlie?"

The matron closed the folder and rose from the straight-backed chair behind her desk. She stood with her back to Christine, gazing out the window at the stretch of green lawn beyond. "It means that he will need to remain here for another month or two until he is ambulatory and able to withstand the sea voyage home."

"And then—"

"Even then he will need to take care not to become tired, or overexert himself." She turned and studied Christine's face for a minute before continuing. "Your brother may never be the same man he was before, Miss Brick."

Fear was a sudden throb in her throat. "But he is out of immediate danger."

An understanding "Yes, he is out of danger."

She heaved a sigh of relief. "Does Charlie know I'm here in London?"

The Englishwoman nodded. "He received your letter a fortnight ago. He's been counting the days until your arrival."

Christine's heart began to pick up speed. "When may I see him?"

"I'll take you along to the ward now if you think you're ready."

Christine struggled to keep her excitement under control. "I'm ready."

They were barely outside in the hallway when the matron issued a warning. "I hope you're not the silly sort of girl who grows faint at the sight of blood, or a man missing an arm or a leg."

She stiffened. "I have done some volunteer nursing back home. I will do my best."

A dissmissive "Let's both hope that your best is good enough, then."

God grant her the strength to see it through, Christine prayed as they walked at a brisk clip down first one gray corridor and then another, their heels clicking on the marble floor of what had once been a rather elite private sanatorium.

The matron struck up a conversation. "Your brother tells me that you've volunteered for Red Cross work."

"Yes. I'll be sailing for France by the end of next week. I've been assigned to canteen service in Paris."

"Cooking and washing up, no doubt."

"No doubt."

The matron opened a double-wide door that was beveled glass on the top half and carved wood on the bottom. As they proceeded through the room filled with beds and discreetly drawn privacy curtains, Christine couldn't help but notice the smell of disinfectant was strong in her nostrils.

"I understand that your young man is a soldier on the Western Front," said the matron.

"He's a lieutenant in the American army."

"I hope you didn't come all this way on the odd chance that you might see him," the woman said without warmth.

Christine felt the color rise sharply in her face. It wasn't the first time she'd heard that particular admonition, of course. It was one of the first things her parents had said to her after she'd told them of her plans to work for the Red Cross overseas. Indeed, she had heard it a hundred times from family and friends before it was all said and done, and her ship had set sail for Europe.

She gritted her teeth and informed the woman beside her, "I volunteered because I wanted to do some small part to help."

The matron sniffed. "Indeed. Well, we shall see, shan't we?"

With an insight that sometimes caught people off guard, she remarked to the woman as kindly as she knew how, "Did you lose your young man in the war?"

The minute the words were out of her mouth Christine very nearly regretted saying them. Her brief acquaintance with the English had made it apparent that they were a bit more reserved than their outspoken and plainspoken American cousins. The woman's face crumpled for an instant, but she recovered almost immediately.

Christine quickly added, "I shouldn't have asked that question. I'm afraid I always seem to be sticking my nose in where it had no business being."

"I don't mind. Not really. And you're right. I did lose my young man in the war. He went to France in August 1915 with the Grenadier Guards, and was killed at the Battle of Somme just over a year later." In a faraway voice she said, "So many were lost at Somme that September, you know. So many. This bloody war has taken a whole generation of young men."

"'. . . and they shall beat their swords into plowshares, and the spears into pruning hooks: nation shall not lift up sword against nation, neither shall they learn war anymore.'"

Christine was startled when the woman laughed softly in response to her recitation.

"Now I know for certain that you're Charles Brick's sister. He's always quoting from the Bible or that volume of poetry he carries around with him."

"That was one of Charlie's favorite verses from the book of Isaiah."

The matron stopped and turned to her. "We're nearly there now. I want to warn you that your brother has lost a great deal of weight and he may not seem to you as he was before."

Christine caught her bottom lip between her teeth. She'd promised herself that she wouldn't cry, that she would have a smile on her face when she saw Charlie again for the first time in nearly eight months. No matter what.

She straightened her back. "I'm ready," she said with all the determination she could muster.

The woman gave her arm an encouraging squeeze. "Good. I know you can do it." With that, she pushed open the door and they walked into the ward.

White. Everywhere Christine looked she saw white. The walls where white, the floors and ceiling, the sheets and the blankets on the beds, the privacy curtains—some open, some closed—the pajamas and robes worn by the patients, the starched uniforms of the sisters. Everything was white.

Bits and pieces of color began to intrude: a man's blond curls against a pillow, a sister's dark hair tucked under her cap, a bunch of yellow posies in a vase on a bedside table, a splash of blue sky through a window, and at the far end of the room—a solitary man sitting in a wheelchair.

She knew at a glance it was Charlie.

"I'll just go ahead and prepare him," said the matron.

Christine slowed her steps, but she never took her eyes from the frail figure sitting there in a spot of sunlight, his back to her. The matron approached and spoke quietly to the man. Then she turned the wheelchair around.

Christine summoned all of her courage. It was the longest walk of her life, she remarked later: the walk she took that day in a London hospital, from the door to the end of the ward where her brother waited for her.

She wanted to run to him and throw her arms around his thin shoulders. But she didn't. She proceeded at a deliberate pace, her eyes straight ahead, a smile pasted on her mouth.

As she came nearer she could see that Charlie was painfully thin and his skin had a gray, unhealthy tinge to it. His eyes were huge and hollow; the flesh was pulled taut across his cheekbones. He had never been a muscular, athletic sort of man, but now he was literally skin and bones. It broke her heart to see him that way.

Then he smiled at her, and it was the smile of an angel.

She began to walk a little faster. She was beside him now. She bent down and pressed her face gently to his and whispered, "Oh, Charlie—"

"Christine—"

It was all either of them could manage before the threat of tears choked off any further attempt at conversation.

After the emotionally charged moment passed, the matron suggested, "Why don't you two go out onto the sun porch? That way you'll have a little privacy for your reunion."

Christine took hold of Charlie's wheelchair and pushed it through the open French-style doors and into the solarium beyond. Once they were alone, she pulled a visitor's chair up alongside his and reached for his hand.

For a few minutes, they simply sat there, holding hands and looking out at the expanse of green lawn and tall trees. The surroundings were pleasant and the day was exceptionally fine for the second week of May.

He turned to her. His eyes were shining. "You're here at last."

"I'm here at last," she echoed, close to tears again. "I can't tell you how good it is to see you."

"You're a sight for sore eyes, yourself," said Charlie, his voice barely more than a whisper.

"The matron said you got my letter."

"Two weeks ago yesterday," he told her.

"And the lap robe from Hannah, I see."

A slightly shaky hand stroked the patchwork blanket covering his legs and feet. Then, apologetic, he said, "I'm afraid the sweater you made for me got misplaced somewhere along the way. I'm sorry to have to tell you that, Christine. I know how much work you must have put into knitting it."

"It doesn't matter," she said, struggling to keep her voice even. "I can always make you another one." At the look of consternation that appeared on his face, she amended, "Perhaps it would be better if I didn't."

"I liked the sweater because you made it for me," Charlie said in a perfectly serious tone.

"I never was any good with knitting needles or a crochet hook."

"Or a needle and thread."

"Or an embroidery hoop."

He laughed and Christine joined in. It was the first sign of the old Charlie she'd seen and it made her heart glad.

Later she told him, "Mama and Papa send their love. Hannah and Thomas Ezekiel, too, of course. Everybody in town has been asking after you, wondering how you're faring."

He patted her hand. "I received a box of sweets in the post from Louise Warren. It was real thoughtful of her." Under his breath, "If I eat all of my dinner the matron allows me a piece of candy each evening as a treat."

That, more than anything else she'd seen or heard that afternoon, made Christine want to weep. She had to turn her head away for a moment while she regained her composure. Charles Jordan Brick, a full-grown man of twenty-six, having sweets doled out to him as if he were a child.

He dug into the pocket of his pajamas and brought out what appeared to be a picture postcard. "I heard from James on Monday. Shall I read it to you?"

An unsteady "Yes."

"He writes, 'Dear Charlie, I hope this finds you in good spirits and improving health. Coop and I got leave and went to Paris last week for a bath and a good meal. We had delicious omelets and coffee at a little café near the Place de la Concorde. You will no doubt be seeing our own dear Christine soon. I envy you that. My love to you both. James.'"

He handed the postcard to her and allowed her to read it a second and third time for herself.

"I haven't heard from James in nearly a month," she said, hungry for any news of him. "There hadn't been an address to post my mail to since I left home. There won't be until I get settled in Paris. Of course, I've been writing to him all along."

"You've no idea what mail from home means to a man when he's away from his loved ones. I've lived for your letters. I'm sure James does, too."

She felt her face flush. "I've written him dozens and dozens of times since he left for Camp Taylor last summer. All of my pocket money is spent on postage."

"James is a lucky man."

She swallowed. "I'm a lucky woman."

"I always thought the two of you were meant for each other. I was in hospital in Paris when I got the news you were engaged. One of the Sisters of Mercy read me your letter right away—she knew it would cheer me up."

A solid lump formed in her throat. Poor Charlie, so far from home and alone as he had been.

He suddenly seemed eager to talk. "What are you doing here, Christine?"

She knew what he was asking. Perhaps of all the people who might ask that question Charlie would best understand her answer.

"I wanted to feel like I was doing something worthwhile," she began. "You were out in France driving ambulances—until you were hurt, of course. James was serving in the army. Hannah was knitting woolens and collecting clothing for our soldiers. Even Louise and Mrs. Warren were holding successful fund-raisers for Liberty Bonds. I seemed to be the only one who was at a loss to know what to contribute."

"What made you decide to volunteer for overseas work?"

"I don't know if I can explain how it happened."

He squeezed her hand. "Why don't you try?"

She smiled uncertainly. "It was one day last winter. I had gone into the attic to get some things Mama was intent on donating to a needy family. While I was up there I started to read more of Elizabeth Banks's diary."

His interest was captured. He sat forward a little. "You and Great-Grandma's diary again."

"But this time I discovered a packet of letters written by her daughter, Mary, on the journey west in 1849." Unbeknownst to Christine, her voice grew stronger and was filled with conviction. "Through her letters I saw our grandmother as a courageous young woman, Charlie. I realized that men and women faced the same dangers in those days because they rode, or walked, side by side into the unknown. It truly meant something when a wife vowed to stay with her husband through the good times and the bad."

"Times have changed, little sister."

"Not so very much, I believe. How could I possibly stay home safe and warm in winter, well-fed and with my family around me while thousands of young men like you and James were giving up everything, even risking your lives, for the rest of us?"

He patted her cheek affectionately. "You always did have a different way of looking at things."

"I simply decided if I was going to call myself a woman, then it was time I acted like one."

"So you volunteered for overseas duty." He shook his head bemusedly. "You always were a determined little soul. Once you made up your mind nobody could get you to change it. Not even Mama or Papa."

"Truth to tell, Mama and Papa were disapproving in the beginning. I think they were afraid for me, as they had been for you. But I explained to them that I was grown up now. I made my own decisions. In the end, they came to respect that. To everyone's surprise I was accepted by the

Red Cross. Even my request to be sent to France was approved.''

He was silent for a moment. Then, ''That was a very brave thing to do.''

''No, dear brother, what you did was brave. All I've done so far is manage not to get seasick.''

''Dear, dear Christine—'' Charlie laughed heartily.

His laugh quickly turned to a hacking cough, and for an instant she was genuinely concerned for him.

''Matron will have my head if I make you ill,'' she said, not altogether exaggerating. ''It's time you rested.''

He didn't argue with her, but clutched her hand and said, ''Promise you'll come back tomorrow.''

''I promise to come back tomorrow and the day after tomorrow and every day until I sail for France.''

That seemed to satisfy him. Charlie allowed her to wheel his chair back inside. He was already nodding off for his afternoon nap when she left the ward.

ItT WAS ON HER THIRD VISIT—they were having tea, and special cakes she'd brought from a little shop around the corner—when the subject of how Charlie came to be shot was finally broached. He came right out and said that he wanted to tell her the whole story, or as much of it as he remembered, anyway.

''I thought volunteer ambulance drivers were kept well back from the front lines,'' said Christine, as they sat together in the solarium, a prettily arranged tea table between them.

''We were,'' Charlie said as he stuffed another cake into his mouth. ''It wasn't the Boche that got me.''

Her teacup stopped in midair. ''The Boche?''

"That's one of the names the British soldiers use for the Germans." Under his breath, "One of the least offensive names, at that."

"I see." Although she wasn't at all sure that she did. "If it wasn't the enemy who shot you, who did?"

Charlie polished off another cake with genuine relish, and casually said, "It was one of our own boys."

Christine was stunned. "I—I don't understand."

He shrugged. "It was the hell of Passchendaele."

"Yes, the matron was telling me about Passchendaele on my first visit here at the hospital."

"The Allied Powers knew the enemy defenses were formidable. The Germans even had specially constructed 'pillboxes.'" She was confused by the terminology. Charlie tried to explain it to her. "A pillbox is a low concrete bunker that houses machine guns and howitzers. Nothing can destroy one except a direct hit by a large-caliber shell."

She shuddered. "How awful."

Charlie continued with his account, his voice low and earnest. "Anyway, the casualties on both sides had been mounting since the battle began on the last day of July. By the time the offensive was called off in November, the number of dead and wounded was astronomical."

"The matron told me that the British alone lost several hundred thousand men."

His voice dropped to a whisper. "It was mass carnage."

Christine saw her brother shiver and she understood why. She, too, found it inconceivable to believe that man was capable of raining such horror on his fellow man.

He went on. "Most of the men who survived were suffering from shell shock and exhaustion. They were close to the breaking point."

Her heart gave a leap. She could guess what Charlie was going to say next. But it was his story to tell, and so she sat quietly and sipped her tea and listened.

She studied his profile as he sat in the wheelchair beside her, staring out the window of the sun porch. "The survivors had seen things no man should ever have to witness. Some of them were half-crazy from it. When they retreated as far back as our ambulance unit we tried to help those who were wounded." He finally turned and looked at her. "One young officer in particular had seen his company of ninety men nearly wiped out. There were less than fifteen of them left alive when the smoke cleared. The others had been killed in the bloodbath and the steady curtains of shell fire."

There was nothing for her to say. She reached out and slipped her arm through Charlie's.

"All of a sudden the young officer brandished his revolver and ordered us to stay away from his men, although some of them were hurt and needed medical attention. We could only think that we imagined us to be the enemy. We tried to talk to him. He wouldn't listen. Or couldn't, was more like it. He fired a shot into the air above our heads, then pointed the revolver directly at us."

"Dear God—"

"I knew then he intended to start shooting. There was a wild kind of look in his eyes that I can't describe even now. I'll never forget it. The poor devil was obviously out of his head. I started toward him, talking in a soothing voice, telling him that we were American and British ambulance drivers who only wanted to help him and his men. I knew it didn't matter what I said as long as I held his attention long enough to get the weapon away from him." Charlie stared into space for a moment and then frowned.

"I almost managed it, too." He sighed and came back to her. "I was only a few feet from him when he shot me."

Christine found she could not speak. She went down on her knees beside Charlie's wheelchair, and rested her cheek on the wooden arm. Then the tears came, hot and heavy.

Her brother reached out and stroked her hair. "You mustn't cry, gentle heart. I'd do it all over again if I had to."

A muffled "I know you would."

He tried to cheer her up. "They claim I saved the lives of five or six of my fellow volunteers that day, as well as a number of wounded men."

"I'm sure you did," she blubbered.

He was almost embarrassed to tell her the rest. "It seems I'm to be awarded some kind of decoration by the British government. It has rather a convoluted name, I'm afraid. Something about conspicuous, or maybe it's distinguished, gallantry." He continued stroking her hair until the tears ceased. "We mustn't blame the poor chap, Christine. He didn't know what he was doing. I suppose he'll spend the rest of his days in a special hospital for soldiers."

She raised her head. "I'm very proud of you, Charles Jordan Brick. It was a wonderfully selfless thing you did that day. You are the bravest man I have ever known."

A tinge of pink washed over his face. "It was necessary, that's all."

"Perhaps so," she said, returning to her chair and pouring them each another cup of tea, "but you were still the bravest man there that day, and don't you forget it."

After a time, "I wouldn't mind having another of those delicious cakes," he said shyly.

She emptied the entire platter of confectioneries onto his plate. "You may have as many cakes as your heart desires, Charlie Brick. It's the very least a true hero deserves."

"I WOULD LIKE TO DEPOSIT a sum of money with you, matron," Christine said, opening her purse. She took out an envelope and laid it down on the desk.

"You have just given me a considerable amount, Miss Brick. What, may I ask, are your instructions concerning the use of the money?" the woman inquired.

"I want it to be used to purchase a few of the niceties for my brother—fresh flowers for his bedside table, tea cakes from the shop around the corner—he's grown very fond of those—a new pair of slippers when his wear out, and anything else you or your staff feel would make his life more comfortable or enjoyable in the time he has remaining under your care."

The matron opened a drawer in her desk and took out a small lockbox. "Naturally we will be happy to oblige. We've all become quite fond of Charles, as you know." She opened the box, placed the envelope inside, locked the box again and returned it to the desk drawer.

Christine softened. "I know you have. That's why I felt I could ask such a large favor of you."

The woman inclined her head slightly. "It's a small enough thing to do if it makes a patient's life more bearable. I will speak to the various sisters and make sure that they keep an eye out for what might please your brother."

Christine was satisfied with the arrangements. She could do without the extras; Charlie could not. At least if she had anything to say about it, he *would* not.

"I understand you'll be leaving us soon," said the matron.

"My ship sails for France tonight."

"This is goodbye, then." She got to her feet and extended her hand to Christine.

"Yes. This is goodbye. I want to thank you for looking after Charlie. It means more to me and all of his family than you know."

"Perhaps not, Miss Brick. Perhaps not."

The matron's smile was genuinely warm as the two women shook hands and parted company.

Christine followed the now-familiar path from the matron's office to Charlie's ward.

A woman's voice rang out cheerfully, "Your brother is waiting for you as usual in the solarium, Miss Brick."

She called back quietly, "Thank you, sister."

An additional thought. "He has a small surprise for you."

She had to admit her interest was piqued. She rounded the corner.

"I'm over here, Christine."

Charlie was standing next to his wheelchair, one hand on the back for support.

"You're on your feet! What a wonderful surprise!" she cried out softly.

He was beaming with pride. "I rather hoped you'd think so."

"Of course, I think so. What an accomplishment!" She gave him an encouraging hug, taking care not to squeeze his chest too tightly. "I do believe you're looking more robust every day. Your color has improved markedly."

"Since your arrival in London, the matron says the change in my health has been nothing short of miraculous. She thinks I'll be able to go home in another month."

Nothing could have pleased her more. "What good news! Mama and Papa and everyone will be so happy to see you."

"Summertime back home in Indiana..." Charlie's voice trailed off for a minute. "Just the thought makes me feel good inside."

She concurred. "Sunshine and clear, blue skies, green fields and wild chickory growing alongside the roads. Mama's home cooking and Hannah fussing over you."

"My rosebushes."

"The blue mist as it drifts across the Happy Valley in the evening."

Charlie sighed heavily. "I've missed it all more than I ever dreamed was possible."

She patted his hand. "You'll be home soon."

"Home." He seemed to take pleasure in just saying the word. A swift frown followed. "We mustn't go on so, or you'll start to feel homesick."

"Homesick? I'm off to see the world," Christine told him, deliberately instilling an enthusiasm into her voice that she wasn't feeling at the moment. "I'm afraid I have to leave early this afternoon."

He nodded knowingly. "Your ship sails for France tonight."

"We leave from Southampton at 7:00 p.m."

His bottom lip visibly trembled. "I don't like goodbyes."

She didn't either, and she wasn't getting any better at them. She said spiritedly, "We won't say goodbye. We'll do as the French do, and say *au revoir*."

He pressed a kiss to her cheek. "God keep you in his care, Christine."

She carefully wrapped her arms around him. "God bless thee and keep thee, dearest Charlie. And may he give thee a safe voyage home."

Christine left her brother there in the sunlight of the solarium and among the caring sisters. Her heart, at least for a time, was at peace.

Chapter Ten

A Rough Crossing

Christine stood at the railing of the long, gray ship and stared into the fading light of day. A westerly wind had come up, and the tang of salt and fish was in the air. She shivered and pulled the collar of her coat more tightly around her throat. Still, she stayed put. She would have to go below deck soon enough as it was.

This was the next leg of her great adventure, she reminded herself. Under the direction of one Miss Margaret Lambert, a woman of great efficiency and superb organizational skills, their small group of Red Cross volunteers had taken the train from Waterloo Station to Southampton, where they had boarded a troop ship waiting to cross the English Channel in convoy. It was on this ship that Christine now stood, breathing in the damp evening air, knowing it was preferable to what she would find below.

For a moment her mind turned to purely practical matters. Once they reached Paris, she must remember to write Mama, or Hannah, and ask one of them to send her several more pairs of heavy, black, silk stockings from home. It was all Red Cross women were permitted to wear, and the stockings cost the equivalent of six dollars on this side of the Atlantic. What an outrageous price!

She watched as several of the other young women came on deck for a last breath of fresh air. She felt slightly the country bumpkin in her high-laced shoes. The women in London—surely Paris would only be more of the same— wore low-cut shoes, even in winter, or so she'd been told.

Not that she could afford to buy a more fashionable pair. Papa was a prosperous man and he had been more than generous with her before she'd left home, but she had given the matron at the hospital in London nearly a third of her money. There was none to spare for her vanity.

" 'Vanity of vanities...all is vanity,' " Christine muttered under her breath.

She would just have to be content with the shoes she had, and be thankful for them at that. She only hoped that Grandmother had been right when she had quoted to her from Corinthians: "The fashion of this world passeth away."

A deep, male voice caught her by surprise. "You'd best be getting below now, miss."

She started. "I—I beg your pardon..." She turned and found a young naval officer at her elbow.

He repeated the warning. "I said, you and the other ladies had best be going below, miss. We set sail in less than half an hour."

"Yes, of course," she said, unable to muster any enthusiasm at the prospect.

She had learned a thing or two about sailing on troop ships during her transatlantic voyage. Even though this journey across the Channel from Southampton to Le Havre, and then down the River Seine to Rouen and Paris, would not be nearly as long, it was bound to be equally unpleasant in many ways. For the air below deck was invariably stale and smelled of human sweat—and, at times, far worse.

She overheard the naval officer conversing with the other Red Cross volunteers. They were, apparently, inquiring as to why the voyage had to be made in a blacked-out ship.

"Is it the fear of zeppelin raids?" one of them asked in an Irish brogue.

"No, miss, not zeppelins, they've not been a threat since the middle of 1915 when poor weather and increasing accidents, not to mention our own fighter aeroplanes, caused the Germans to cancel their airship raids over England. It's the Gothas we have to watch out for now."

Gothas. The very word struck terror into the hearts of anyone who had witnessed the indiscriminate death and destruction wreaked by the twin-engined enemy biplanes that dropped their bombs on the English countryside, and even on London itself. There had been a Gotha raid only last week while Christine and the others were quartered in the city. Six of the German bombers had been shot down by British fighters and an astounding barrage of 30,000 antiaircraft shells. There had been little sleep for any of them that night.

"What about the danger of submarines?" asked another woman.

"Can't imagine there's a U-boat in the entire German fleet that would dare to show its head in these waters, not since we went to traveling in convoys. Besides, the tides are full of irregularities. That's why we have double high tide here at Southampton Water, and prolonged stands at high tide on the other side at Le Havre. And you have no doubt heard that the Channel is noted for its rough seas and bad weather."

They seemed comforted by the fact. Christine knew better. Rough seas and bad weather meant only one thing: seasickness.

"Rest assured, ladies—" the officer gave a little bow before he went about his duties "—you're safe with the Royal Navy looking after you."

It was time to go below. Christine and the other women made their way to their assigned cabin. The quarters were cramped. There were nearly a dozen of them, including Miss Lambert, in a space intended for less than half that number.

The cabin was warm and noisy; it was a plethora of accents, some of which Christine had difficulty understanding. For their group consisted of English, Irish, Welsh and Scottish, in addition to herself, the solitary American.

She sat down on a bench beside a girl named Irene, and unbuttoned her coat.

"Bit warm in here, isn't it?" commented the girl as she took to fanning herself with her purse.

Christine agreed. "Yes, it is."

"You been up on deck getting a breath of fresh air?"

She nodded.

"You're an American, aren't you?"

She nodded again. "I'm from Indiana."

Irene frowned, then broke into a cheerful smile. "Never heard of Indiana myself, but you can always tell a Yank from the accent."

"Where are you from, Irene?"

"I come from the North Country. Northumbria. Just a stone's throw from Hadrian's Wall. My people have lived there since the time of Bloody Mary." For Christine's benefit she went on to explain, "That'd be four hundred years, give or take a year."

"Hadrian's Wall," repeated Christine. The words were pure magic to her ears. "To think that the Roman Emperor Hadrian had the Wall built nearly eighteen centuries ago and it's still there today. How exciting it must be to live smack-dab in the middle of all that history."

Irene cast her a skeptical look. "Don't know about that. I always think of the North Country as being mostly empty. London. Now that's what I call exciting." She stopped fanning herself long enough to open her purse and take out a small tin of licorice candy. "You care for a piece?"

"No, thank you."

Irene shrugged and helped herself. "What's this Indiana of yours like?"

Christine was happy to enlighten her companion. "It's farm country mostly. Rolling green hills and fields of corn and wheat as far as the eye can see. My great-grandparents settled in the region about one hundred years ago. Before that it was pretty much thick forest and a few Delaware Indians."

Irene allowed, "Sounds like pretty countryside."

"We think so. Our farm is situated just outside the town of New Castle. Some folks say the town is named for Newcastle upon Tyne."

"Why, that's up in our part of the country, it is," Irene exclaimed. She shook her head from side to side. "They keep saying it's a small world. I guess they're right." She held out the tin of candy. "Sure you won't change your mind and have a licorice?"

Christine had no wish to offend her newfound friend. "All right, I will. Thank you."

All conversation ceased in the crowded cabin when the women heard the powerful engines start up somewhere deep within the bowels of the ship. Their journey across the English Channel was about to commence.

Unfortunately Christine's suspicions were, all too soon, proven correct. They were only an hour out from the Isle of Wight, two at the most, when they encountered the rough seas and bad weather ably predicted by the naval officer.

The ship was tossed to and fro on the Channel waters like a child's toy boat. Several of the women became sick; Christine could hear their piteous moans. Once again she was thankful for her seemingly cast-iron stomach, which had stood her in such good stead crossing the Atlantic. But even she had been wise enough to take only tea and toast before they'd sailed from Southampton, the licorice candy from Irene being the only exception.

She tried to help the others, but there was little she could do beyond dispensing sympathy, holding their heads when they were ill and, afterward, washing their hands and faces with a clean, damp cloth.

It was sometime later that evening—perhaps in an attempt to take their minds off the unpleasant conditions below deck—that one of the young women began to sing. The song was quiet and sad. Yet, Christine didn't think she had ever heard a voice so sweet and clear. She leaned her head back against the wall and listened.

"Black, black, black is the color
    of my true love's hair.
His lips are something wondrous fair
The purest eyes and the bravest hands,
I love the ground whereon he stands.
Black, black, black is the color of my true love's hair.
I love my love and well he knows,
I love the ground whereon he goes

And if my love no more I see,
My life would quickly fade away.
Black, black, black is the color
   of my true love's hair.''

Christine closed her eyes. She could see the image of James's face in every detail, as if he stood right there in front of her. His hair was dark, nearly black in color. His eyes were flecked with green and gold and brown. His features were handsome and rugged.

She raised a finger to trace the outline of that intelligent brow, that wonderful, slightly imperfect nose with the bump in the middle—she remembered when that nose had been broken during football practice during his freshman year and he had come home from college with a white bandage across the bridge, much to his mother's dismay and hers—that mouth with its full bottom lip and sensuous curve, that noble chin seemingly chiseled from fine marble.

She could almost *feel* him there.

Christine remembered a fine summer night several years before. She had been sitting on the front porch of the Brick farmhouse with Hannah and Charlie, enjoying the cool of the evening after the heat of a long day. James had driven up in his father's new automobile. He had just arrived home from a trip to New York City, and had come over to tell them all about his adventures.

A short time later Hannah had excused herself and gone to the kitchen to prepare a pitcher of lemonade for them. Charlie had wandered out into the gravel drive to check over the new vehicle. He'd been far more interested in its engine than in any stories James might have about New York. For a few minutes the two of them had been left alone.

Christine remembered the tingling sensation, the heightened awareness she'd had of James that night. His voice had been low and rich and he'd talked and laughed and related his amusing tales of life encountered in the big city. She couldn't recall a single thing he'd said to her, but she had never forgotten the timbre of his deep baritone, the sense of how near he had been, how the tiny hairs on her arms had stood on end when he'd moved closer to her on the porch swing, the distinctive scent of him: slightly spicy and masculine and entirely James. She had been aware of him that night in the way a woman was aware of a man.

She could almost *feel* him there beside her now.

Suddenly, without warning, Christine began to weep.

Day after day, week after week, for months on end she had been without James. Yet, not an hour passed awake or asleep that he was not on her mind. He dwelled in her night dreams as surely as he did in her daydreams. There was a kind of awful ache inside of her chest that never went away. She was heartsick for the lack of him.

She missed him in a hundred ways and more. She longed to hear the sound of his voice and his laughter. She yearned to feel the strength of his hands, the caress of his fingertips, his kiss on her lips.

"Oh, James, I miss thee so," she whispered, miserable and lonely as she curled up in a dark corner of the cabin and stuffed her fist into her mouth to stifle the sound of her sobs.

Her only comfort was the postcard Charlie had given to her before she'd left London. She clutched it to her breast. She knew the message by heart. "Dear Charlie, I hope this finds you in good spirits and improving health. Coop and I got leave and went to Paris last week for a bath and a good meal. We had delicious omelets and coffee at a little café near the Place de la Concorde. You will no doubt be seeing our own dear Christine soon. I envy you that. My love to you both. James."

Coop and James had gone to Paris. How she wished that she were going to Paris with James! Paris: the city of lovers, the city for lovers.

Paris and the legendary Bois de Boulogne, the outdoor cafés along the Avenue des Champs-Elysées, the Tuileries, the Louvre, Notre Dame and the climb up the holy hill to Montmartre where the view of the city was said to be incomparable on a clear summer night. Yes, how she longed to see James and Paris!

It was with James's name on her lips that Christine finally drifted into a fitful sleep later that night.

In the gray light of dawn she went up on deck again. The throbbing vibration of the ship's engines could be felt somewhere far beneath her feet. She could make out the ghostly shapes of the other ships and smaller boats all around them. The sea was darker than the sky; the water churning and foaming. The wind tore at her clothes. Her hair came loose from its combs and whipped around her face and shoulders like the slash of a sail against the mainmast.

There was an unreal quality about the ship, the wind and the sea all around her. As her great-grandmother had written in her diary, Christine knew what it was to be a Stranger in a Strange Land.

Dear God, what was she doing here on the deck of an English troop ship on her way to France? She was half a world away from home and she was all alone. Alone and afraid.

"Remember. Remember. Remember." Over and over again Christine repeated the word out loud to herself.

For whenever she began to feel sore afraid and her courage seemed about to fail her, she thought of Elizabeth Banks and Mary Long: two courageous women who had gone before her, pioneer women who had once ventured into the dangerous unknown. As she was now.

It was time she gave herself a good talking-to, Christine decided.

She liked to think that she was a pioneer woman in her own way. Well, no one had promised her it would be easy. No one had said she wouldn't feel lonely and tired sometimes, or cold and hungry. It wasn't enough to simply say that she believed; she had to act on that belief. And there was always a price to be paid.

A hand flew to her mouth, but not before a small cry escaped her. Wasn't the price she was paying cheap in comparison with that already paid by her brother? Sweet, brave, heroic Charlie. He had, indeed, paid dearly for his beliefs.

And hadn't James paid a price, as well? Separated from family and friends, his letters told her that he had been lonely and tired during the long weeks spent training at Camp Taylor. It wasn't going to be any easier for him now that he was in France and about to become embroiled in the thick of the fight.

Christine was suddenly ashamed of herself. She took a deep breath of air and cleaned out her lungs. If her grandmother and great-grandmother had met the challenge, then so could she! If Charlie and James were willing to pay the price, then she could as well.

It was a quarter of an hour before dawn when there was a movement behind her, and Irene joined her on deck.

"Are you feeling better this morning?" Christine inquired kindly.

"Yes, some." But the other girl was still noticeably pale. "Is that land I spy?" She pointed toward the horizon.

Christine peered into the fog. "If so, it must be Le Havre."

"Dry land," said Irene. "It can't be soon enough for me."

Christine stood a little taller. "France." The last leg of her long journey, she thought, greatly heartened. With it came a swiftening of her pulse, for she knew that James was somewhere out there. Ahead was France and the man she loved.

THE DAY WAS BRIGHT and sun-filled when they sailed down the Seine toward Rouen and on to Paris. Along the way soldiers and nuns and excited schoolchildren crowded along the river's banks, and waved their handkerchiefs and caps and shouted to them. The women aboard ship waved and shouted back, although most of them didn't understand a word of French.

They arrived in Paris on the morning of the fourth day since setting sail from Southampton. An *autobus* met them at the quay and took them from the ship to the house where they would be living for the next few months.

When Miss Lambert informed her group of volunteers that they must double up, Christine and Irene Chandler agreed to share a room. Theirs was on the third floor. It was small and cramped. There was just enough space for two narrow beds, a single bureau and a tiny closet.

"Lordy, we'll meet ourselves coming and going!" exclaimed Irene as they stood in the doorway and took stock of their new surroundings.

"It's not very large, is it?" said Christine.

Irene set her suitcase down. "I suppose we'll make do."

"I suppose we'll have to ."

"A good scrubbing from top to bottom is what this place needs," stated the North Country woman as she rolled up her sleeves. "Some bright curtains at the windows, a vase filled with fresh flowers from one of the vendors we saw on the street corner, maybe a picture or two on the walls and it'll seem real homelike. You wait and see if it doesn't."

"You're a good soul, Irene Chandler," Christine declared. "You make me believe that anything is possible with a little elbow grease and a great deal of faith."

The good-natured woman stuck her head around the corner. "I'm afraid all the faith in the world isn't going to change the fact that there is only one WC at the end of the hall for the ten of us."

Christine sighed and set her valise on the bed. "Hot baths are going to be a genuine luxury, I can tell already."

She had just finished unpacking her few belongings when a knock came on their door. It was Miss Margaret Lambert.

"I see you ladies are settling in."

Nearly in unison, Christine and Irene said, "Yes, Miss Lambert."

"The two of you are assigned to canteen duty in the morning. Please report to the head cook by five o'clock sharp."

They nodded their heads and groaned silently. There would be no sleeping in for them.

On her way out the door, Miss Lambert stopped and spoke to Christine. "You handled yourself well aboard ship, Miss Brick. Especially with those who were indisposed."

Compliments were rare. "Thank you, Miss Lambert."

"I was told that you've had some nursing experience," the woman went on.

"I don't know if I'd exactly call it nursing experience. Before I left home I'd been helping out in the office of a local doctor for a few months," Christine clarified.

"I see. Well, I'll keep that in mind, Miss Brick. You've got a level head on your shoulders for one so young. I like that in my volunteers,"

"Mademoiselle, pardonnez-moi."

Miss Margaret Lambert turned to the young French girl who served as housemaid, kitchen help and sometime translator to the Red Cross volunteers. "Yes, Viviane, what is it?"

"A monsieur is here to see Mademoiselle Brick."

Frowning, Margaret Lambert repeated, "A gentleman?"

"Il est un soldat."

"Where? *Où?*"

Viviane shrugged. "I have placed him in the *parloir*. *"Bien."*

Miss Margaret Lambert turned back to Christine. "There is someone here to see you."

She was speechless for a moment. "But I don't know anyone in Paris."

A raised eyebrow. "According to Viviane, your visitor is a gentleman and a soldier."

Irene Chandler blurted out, "Isn't your fiancé in the army, Christine?"

For an instant her heart stopped beating. "James? James is here?" It didn't even sound like her voice.

"Did the monsieur tell you his name, Viviane?"

The girl sighed and murmured, *"C'est un bel homme avec les cheveux noirs."*

Margaret Lambert appeared to give up on the prospect of learning their visitor's name. "Viviane says he is a handsome man with black hair."

Christine's hands suddenly became like ice, and they were trembling. But then she had begun to tremble all over. "It must be James. My fiancé is Lieutenant James Warren," she related to the older woman, telling herself to stay calm, that it might *not* be James, after all. "He's with the American army and has been stationed in France since last winter. I haven't seen him in six months."

Hesitation. Then a smile. "In that case, you'd best get downstairs and greet him, hadn't you?"

It was the last thing any of them expected of Miss Margaret Lambert. But then the world was full of surprises, as Christine was discovering.

She flew past the woman and Viviane, calling over her shoulder, "Thank you, Miss Lambert. *Merci*, Viviane."

"Miss Chandler—" Irene snapped to attention "—you go along with Miss Brick, just to make certain that she is properly chaperoned."

Irene Chandler followed her roommate to the formal if shabby parlor on the first floor. She peeked inside just long enough to make certain that the *bel homme* was the right *bel homme*, and then quietly closed the door. For Irene had a truly understanding heart. The last thing Miss Christine Brick needed right now was a chaperone.

CHRISTINE STEPPED INTO the parlor. A man dressed in military uniform was standing at the far end of the room looking out the window. His back was to her.

She opened her mouth to say his name. No sound would come out. She wanted, desperately, to run to him, but her legs were suddenly the consistency of quince jelly.

James turned around.

Christine could only stand there and stare at him. She'd forgotten how tall he was. She didn't remember his hair being quite so dark or so short. He had a cigarette in his hand; she'd never seen him smoke before. His face was older. His eyes were older yet.

Then James smiled at her and it was all there in his handsome face for her to see. It was as loud and clear to her as if he'd shouted it from the rooftops of Paris itself. He *had* missed her terribly. He *had* been living for the next moment he would see her. His world *did* begin and end with her. But most of all, he loved her.

He dropped his cigarette into the *cendrier* on the table. Then, "Christine—"

No one said her name the way James did.

Wordlessly, she flew into his arms.

For an eternity or two, neither of them spoke. They simply stood with their arms around each other, oblivious of everyone and everything in the world. They were each other's world.

There would be a time for whispered endearments, tender caresses and impassioned kisses, but this was *not* the time. This was a time to be thankful; they were alive and they were together. For the moment, nothing else mattered. For now, it was enough.

Christine didn't have any idea how long she stood with her arms entwined about James's waist, her face pressed against his chest. It could have been five minutes or five days. For the first time in a very long time, time itself had no meaning for her. She was content. She was happy. She wanted nothing more from life than this moment.

Beneath her cheek she could feel the steady rhythm of James's heart, and she was grateful for every life-giving beat. She could feel the strength in his arms and legs, and she was relieved to find that he was healthy and whole.

She put her head back and gazed up into his eyes, and she thanked God for the love she saw there.

"I can't believe you're here," James said at last.

"I can't believe I'm with you," she murmured, still half dazed.

His voice was strangely hoarse. "It's been so long since I've seen you, held you . . ." He could not go on.

Christine raised a trembling hand to his face. She needed to reassure herself that he was real, that he was flesh and blood, and not a figment of her overwrought imagination and desperate desires.

"I am real. You are real," James assured them both.

"Yes!" she cried out softly.

"I can feel the wild, frantic beating of your heart." He pressed a fingertip to the small hollow at the base of her throat and counted quickly, "One, two, three, four . . ."

"My heart beats faster only for you, James."

He came closer. "I can feel the heat of your breath on my skin."

"You take my breath away."

Closer still. "A man could get lost in your eyes."

"I would always be there to help you find your way."

He took her face in his hands. "It's been so long since I kissed you."

"It seems like forever."

"I'm afraid once I start I may not be able to stop."

She confessed, "I'm shaking from head to toe."

"So am I."

Tears welled up at the edge of her eyelids. "Kiss me, James, before I die from wanting you."

"Dearest Christine—" He broke off and crushed her mouth beneath his.

It was a kiss unlike any James had ever given her. It was a time and place unlike any they had ever known. They were not the same boy and girl they had once been. They were a man and a woman who loved each other in the midst of a world gone mad.

"I love you," she said, clinging to him.

"And I love you more than life itself," he declared with an intensity that frightened her.

She spoke her dearest wish aloud. "I wish we could be alone."

His eyes were dark and dangerous. "So do I. We'd find a place where it would be just the two of us."

She was nearly swept away by his passion, and her own. "Oh, how I wish we could . . ."

Almost imperceptibly, his arms tightened around her. "One day, my love. Someday."

Some semblance of sanity returned. "But not today, not when we've just arrived."

"And not today when I have only a short time left in Paris." Reluctantly James let her go. "How was your voyage across the Channel and down the Seine?"

Christine took a seat on the sofa and pulled him down beside her, not wanting him out of her reach. "The crossing was rough, but I never seem to get seasick. I would have made an excellent sailor."

That made him laugh. "Can you imagine women serving in the navy?"

"Why not?" she said spiritedly. "We have women serving in the army as Signal Corps telephone operators."

He was conciliatory. "We men couldn't do without you women." He reached behind her and casually caressed the back of her neck. "I know I could never do without you."

Christine softened. "In that case, it's a good thing you'll never have to."

"Do you mind if I smoke?" he asked.

"No, I don't mind."

She watched as James struck a match and held the flame up to the cigarette he'd put in his mouth. She tried not to stare, but she couldn't help but notice how his hands shook. Something wasn't quite right and she didn't know what it was.

"I can't tell you how much your letters have meant to me," James went on.

"Charlie said the same thing to me when I saw him in London last week."

He frowned. "Charlie's doing better?" It was more of a question than it was a statement.

She nodded. "In fact, the matron at the hospital said his health has made such a dramatic improvement that he may be on his way home by the end of the month."

"That is good news." He crushed his cigarette out in the ashtray at his elbow.

"Charlie received the postcard you sent him. It was good of you to write." She added, "You must have received my letter with our travel plans for crossing the Channel."

James indicated that he had. "There was no way for me to let you know that I was able to wangle a short leave, so I decided to surprise you."

"It's the best surprise I've ever had."

"I wasn't sure you'd feel that way," he admitted.

Christine was puzzled. "Why ever not?"

James ran a nervous hand along his pant leg. "We haven't seen each other in six months. People's feelings can change."

She was adamant. "Not mine. Not ever."

He gently reminded her, "But people do change, Christine. The war has seen to that."

James wasn't asking her something, he was trying to *tell* her something. Something important. She had to find out what it was.

She stared first at his larger hands and then down at her own. "You're right, of course. People do change. The war has seen to that as we knew it would." She sighed and admitted, "I have changed." He stiffened beside her. "I'm not the same girl you proposed to last Thanksgiving, James. I'm skinny—" she laughed but there was no mirth in the sound of it "—and I'm tired and sometimes I feel like an old woman."

He relaxed and reminded her with a crooked smile, "You are almost nineteen."

She sighed and told him in the spirit of camaraderie, "I've spent days—weeks—on troop ships that smell like outhouses."

"You can't imagine the stink of the latrines they dig in the trenches," he chimed in.

"I've eaten tinned food that I wouldn't feed to a dog."

He went on to tell her, "You only hope and pray that the water cart doesn't get stuck in the mud and the muck. Otherwise, God knows what kind of germs and disease are floating around in the stuff you find to drink."

"I've worn the same two pairs of stockings since I left home and I'm lucky to get a hot bath every other week."

"Coop and I had to go to Paris to get a decent meal and the first soak in a tub that we'd had in a month."

She became deadly serious. "I've witnessed the destruction that the enemy bombers leave in their wake—whole buildings gone, streets destroyed, houses that end up a pile of rubble."

"I've seen miles of trenches and barbed wire and crater-filled No-Man's-Land as far as the eye can see in either direction. And men, dead."

Her voice was scarcely above a whisper. "I've seen soldiers in the hospitals without arms, without legs, without faces. I close my eyes and I still see them. I've lost some of my faith in the goodness of man. There are times when I can find no joy in living when so many are dying. It's all such a waste." She looked up at James with tears brimming in her eyes. "I won't ever again be that sweet, innocent girl you knew and loved last summer." A sob caught in her throat. "I wish we were children again and the world was all shiny and new."

He pulled her into his arms. He held her as if she were precious to him beyond measure. He stroked her hair. He soothed her fears. And, in the end, he dried her tears as well.

"You will always be the girl I love, Christine."

"And you will always be the man I love," she reminded him.

He sighed resignedly. "We're both a long way from home and we've seen things we never imagined in our worst nightmares. But we will see it through, together."

Christine knew then what James had wanted, *needed*, to tell her. He wasn't the same man he had once been. For better or worse, the war had changed him. And, in her own fashion, she had found a way to reassure him that she understood. That she, too, had seen what war could do to a man's spirit. Indeed, to his very soul.

"I must be going now," James said some time later. "I have to report back to my commanding officer by midnight."

"Take care of yourself for my sake," she told him when he was ready to depart.

He kissed her tenderly, and it was bittersweet.

"I promise to come to you as soon as I can wangle another leave," he said. "I don't know how or when but I'll manage somehow."

"I will be here waiting for you," she said, hiding her fears and concerns from him.

He brushed his lips across hers and whispered, "*Au revoir*, my love, until we meet again."

"Until we meet again," she murmured.

After James had gone, the last lines of the song she'd heard aboard ship kept playing over and over in her mind.

And if my love no more I see,
My life would quickly fade away.
Black is the color of my true love's hair.

Chapter Eleven

Till We Meet Again

Christine had been in Paris for a month when she received a summons to Miss Margaret Lambert's office. It was a small room on the first floor, tucked between the rather shabby front parlor and the big, old-fashioned kitchen in the rear of the residence occupied by the Red Cross volunteers.

Christine knocked and waited for a response.

"Entrez!"

She opened the door and entered.

Miss Lambert was seated at a wooden table—it was obviously being used as a desk—poring over a sheaf of papers and work schedules. She did not immediately look up.

"Yes?"

Christine straightened her posture. "Miss Brick reporting, as requested."

Gray eyes peered at her over wire-rimmed spectacles. "Ah, yes, Miss Brick," murmured the woman. "I wanted to speak with you." Miss Margaret Lambert rifled through the papers in front of her until she apparently found the one she was looking for. "I have a special assignment for you."

That captured Christine's attention. She waited anxiously to hear the details.

"There is a small village some distance from Paris called St. Jean. The Red Cross hospital there is critically short of nurses at the moment, and I cannot get them a replacement from England for another several weeks. I would like you to temporarily fill in."

"But—"

Miss Lambert held up her hand, the palm facing Christine, and brushed aside any objections she might have with "I know. You aren't a trained nurse. But you have worked as a volunteer in a clinic and you're a level-headed girl. That will suit my purposes until I can get a professional."

"But—"

"No buts about it, Miss Brick," the woman said in her usual no-nonsense tone. "All I ask, all anyone will ask, is that you do your best."

What choice did she have? Christine capitulated with as much grace as she could muster. "Yes, Miss Lambert."

"You'll want to go to your room now and pack your things. There is a shipment of medical supplies going out to St. Jean this morning. I have arranged for you to ride along with the truck driver, Pierre. Any other details will be seen to once you arrive in the village."

"Yes, Miss Lambert."

The woman's parting words of encouragement were: "Chin up, my girl. You'll do just fine."

"WHAT IN THE DICKENS IS Miss Lambert up to now?" inquired Irene as she watched her roommate take a suitcase from beneath the bed and begin to pack her belongings.

"I've been temporarily assigned to a hospital in the village of St. Jean. It seems that they're a bit short-handed."

"Well, I'll be!" exclaimed the North Country woman.

Christine took her spare uniform from the closet and placed it in the suitcase; a pair of black stockings followed, then her nightgown and hairbrush and personal effects. "Viviane tells me that St. Jean is about forty miles from the front lines, and that American and British officers go there for a hot meal and a glass of local wine when they can get a pass." She handed an envelope to the other woman. "I'll be at the Red Cross hospital. I've written it all down in this note. Would you mind posting it to Lieutenant Warren for me?"

"Course I don't mind."

She explained further, "I don't know whether James will be able to procure a pass, but, all the same, I want him to know where I'll be."

Irene Chandler assured her, "I'll see to it that your letter is sent off this morning, I will."

"Thank you, Irene. I knew I could rely on you."

"Going to miss having you around, though," the woman confessed in a gruff voice. "When do you think you'll be coming back?"

Christine closed her suitcase and straightened her cap. "Miss Lambert said it would only be until she can get a regular nursing sister from England."

There was concern in her friend's voice. "You take care of yourself, Christine. Mind that you don't let them work you too hard. And don't forget to eat a proper supper every night."

"I won't forget." She gathered up her case and paused in the doorway of their room. "As Miss Lambert says, 'Chin up, my girl.' It will only be for a week or two."

The truck driver, Pierre, was waiting in front of the Red Cross building. He was middle-aged and very French.

He doffed his hat and called out, *"Bonjour, mademoiselle,"* as Christine climbed into the truck with the familiar red cross painted on the side. He stowed her suitcase in the back and got behind the wheel.

She inclined her head slightly. *"Bonjour, monsieur."*

Immediately the man brightened and gestured vigorously with both hands. *"Ah, parlez-vous Français, mademoiselle?"*

She knew enough to shrug her shoulders and admit, "No, I'm afraid I don't speak French. Only a few words, anyway. *Un peu,"* she tacked on when she realized that the driver spoke even less English.

Their lack of a common language didn't seem to discourage Pierre; he chattered nonstop to Christine as he maneuvered the ancient truck in and out of the intricacies of Paris traffic. As they rounded the next corner, a horse-drawn wagon filled with cabbages pulled out in front of them.

Pierre slammed on the brakes and leaned his head out the window. *"Quelle stupide!"* He motioned to the other driver to get out of their way and shouted, *"Bougez! Bougez!"* Turning to his passenger, he was all smiles and apologies. *"Excusez-moi, mademoiselle."*

Christine gave him a polite nod and bit the smile from the corners of her mouth. It would not do for the man to think she found him comical. But he did remind her just a little of Charlie Chaplin.

The morning passed pleasantly enough once they were out of the city and driving east on the road toward St. Jean. The sky was a clear summer blue; the trees and the countryside were lush and green. It did not seem possible that a war was going on.

Hoping that the driver would comprehend her meaning if not her exact words, Christine remarked to him, "Your country is very beautiful, *monsieur.*" She searched for the French word; she'd picked up only a smattering of the language from Viviane. *"Beau. Très beau!"*

"Oui, que c'est beau!" the man agreed, beaming at her.

It must have been close to noon when Pierre pulled the truck to the side of the road and took a small basket from behind his seat. Inside was a loaf of dark bread, a round of thick, yellow cheese and a bottle of wine.

A growling in the pit of Christine's stomach reminded her that breakfast had been many hours ago and that she had made no provision for her own lunch. She realized she was hungry and thirsty. She tried to swallow the dry lump stuck in her throat. Perhaps there was a farmhouse or an inn nearby where she could at least buy a cup of coffee.

The Frenchman seemed to anticipate her request. He patted his belly and said, *"Avez-vous faim?"*

Christine's empty stomach answered for her by growling even louder.

With that, Pierre tore off a sizable chunk of bread and held it out to her.

She accepted with a heartfelt *"Merci."*

Next he took a small knife from the basket and carved the cheese into thick slices, urging her to help herself to as much as she could eat. Then he uncorked the bottle and offered her the first swig of deep red wine.

Christine didn't think she'd ever tasted anything quite so wonderful as the dark bread and yellow cheese and unaccustomed wine she had for lunch that day. She never forgot the journey made along the country road between Paris and St. Jean. And she always remembered the kindness and generosity of a Frenchman named Pierre.

Still, she was relieved when they finally arrived at the Red Cross hospital in St. Jean and a sister with a crisp British accent said to her, "Would you like a cup of tea, Miss Brick?"

"Yes, I would. Thank you," she said wholeheartedly.

As she sat sipping her tea a few minutes later Christine thought about what an oddly peaceful day it had been. It wasn't until they'd come upon the first bombed-out buildings and platoons of weary troops not far outside the village that the war had become all too real.

All too real, indeed, with the small hospital filled to capacity with wounded soldiers. Most of them had been brought there from makeshift facilities on the Western Front and would soon be transported to a *hôpital* in Paris and eventually on to England. Much as Charlie must have been, Christine realized.

Some of the men, of course, would recover sufficiently to be sent back to the front lines. But the majority were out of the fighting for the duration.

And, as always, she thought of James, wondering where he was and how he was doing. Was he well? Was he safe? Was he missing her as much as she missed him? The questions swirled around in her head like bits of paper caught up in a dust devil.

"If you're finished with your tea, Miss Brick, I'll give you a quick tour of the hospital and show you what your duties will be," the sister told her.

After that, Christine found she had little time to think of anything except getting up before dawn, working all day in the wards giving baths, changing bandages, making tea for the sisters and the doctor—they were even more overworked than she—and falling into bed at night in the tiny room she'd been given at the inn nearby. Only the nurses on duty slept at the hospital; every spare bed was needed for the wounded.

Truth to tell, there were some evenings when she was simply too exhausted to eat a "proper" supper, despite Irene's parting admonition. The chance to grab an extra half hour of sleep was far more important to her than food when she'd been on her feet all day.

It was the beginning of Christine's second week in St. Jean when the word raced through the wards like a brushfire: more wounded were coming in. They were fresh from a major battle, and some of the men were in critical condition.

The staff was alerted only minutes before the first ambulances came rumbling into the hospital yard. Before the dust had even settled, stretchers were unloaded directly onto the ground by uniformed orderlies. Soon there were wounded everywhere: men with makeshift bandages draped around their heads like turbans, arms in slings, bloodied puttees wrapped around legs and feet.

It was utter chaos.

Shouts.

Piteous moans.

Occasional shrieks of pain.

"Sister, come with me!" barked the doctor. "We'll see to the worst cases first." He turned to Christine for an instant. "Do what you can for the others, Miss Brick, even if it's only offering them a cigarette."

She simply stood there in the midst of the nightmare and wondered what in the name of God she should do.

"Sister—"

It took Christine a moment to realize that the wounded soldier at her feet was speaking to her. She knelt down beside him.

"I'm not really a—"

"Sister—" Just the way he said the word told her that it didn't matter in the least to him whether she was a professional nurse or not. He was a human being in need and she was the only one there to help him.

"Yes, soldier."

She could see the suffering in his eyes. But he managed to smile and say, "Hey, you're an American, too, aren't you?"

She smiled back at him. "Yes, I am."

"Where are you from?"

"A small town in Indiana. And you?"

"Philadelphia."

The young soldier closed his eyes and Christine could discern the grimace of pain on his face. She did not want to stare at his chest but she had caught a glimpse of a bloodied bandage and wondered how bad his wound was.

His eyes opened. "Light a cigarette for me, nurse?"

"Of course." With hands that trembled, she reached for the pack in his pocket. She took one out and put it between his lips, then struck a match and held it up to the cigarette for him. He took a couple of grateful puffs.

"Thanks."

"You're welcome."

His mouth moved painfully. "What's your name?"

"Christine."

"Pretty name. Pretty lady."

She hadn't thought of her appearance in a very long time, Christine realized. She didn't give it a second thought now, but asked, "What's your name?"

"Harry." He coughed. "Harry Radford."

"You're a long way from home, Harry Radford," she murmured.

"We're both a long way from home, pretty lady," he said, and coughed again.

She quickly took the cigarette from his mouth and tossed it to the ground.

Then he began to cough in earnest and Christine spotted the first dribble of bright red on his lips. The man was choking on his own blood. He tried to sit up, but he couldn't manage. She put her arms around his shoulders and tried to ease the spasms. It was to no avail. She glanced down at her hands and saw that they were covered with blood: Harry Radford's blood.

"Doctor—" Christine raised her voice and repeated urgently, "Doctor."

"Sister, over here!" shouted the doctor when he saw that Christine had an emergency case.

The doctor and nurse went to work on the man, and Christine knew she would only be in the way if she stayed. She stepped back and looked down at her blood-covered hands.

The words uttered by her grandmother long ago ran through her mind. They'd been quilting together and Christine had pricked her finger with the needle.

"*But, Grandmother,*" she had protested as a child of six, "*My finger is bleeding.*"

"*Does thy finger hurt, my child?*"

"*No, Grandmother.*"

"*Then wash the blood from thy hand, Christine, and begin again.*"

Wash the blood from thy hand and begin again.

"Nurse—" came another voice nearby. "Nurse, can I have a drink of water?"

Christine knew that someone else needed her. She wiped her hands on the skirt of her uniform and turned to the next wounded soldier.

Day merged into night and then into day again. They were all working round the clock, stopping only to grab a cup of tea and a ten-minute nap when they were literally falling asleep on their feet. By the third evening the emergency was over; there were no new cases to be dealt with. Christine was sent back to the inn for a hot meal and a good night's rest.

Despite the warm summer night, she was thoroughly chilled. She pulled a chair up in front of the inn's solitary fireplace and lit a match to the logs on the grate. The innkeeper brought her a bowl of potato soup and a chunk of coarse bread. She had only enough energy to take a bite or two. Before she knew what had hit her, her chin dropped to her chest and her eyes closed.

Was she dreaming?

She could hear voices close by.

The first one said in a slurred tone, "What's happened? Has she fainted?"

The second voice was calmer. "I don't think so. My word, James, I believe she's fallen asleep over her supper."

Christine tried to open her eyes and couldn't. She wanted to move her arms and found that she had no control over them. Then someone took her hand and held it gently. It was a man. She could tell from the size and strength of the fingers and the calluses on the palms.

She opened her eyes a fraction of an inch. There was a soldier leaning over her.

For a moment Christine was reminded of another time and another place when she had awakened and found a soldier bending over. Had that been a dream? Was this a dream, too?

She moved her lips and whispered, "Is that you?"

This time the soldier answered, "Yes, dearest, it's me."

Her eyes opened wider. Her heart skipped a beat. She was tempted to pinch herself to make sure she wasn't dreaming. She reached out and touched the face in front of hers. "James, is it really you?"

"Yes, dear girl, it really is me," he reassured her in a familiar, husky voice.

Wordlessly he removed the bowl of soup and the chunk of leftover bread and placed them on the table beside her chair. Then he held out his hands. She put hers in his and was swept to her feet and into his waiting arms.

James held her so tightly that Christine feared for a moment that he might crack her ribs. Not that she cared. She'd never been so happy to see anyone in her whole life! James was here. It was true. It was no dream.

She clung to him.

It was some time before she became aware of the other officer in the room. She untangled her arms from around James's neck and tried to make herself presentable before turning around.

"I'm an awful sight," she stammered, smoothing the skirt of her uniform. There was nothing she could do about the wrinkles or the bloodstains, she recognized. "We've had an emergency at the hospital for the past three days. I haven't had a chance to change...."

"It doesn't matter," James assured her. "You look wonderful to me."

"And to me." The man accompanying him stepped forward and introduced himself. "Robert Hershel Cooper, at your service." He smiled at her unreservedly. "I've wanted to meet you for a very long time, Miss Brick."

"Please, call me Christine," she told James's friend and fellow officer.

"I'd be honored if you would care to use my nick-name—"

"I shall call you Robert."

He agreed with her. "I'd like that even better."

Christine was wide awake now. She fired one question after the other at her visitors. "How did you two get here? Are you on leave? How long can you stay?"

"All in due course," James told her. "But, first, I insist you have a bowl of hot soup and some fresh bread. Then I promise to answer your questions."

Once he'd made certain she had something to eat, he went on to explain, "We're not really on leave."

Between bites, she mumbled, "You're not?"

"No. We're on an errand for our CO." She frowned and James expounded, "Our commanding officer."

Coop decided to help his friend out. "You see, Christine, when James got your note telling him that you were going to be here at the hospital for several weeks, he knew he had to find an excuse—"

"—a reason," corrected James.

"—a reason to make the trip to St. Jean."

She looked from one man to the other. They were wearing the same sheepish expression. "I see." But she didn't. "And how did you manage to find an excuse? Or should I say, a reason?"

James scratched his head. "Well..."

Obviously pleased with himself, Robert Cooper confessed, "Well, to tell you the truth, I kind of arranged that part."

She looked at him over the edge of her raised soup spoon. "You did?"

"Yes. You see, our CO is very fond of his brandy. And it seems that he recently 'misplaced' his last remaining bottle. As luck would have it, the nearest place that we could find any was right here—''

"—in St. Jean," the three of them finished in unison.

"So James and I volunteered to drive over and pick up several bottles for him."

Christine reached out and gave Robert Hershel Cooper's hand an affectionate squeeze. "Thank you. James and I are very lucky to have you for our friend."

Coop was temporarily nonplussed. It was a minute or so before he managed in a slightly self-conscious tone, "James is always telling me what a lucky man he is. Now that I've met you, I'd say that he's very lucky, indeed."

A man's choice of friends said a great deal about the man himself. James had chosen well.

Lieutenant Robert Cooper twisted the cap in his hand. "Since we have to start back to camp tonight, I'd better go speak to the innkeeper about the CO's brandy." To Christine, he said, "I had to come halfway around the world to finally meet you. It was well worth the journey." To James, he added, "I'll see you out front in a half hour."

Once they were alone Christine turned to James. "That's all the time we have? A half hour?"

He gazed down at her. "I'm afraid so, dearest girl."

After a pause, she inhaled deeply and whispered, "It will have to be enough."

James's face momentarily darkened. "How can a half hour be enough when even eternity itself seems too brief a time for me to love you?"

He stepped into the shadows and pulled Christine along after him. For a moment they were kiss against kiss, heart against heart, thought against thought. It was sweet, silent love. It was desperate and lonely love. It was until-death-us-do-part love.

Christine was trembling with emotion. The events she had witnessed the past few days had not only brought death closer, but taught her to appreciate each moment of life. If this was all she could have of James—these few brief minutes with his arms around her, strong and sure; his lips on hers, taking her fear and despair, and turning them into passionate desire—then she would savor every touch, every caress, every second with him. If this was what she was given, then she would gladly take it!

Fate could be cruel to lovers. For their time together went so quickly, while the days and the weeks and the months they were apart seemed like forever.

"I have to go, my dearest love," James finally whispered against her mouth.

Christine put her head back and stared searchingly at him. "I know you must."

He repeated his promise of a long ago autumn day. "One day, Christine. Someday, we will be together."

Her tongue was thick in her mouth as she repeated the words. "We will be together, James."

He touched her lips with the tip of his finger. "Till we meet again."

She took one last deep breath, masked her despair and sent him on his way with "Until we meet again, my love..."

Chapter Twelve

A Time of War

"Let's try it again, Coop. Only this time I'm going to throw a long, high pass so you had better move back a few yards," James warned his friend.

Lieutenant Robert Hershel Cooper stood in the middle of the barren churchyard, his hands planted on his hips. "If I move back any farther, James, I'll be lucky not to fall into a damned shell hole and break my neck."

That brought an amused chuckle from the first man. "Those are the risks of the game, old chap."

Coop muttered under his breath, "Assuming that one wants to play this Neanderthal game in the first place, *old chap*."

"Are you ready?"

"As ready as I'm ever likely to be," he mumbled.

The question was repeated in a booming baritone that had been known to carry the length of a football field. "I can't hear you, Coop. Are you ready?"

"Yes," he said, this time loudly enough to be heard. "But let's bear in mind that my sport in college was tennis. And one is rarely tackled on the tennis court."

"Don't worry. I'll go easy on you," James promised, taking the makeshift football back for the pass.

The patched-up job of rubber and twine sailed through the air for twenty or thirty yards, then tumbled end over end and plopped to the ground several feet from Robert Cooper's boot.

"Dead ball!" he shouted to his companion.

James shook his head and started across the deserted churchyard toward his receiver. "Let's not get technical. We're hardly playing by official rules here."

Coop bent over and retrieved the deflated piece of rubber. "I meant 'dead ball' literally. The darned thing has fallen apart again." He handed what remained of it to James.

The former college star acknowledged grudgingly, "I guess that's the end of our game for this afternoon."

Robert Coop uttered a solemn "Bloody shame."

James put his head back and let out an uproarious laugh. "If you're that disappointed, we could always try to fix it."

The man's expression was perfectly bland. "Actually I think I'd rather have a smoke, if you don't mind."

James reached into his pocket. "Here. Have one of mine."

"What have you got? British? Turkish? American?"

"American, of course."

They lit their cigarettes and strolled along the flagstone path leading toward the front entrance of the small cathedral. There was a huge, gaping hole where the door should have been. The church was in ruins.

"Must have taken a direct 155 mm shell or larger," Coop speculated as they looked at what was left of the building.

"It would only take a couple of strategic hits to level an entire village," James pointed out as they studied the devastation surrounding them.

"This is a no-man's-land for sure," said Coop. He dropped his cigarette to the stone path and ground it out with his heel.

James shook his head in disbelief. "I never thought we'd get to the Western Front, Coop, and find that a steady diet of canned food and plain, old monotony were two of our biggest problems."

His friend and fellow officer spoke up. "Even *I* would rather play football than sit around in the trenches all day, or that dugout they call our officers' quarters. The damned place is crawling with vermin."

James stopped and scraped the mud off his boots. "Have you been deloused yet this week?"

A nod. "For all the good it does. The bloody lice are back in action before we are."

Stuffing his hands into his pockets, James wondered aloud, "Maybe we'll see a little action tonight."

"Maybe."

"It hasn't turned out to be much of a war when all we do is sit and wait for the Boche to fire their artillery at us." He kicked at the smaller stones on the path. "Heard we lost half a dozen men last night, though."

Coop was sympathetic. "It does make one feel a bit like a sitting duck." He tried to cheer up his companion. "I keep telling you, James. You ought to use the time to catch up on your reading."

He cracked a smile. "What is your recommendation for this week, professor?"

"I'm rereading Plato's *Apology*, myself."

James arched an expressive eyebrow. "You do have the mind of a schoolteacher, Coop."

It was taken as a compliment. "That's what I intend to do when this whole crazy business is over—go back to Ohio and teach literature."

"You'll make a fine teacher, too," James said as they headed in the direction of their quarters.

"What are your plans? Are you and Christine still going to get married when this is all over?"

"We hope to." He gazed off toward the horizon. "But I've got to tell you, Coop. I don't like to see her work so hard. You saw how thin and tired she was that night at the inn." His expression was grim. "Christine was worn out and so slender that I could get my hands clear around her waist."

"She's a very brave woman."

He grunted. "Determined, too."

"Yes, brave and determined."

James frowned. "Christine has always had a mind of her own, ever since she was a little girl."

The other man smiled. "I asked you once before, would you want her to be any other way?"

After a moment a softly spoken "No."

They strolled by a sizable pile of rubbish thrown out by the Germans, mostly cans with American labels.

"I wonder what's for dinner tonight," said Coop.

James repeated something Christine had once said to him, "Tinned food that you wouldn't feed to a dog."

"Ah, another gastronomical treat."

Both men were in surprisingly high spirits as they walked back toward the trenches.

THEY HAD NAMES LIKE Devon Lane, Savile Row, Cromwell Road and Little Willie. On the Western Front the trench system was nearly five hundred miles long, stretching from the English Channel on the coast, across a corner of Belgium, through the Champagne region of France, all the way to the Swiss border. What began as little more than a series of holes dug into the ground in

1914 had become an elaborate system of reinforced bunkers by the summer of 1918.

Lieutenants James Warren and Robert Cooper shared their dirt-floored dugout with three other officers. The cubicle measured ten by twelve feet, spacious by bunker standards. There was room for their bedrolls against the outside walls, a brazier for boiling water in the middle and precious little else—except for the lice and the odd rat or two.

It was later the same afternoon as their football match. The blanket covering the entrance to the dugout was pushed to one side to allow the sunlight and the fresh air in. Coop was sitting on a waterproof sheet he'd scrounged from somewhere. He wouldn't tell even James exactly how it had come into his possession, but he was the envy of them all.

He was reading. James had just completed a letter to his parents. The other men were on duty.

"I think I'll wander over to Tin Pan Alley before dinner and see if that sergeant was able to get me the chocolates I asked for," James remarked to him. "Do you want to come along?"

Coop looked up. "What time is it?"

"Don't worry. You don't go on duty for another two hours. We can get over there and back, and still have ample time to dine at our leisure before you have to relieve Jenkins."

He shrugged. "I think I'll pass. I'd like to finish this chapter before duty calls."

"Suit yourself, professor."

James took his leave and stepped out of the bunker. The sky overhead was a clear blue; there wasn't a cloud to be seen. He took off along the American sector of trenches, whistling softly under his breath and remembering to keep his head down. A tall man was an easy target for a sniper.

He'd gone several hundred feet when a series of thuds could be detected in the distance. He muttered to himself, "Damned Boche artillery's starting early today," and kept going.

A second salvo of shells whistled and moaned as they shot through the air. This time they were louder and closer. James had no trouble pinpointing their location when they landed only ten yards in front of the trench where he had flattened himself against the side!

The bombardment continued to get closer and louder; it was one earth-shaking explosion after another. Crash! Crash! Crash! A fierce screech, a vivid flash of light, another big explosion followed by a spray of earth and stones and metal fragments that rained down on their heads. Men were taking cover wherever they could find it. Faces where white with fear. Hands were clasped over their ears. The noise was deafening.

In the early years of the war it wasn't unknown for a bombardment of thousands of guns to go on for days, James reminded himself. Little wonder so many of the soldiers at the time suffered from shell shock and battle fatigue.

There was another huge explosion down the line.

Then silence.

James stood up and looked back. He could see smoke and flames shooting up from one of the bunkers. He turned and started to run as fast as he could in the direction he had just come from. His heart was pounding in his chest. His lungs felt as though they would burst.

Coop!

"Coop!" he shouted as he neared their bunker. "Coop, are you in there?"

He glanced down at his feet. The blanket that had covered their doorway only minutes before had been reduced to a small bit of smoldering cloth lying in the dirt. The doorway was a mound of caved-in timbers, smashed sandbags and loose earth. The bunker, itself, no longer existed.

Frantic, James began to dig through the rubble with his bare hands, calling out to his friend, "I'm coming, Coop. Hang on, pal, I'm coming!"

He dug until his fingers were filthy and bleeding where the flesh had worn off. He dug until the muscles in his arms cramped with exhaustion, and yet never once did he consider stopping. Coop was under there somewhere and he needed James's help.

Someone tried to stop him; he pushed them aside.

His name was being shouted nearby, but he refused to listen. He blocked out everyone and everything except the attempt to save his friend.

"Lieutenant Warren!"

Another voice. "James!"

Someone finally got through to him. He felt a restraining hand on his arm.

"James, it's no good. He's gone."

"Gone?" His voice was a hoarse whisper. His eyes began to focus. He could make out the blurred features of one of the other officers, then the detail of men who had gathered around what was left of the bunker.

"We have to start digging right away," ordered James. "Coop may not have much air left. He could be hurt. We've got to get him out now."

"It's no use digging. There won't be anything left," the officer told him as gently as he could.

James didn't understand. "Anything left?" he repeated.

"The bunker with Lieutenant Cooper inside took a direct hit. We won't find any trace of him, I'm afraid. He would have been blown to bits."

It finally registered somewhere deep inside his brain. James staggered backward and leaned against the side of the trench wall. "Sweet Jesus," he said, and covered his face.

IT WAS LATER that he got angry. He was sitting in front of a small fire, nursing a cup of whiskey that someone had pressed into his hand. He'd asked to be left alone.

"Why in the hell didn't you come with me, Coop? Why did you have to stay behind to finish that damned chapter? Who reads Plato in the middle of a war?" he said aloud, shaking his head in utter despair.

"A man like you should never have been sent to France in the first place. Men like you and Charlie Brick. You weren't meant for war. Either of you. You don't have a violent streak in you like the rest of us do, like I do."

James polished off the cup of whiskey and poured himself another one. He pulled a blanket around his shoulders and huddled near the fire. He was cold and miserable despite the warmth of the summer night.

"All you ever wanted to talk about was poetry and the classics and philosophy. Well, I'll quote you a poem, Coop. One that's short and sweet: 'The good die young.'" With that, James lifted his cup in a toast and downed the liquor in a single gulp.

He tossed the tin cup aside and grabbed the bottle of whiskey. For the first—and what would be the last—time in his life, James Warren intended to drink himself into mindless oblivion.

"I don't believe it's God's will that one man dies and another lives," he ranted, his voice echoing in the empty bunker. "It's all a ridiculous game of random chance. You were in the wrong place at the wrong time, old chap, and—boom! No more Robert Hershel Cooper. No more loving son. No more summa cum laude graduate of Oberlin College. No more future teacher. No more loyal friend."

James staggered to his feet. "It isn't right, Coop. You deserved to live if anyone did."

The half-empty bottle of whiskey fell with a thud to the dirt floor, forgotten. The blanket was shoved aside. The afternoon was long gone, and it was dark outside the bunker.

James made his way up the steps and into the star-filled night. He put his head back and gazed up at the sky. There was the North Star and Scorpius and Ursa Major, the Big Dipper. He suddenly wanted a closer look.

He bumped into a sentry standing at a corner where two trenches intersected.

"Sir!"

"Excuse me, soldier," he grunted, and followed the path that led off toward the north.

The crisscross of trenches through the French countryside was like a labyrinth, James concluded. They reminded him of the garden mazes he'd seen while he was in England. He walked along at a leisurely pace, almost enjoying the nighttime stroll.

He ran into a dead end. Beyond this point there was only barbed wire and a crater-filled landscape known as No-Man's-Land. He climbed out of the trench, found a gap in the barbed wire and continued on his way.

He stumbled over something in the dark and wasn't sure he wanted to know what it was. He went on.

He'd gone another twenty yards when suddenly the small hairs on the back of his neck stood straight on end. He stopped dead in his tracks.

Silence.

Then came a burst of enemy gunfire and the ground around James's feet spit with bullets, the dirt erupting with small explosions.

Zing! Zing! Zing! More bullets flew past his ear. He threw himself to the ground and covered his head with his arms.

"What the—" He instantly sobered.

He raised his eyes a fraction of an inch. He was lying flat on his belly in the middle of No-Man's-Land—that stretch of deserted, barren battlefield between the Allies' frontline trenches and those of the Germans. He was pinned down by enemy gunfire, and there was no way out.

He was doomed.

His teeth started to chatter and he was shaking all over. He'd thought about dying. Every soldier had. But he had never imagined it to be like this—on his belly like a snake.

Then he thought of Christine.

He closed his eyes for a moment and the image of her lovely face appeared in his mind. He could smell that distinctive sweet scent that was hers alone. He could taste her warm lips. He could feel the promise of her slender body. She was everything he had ever wanted in a woman. She was all of his dreams come true.

But there were so many things he had never done in his short lifetime. He had never been to California. He had never seen an eclipse of the sun. He had never owned his own home or walked the land, knowing that it was his.

He had never told Christine that she was the most desirable woman in the world to him. He had never admitted to her that she set his blood on fire. He had never made love to her. He had never watched his child grow within her beautiful body.

A sob caught in James's throat. He would never know what it was to grow old beside the woman he loved. He would never see his children or his grandchildren or his great-grandchildren come into this world.

To never again see the summer sun on a perfect July day as it filtered through the golden blossoms of the Raintree atop the hill.

To never again see Christine's sweet face, to lose himself in the endless depths of her blue eyes, to bury his face in the sweet fragrance of her hair. How could he never again do these things?

Besides, he had made Christine a promise. He could clearly hear the words:

"I will always come for you, Christine."

"And I will always be there, James."

It was a solemn vow they had given to each other on that summer afternoon. Could it be only a year since the day they all picnicked together beside No Name Creek: Christine, Hannah, Charlie, Louise and he? It seemed a lifetime or two ago.

James Wilson Warren was a man of his word. He knew that he had to find a way out of his present predicament. He knew he had to choose life and not death. He had promised Christine, and he would keep that promise whatever the cost.

He began to inch his way backward, biding his time, waiting for just the right opportunity. During a momentary lull in the gunfire, he jumped to his feet, turned and sprinted toward the safety of the Allied trenches. Bullets whizzed by him but he never hesitated. He scrambled through the gap in the barbed wire and dove headfirst into the nearest trench. He landed hard on the ground with a resounding thud.

LIEUTENANT JAMES WARREN awoke with the first gray light of dawn and wondered why he was lying in the bottom of a remote trench, his uniform covered with dirt and specks of dried blood. He tried to move and discovered that every bone and muscle in his body ached.

Then it all came back to him in a rush. The chocolates. Coop. The shelling. The bunker blown to smithereens. The whiskey. Sobering to find himself under enemy gunfire. Hopelessness. Christine. In the end, always Christine.

He sat up and patted himself. He was alive! Thank God, he was alive!

He put his head back against the dirt wall of the trench and he began to laugh. Quietly at first, and then loudly enough to be heard on both sides of No-Man's-Land. He laughed so hard that the tears came to his eyes and rolled, unchecked, down his cheeks. He laughed until his sides hurt. He laughed until he thought he would die.

And then there was no more laughter. He buried his head in his hands and he wept.

CHRISTINE AWOKE with a start and sat straight up in bed. Her heart was pounding in her chest and her skin was damp with perspiration. Her breath was coming hard and fast, as if she'd been running. Her whole body was trembling.

She arose from her bed and stood in front of the solitary window in the room she shared with Irene Chandler. She looked out. It was nearly dawn. There was a hint of light on the horizon. But Paris still slept.

The perspiration dried on her skin. She shivered and reached for the blanket at the foot of her cot. She pulled it closely around her.

What had awakened her? She couldn't remember. Perhaps it had been a dream. Perhaps a nightmare.

Suddenly she sensed that something was wrong. Terribly wrong. It was James. She knew it. He was in trouble. She wrung her hands, angry and frustrated that she could be of no help to him.

Then Christine closed her eyes tightly and concentrated. She whispered into the darkness: "We can survive anything as long as we love each other. In your darkest hour, remember that, my love. You promised, James. You promised to always come for me. And I will always be here waiting...."

Chapter Thirteen

To Love and Honor

Christine was nearly beside herself with excitement. She had been back in Paris for a month when she received word from James that he had been granted a special leave.

She was excited and relieved. Her fears of the past several weeks had been for nothing, she told herself. Her worries were groundless. James was fine. In fact, she had rarely seen him in such good spirits as he gave her his arm that morning and promised to show her the sights of the *Ville de Paris*.

"You've been in France for how long, Christine? Three months? Four?" he said as he hailed a taxi. An answer was obviously not expected of her. "What have you seen of Paris, the City of Light? I will tell you. The street where you live. The vendors where you buy an occasional bunch of flowers for your room. The canteen where you bake five hundred doughnuts before the first light of day. You work too much and you play too little. Today that is going to change."

She was about to remind James that she hadn't been sent to France to play, but thought better of it. Why spoil his mood? Or her own for that matter? For the first time in months, she felt lighthearted, even gay, and she was going to enjoy it! She was young, she was in love and she was in Paris. Surely that spelled magic if anything did.

There were so many wonderful sights to see and things to do from one end of the city to the other. She knew them by heart from her conversations with the effervescent Viviane.

"You should have seen Paris before *la guerre. Magnifique!* I fear it will never be the same, *mademoiselle*," Viviane had sadly concluded one day, shaking her head.

"Nothing has been the same since the war," Christine had agreed, "but your city is still *magnifique*."

On another occasion Viviane had laughed and boasted to her, "They say that 'God invented the *Parisien* to prevent foreigners from ever understanding anything about the French.'"

The statement had left Christine puzzled.

Whether she understood the Parisians or not, she could enjoy their city and bask in the warmth of the summer day, Christine decided as she and James climbed into a hired carriage.

"Oh, James, I never thought that you and I would be taking a carriage ride through the famous Bois de Boulogne in Paris," she exclaimed, slipping her arm through his. She knew her eyes must be shining with the excitement she was feeling. "Home seems so far away."

He gazed down at her and smiled. "Home *is* far away."

On either side of them were vast expanses of green lawn and brilliant flowers and thick woods. "Even the war seems far away today," she murmured.

"The war doesn't exist today, Christine. Not for us," he promised.

James kept his promise.

They viewed the city from the Eiffel Tower. They lunched in an outdoor café along the Champs-Elysées.

They strolled through the vast gardens at the Tuileries. They crossed to the Île de la Cité and stood gazing up in wonder at the massive towers of Notre Dame, and then took a taxi north to Montmartre, where James had arranged for them to dine at one of its most famous restaurants: Restaurant du Coucou—the cuckoo.

The Restaurant du Coucou was small and crowded and noisy. There were red-and-white-checked curtains at the windows and green shutters on either side of the narrow doorway. They were greeted by Vincent, the proprietor, and escorted to a tiny corner table.

Christine hadn't realized how hungry she was until a plate of steaming food was set in front of her. She inhaled. It smelled spicy and delicious.

"What is it?" she asked James as the wide noodles and tomato sauce melted on her tongue.

"Something called lasagna. It's Italian," he explained, and laughed as a string of cheese caught on her chin.

They filled up on lasagna and hot, crusty bread. They drank glasses of dark, red wine and gazed at each other by candlelight. They listened to the conversations all around them, understanding little and yet more than they expected to. And then they climbed to the top of Martyr's Mount—Montmartre—and stood looking down on the city of Paris.

They were all alone. James slipped his arms around her waist, and it seemed the most natural thing in the world to her, Christine realized. She leaned her head back against his shoulder.

She sighed contentedly. "When I was a little girl, your sister showed me a splendid new toy she had received for her birthday. It was a cylinder fashioned of polished wood, and it was filled with bits of colored glass. I re member thinking what a disappointment it must have been for Louise to receive such an oddity as a gift, until she showed me how to hold it up to the light." Her voice shimmered. "It was pure magic. I had never seen anything like it before in my life. It opened up a whole new world for me, James, and in a strange way I was never quite the same again." She turned in his arms. "Seeing Paris with you has been like gazing through that kaleidoscope—a wondrous and magical world has been unfolded before my eyes. I will never forget this day as long as I live."

"Neither will I, my dearest girl. Neither will I."

Then, with the stars overhead and the lights of Paris below, James bent his head and kissed her.

It was a gentle kiss at first. His lips were warm and sweet and tasted of the wine they had sipped with their dinner. She found herself feeling slightly light-headed and wondered if it was the wine or James.

She laughed a little and pulled away, but he brought her back into his arms and kissed her again. This time his mouth was hard and hungry. He was devouring hers. She could feel his tongue on her lips, her teeth. It created the oddest sensation inside her, unlike any she had ever known.

She thought of that night at the tiny inn in St. Jean when she had last seen him. They had had only a brief time together before he'd had to return to camp. There had been a desperation to their kisses, to their caresses. Every moment was precious when the next moment might be their last together.

Christine realized she was holding herself stiff beneath his kiss. She relaxed her lips, giving in to the temptation to taste his mouth, to take a little of him for herself.

She could sense an immediate change in James. Desperation became desire. Demand became a kind of lovely seduction. It was indefinably exciting to sense his response through her mouth and fingers and body.

Before she could decide what to do about the undertow of passion ebbing to and fro between them, James took a step back. He stood there for a moment, staring at her, his chest visibly rising and falling with each breath. Then he seemed to make up his mind about something.

"Perhaps it would be best if we resumed walking," he said in a slightly husky voice and took her hand in his.

Part of her knew he was right. Part of her was frustrated by the logic of his actions. She wanted him. He wanted her. How could it be wrong when it felt so right?

After they had gone some distance she asked, "How long is your leave this time?"

A restrained "Four days, including today."

She had him for another three whole days. The exquisite joy of it! "I have been saving up my days off all summer."

James turned to her. "Will you consent to spend tomorrow, and the day after tomorrow, and the day after that with me, my dearest Christine?"

"Of course," she said happily, squeezing his hand. As an afterthought she added, "What will your friend Coop do if you spend all your leave with me?"

The instant the words were out of her mouth, Christine knew something was wrong.

James froze in place. He looked down at her, and his features were unreadable. After a slight hesitation, he spoke. "Coop didn't come to Paris with me."

She was almost afraid to ask, "Couldn't he get leave?"

Beside her, James grew rigid. His face darkened. Even in the pale light of evening, she could clearly see the change in him. Her fears of the past several weeks returned. Her worries no longer seemed groundless. Something was wrong, dreadfully wrong.

"James, what is it?" she asked gently.

He bowed his head and could not speak.

"Is it something to do with Coop?"

He nodded.

She swallowed hard. "Do you want to tell me about it?"

It was some time before he lifted his head. She could see the pain in his eyes. "I wasn't going to tell you. At least not right away. I wanted us to have a few days together...."

There was a terrible ache around her heart.

James finally said the words she'd been dreading to hear. "Coop was killed three weeks ago."

"Robert dead?"

She hadn't realized that she'd said the words out loud until James responded with "I could have easily died with him. I would have if it hadn't been for you."

"I don't understand," she said in a trembling voice.

His brows congealed into a scowl. "We'd been in the churchyard playing football." He laughed sadly. "Coop hated football. But he was always such a damned good sport about it. We saw this bombed-out church."

He was talking in bits and pieces that made little sense to her, but Christine didn't interrupt him.

"Later we walked back to the trenches. Coop spent the rest of the afternoon in our officer's dugout reading Plato. I decided to go see a sergeant about some chocolates he'd promised to get me." James's face was masked by darkness. "I wanted to surprise you."

"The chocolates were for me," she said quietly.

His voice was deep and his words slowly spaced. "Yes." Then, "I asked Coop if he wanted to come along while I saw the sergeant. He declined, saying he wanted to finish the chapter he was on before he went on duty."

James opened his mouth and closed it without speaking. He was unable to go on.

Christine placed a gentle hand on his arm. "You don't have to tell me any more if you don't wish to."

His gaze brushed her face like a touch of need. Maybe he didn't have any choice in the matter, maybe he *had* to tell her. "I was a few hundred feet from our bunker when the enemy shelling began. I remember thinking to myself, 'Damned Boche artillery's starting early today.' But I kept going, all the same. The explosions came closer and closer. I flattened against the wall of the trench. The noise was deafening. One loud crash after another—like the world was coming to an end. There was one more big explosion down the line and the shelling stopped."

Christine could see his eyes: they were fixed on the horizon. There were beads of sweat on his upper lip; he wiped them away with the back of his hand.

"It can be like that in the trenches," James said breathing through his teeth. "Earth-shattering noise one minute and silence the next. It's damned eerie sometimes."

She waited quietly, patiently, while he relived those awful moments.

"I looked back and I could see the flames leaping above one of the bunkers. In my gut I knew it was ours. I turned and started to run. By the time I reached our dugout, it was a pile of rubble."

"Dear Lord in heaven," Christine whispered, staring into his eyes with sudden comprehension.

Then the words came in a rush. "I started to claw at the dirt with my bare hands. I knew Coop was under there, buried under all that earth and splintered wood and sandbags. I could hear somebody calling my name and realized it was another officer from our unit. I shouted to him that we needed men with shovels to start digging immediately. We had to get Coop out. He said it was no use. No use." The fatigue and strain of months in combat had shorn James of his defenses. The tears brimmed in his eyes. His voice was sharp with pain. "There was nothing left of Coop. He'd been blown to pieces."

Christine could not bear the sight of his suffering. Wordlessly she reached for him. Her arms went around him and she held on tightly, as if she would never let him go. He buried his face in her hair and held on for dear life.

Later she murmured, "I am so sorry, James. I know what your friend meant to you."

He pulled himself together with a visible effort. "It's such a damned waste, Christine. Coop wasn't a soldier—he never wanted to hurt anyone. He was a kind, gentle, peaceful man. All he talked about was going back to Ohio and teaching literature."

"I know. I know."

His anger began to surface again. "Why in the hell did Coop have to stay behind to read that book of his? He'd still be alive today if he'd gone with me." He turned to her and his bitterness was like an open, festering wound. "Tell me, Christine, why does one man live and another man die? I don't believe it's God's will. I refuse to believe that God has anything to do with this bloody war."

"James—" Her blood ran cold. What was, simply was. But those were not comforting words, and what James needed right now was comfort.

He agonized, "Why did I live and Coop die?"

It was the question to which neither of them had the answer. She had no magic words to take his pain away, to soothe the anguish in his soul. She had only her presence, her arms around him, her love, always her love for him.

"Your friend has died and you are grieving for him and rightly so. I do not know what purpose his death will serve. Maybe it will make sense someday. Maybe it won't. War often doesn't make sense. You know that better than I do." She gripped his arms tightly and stared up into his eyes. "I only know that if you live, I live. And if you die, then I will cease to exist as well. You are my heart, James. I cannot live without you."

His voice was hoarse as he echoed, "And I cannot live without you."

Christine shivered and burrowed into his side. She had come very close to losing James. It frightened her. Indeed, it made her afraid as she had never been afraid before. Suddenly she realized that this moment, this night, was all they had promised to them. Who could say what the morrow would bring?

What if they should die before they had even begun to live? The question plagued her.

She had known for a long time that this moment would come. "James, I don't want to be alone tonight."

He stepped back and held her at arm's length. "Christine—"

She looked at him squarely in the face. "Where are you staying?"

Almost by rote, he said, "I've taken rooms at a hotel not far from your residence."

Her eyes pleaded with him. "Please take me back with you. Only Irene will know that I haven't returned and she has a kind, generous heart. Please, James, I want to be with you."

He gazed down into her face. "Are you certain?"

"Yes. I want us to have this night together."

She was firm in her resolve. This was right. She knew it. She could feel it. She and James had always been right for each other.

Reverently he brought her fingers to his lips. "I once said to you, 'come with me and be my love.' Do you remember?"

She could scarcely catch her breath. "I remember. It was last fall and we were in the old red barn."

Suddenly his voice grew softer; he was almost caressing her with his words. "I will say it again. Come with me now and be my love, Christine."

"Yes, James."

They joined hands and walked down from Montmartre until they found a taxi to take them to his rooms.

Christine stood in the foyer and marveled at the luxury that met her eyes. James's suite was elegant. There was a sitting room with chairs and a sofa and a small balcony overlooking the city. Down another passageway was a private bath and a large boudoir with a damask-covered bed.

"I do believe that the room Irene and I share is half the size of your sitting room."

She did not see the frown her statement brought to his handsome face.

"I do not like to think of you living in that cramped attic," he said disapprovingly.

She shrugged. "We make do, Irene and I. With bright curtains hanging at the window and pictures on the walls, it is quite pleasant. We could never afford accommodations like these. I keep forgetting that you are a wealthy man, James."

He came up and stood behind her. "I know you do. It's one of the things I love about you."

She was suddenly, vividly, aware of the smallest detail. Off in the distance she could hear the rattle of carriage wheels on the cobblestones, the clip-clop of horses' hooves as they ambled by in the street, the horn of an autobus, the sounds of people laughing and talking. Paris by night.

The breath from James's lips gently stirred the wisps of hair that had escaped at her nape. The wonderful masculine smell of him filled her nostrils, as surely as his presence filled the room. Every nerve ending in her body seemed attuned to him; she knew where he was every moment. Then she felt his touch on her hair as he wound a strand around his finger.

Her voice came out husky and half expectant. "I will take my hair down, if you like."

Placing his hands on her shoulders, he said meaningfully, "I will do it for you."

He guided her to the gilt-edged mirror above the bureau in the boudoir. Mesmerized, she watched as he carefully removed the combs and pins. When he was finished, her hair fell into a wild tangle of curls about her face and shoulders.

"I have dreamed of taking your hair down," he confessed as he ran his fingers through the thick swath of gold. "When I was a boy I cursed your braid because it caught on a log and nearly caused you to drown. When I was older I watched your hair flow about you like a silken mantle and it made me realize you were no longer a child. Now it reminds me that you are a beautiful woman. Your hair has always fascinated me."

James picked up a hairbrush from among his personal effects on the bureau, and began to stroke through the long, blond tresses.

Christine closed her eyes and gave in to the pleasure, the purely physical sensation, of having him brush her hair. It was a personal and intimate act. She could feel her entire body beginning to relax and wondered if she could stay standing on her feet.

Opening her eyes, she gazed at her reflection in the mirror. She had never seen herself like this before, her complexion rosy and all aglow. She had never watched as a man touched her. She had never witnessed the wild blue fire in her eyes.

"Christine... Christine..." James said her name over and over. It was like a whisper on the night wind. "I love the way you look. I love the way you smell. I love the way you feel." he murmured as he bent his head and trailed his lips along one shoulder.

A shiver of awareness ran down her spine, creating a sense of expectation that left her shaking. She watched as his mouth slowly moved from her shoulder to her neck and on to the curve of her ear. Her lips parted a fraction of an inch. It took every bit of willpower she possessed to swallow the small, keening sound that quivered deep in her throat.

James looked up and they stared at each other in the mirror. It was their reflection and yet it wasn't.

Christine raised a trembling hand to her mouth. "Can it be me?" she asked in a bemused whisper. "Can it be you?"

"Yes," he answered huskily.

She turned in his arms. "Kiss me, James."

He kissed her and she opened herself to him. She held nothing back. She revealed her vulnerability, her innocence, her passion, her desire for him. She would have no secrets from him before the night was over. She would become such a part of him that if he cried, she would taste the salt of his tears on her lips. If he was hurt, she would suffer his pain. Wherever he went, she would go also. He was the other half of herself, and now she would know for the first time what it was to be whole.

He kissed her and all the emotions, all the latent tensions, all the strains of the past few months gave way to kiss after kiss until they both burst into flames and burned—burned hot and dangerous.

He tasted her ears, her throat, her mouth, again and again as if he could not get enough of her, as if he never would. He took her breath away. He devoured her sweetness, drank from her lips.

He brought his hands up to splay across the undercurve of her breasts. She could feel the heat of his palms through her blouse and shift. She could sense the slightest movement of his fingers.

Then she was crushed to him and her heart slammed against her ribs. The warmth inside her flowed like thick, sweet honey left out in the summer sun. There was no denying the changes in her body. Nor those in James's. She could feel his heart hammering in his chest. His body was tensed and hardened.

He reached for the buttons at her throat and began to undo them one by one. His hand was shaking. She could feel the heat of his flesh as it brushed along her bare skin.

He removed his military tunic and shed his shirt as she slipped out of her clothes. She stood there in her cotton shift and watched as he undressed. It was a new experience for her. She marveled at the muscles of his arms and chest, the flat belly, the length of his legs.

James pulled back the bed covers and they slipped beneath the sheets. She turned and was gathered gently into his arms.

"Remember that day last autumn when you were home on leave from Camp Taylor and we went for a walk with Hannah?"

"Of course, I remember. It was the day I proposed to you. A man doesn't forget something like that."

She pressed a quick buss to his shoulder. "We climbed up into the hayloft. We kissed and then we stopped. You said that one day we would not stop, that you would not leave me. I want this to be that day, that night, James. We don't know what tomorrow holds for us. But I want to love you, and know what it is to be loved by you."

He faced her and spoke as if it were a solemn vow. "You are my heart and soul, Christine Brick. You are my only love. I promise to honor and cherish you as long as we both shall live."

"And I will love and honor you for this night and for whatever comes after, James Warren."

They sealed their vows with a kiss. It was a kiss that said they would learn how to love each other together.

Then Christine felt his touch on her skin, her heart in the palm of his hand. There was only this then in all the world—his touch on her, caressing her, shaping her to his will. He created a wild song that echoed through her veins.

She looked deeply into his eyes. "I want to touch you, too, James."

Her hands moved across the surprisingly smooth skin of his body, the soft curls of dark hair scattered along his chest, the taut muscles. He was beautiful. And when she caressed him she heard the air catch in his throat, felt the thundering beat of his heart.

They reached instinctively for each other and it was a joyous proclamation of life. They had been one in spirit for many years; now they were one in flesh as well. Theirs was a union of heart and soul and body. James had found the missing half of himself. For the first time in her life, Christine was whole.

CHRISTINE AWOKE and stretched her arms above her head. She slowly opened her eyes. The early morning sun peered into the room through gossamer-thin curtains, highlighting the bed with its damask spread trailing along the floor, the luxury of the soft sheets covering her body, the fine, dark down of hair on the muscular arm that lay across her stomach.

She turned her head and saw the face on the pillow next to hers. James. He was still sleeping.

She watched him, studying each feature in repose: the dark eyebrows relaxed in sleep, the even darker eyelashes outlined against the tanned skin, the well-shaped ear that lay close to his head as an ear ought to, the patrician nose with the slight bump on its bridge, the mouth softened by slumber, the strong jut of his jaw, the stubble of beard on his chin. She was fascinated by even the smallest detail of his appearance.

Somehow he seemed younger while asleep, she realized. Almost like an overgrown boy. She wondered if it were true for all men. Did they all seem younger and more vulnerable when they weren't so busy wearing a mask of maturity and strength?

James stirred but did not awaken. He turned onto his side and for the first time she could clearly see his hands against the white backdrop of the sheet.

Christine frowned. The skin on the tips of his fingers was a different color and texture than the rest of his hand.

It was pink and new and appeared tender to the touch. Then she noticed the blood-red scratches and deep gouges on the backs of his hands. Scratches and gouges that would, in time, fade to white scars.

How could she have missed seeing them yesterday? Then a flesh-colored bandage, a pair of dress uniform gloves, a sleeve that partially covered his hand came to mind.

Tears suddenly blurred her vision. She covered her mouth until the urge to cry out had passed. She remembered what James had said to her last night when he'd told her about dear Coop's death: "I clawed at the dirt with my bare hands. I knew Coop was under there, buried under all that earth and splinterd wood and sandbags."

She had not thought it possible for her to love James Warren more than she had loved him last night. She was wrong. She loved him more at this moment. He had tried to save his friend and he would carry the scars for the rest of his life—both those on his hands and those in his heart.

There was a movement beside her in the bed. She looked up and found James watching her, watching her with those beautiful, perceptive eyes of his.

"You have tears on your face," he said, still half asleep.

"Do I?" She sniffed and tried to brush them away.

He pushed himself up on one elbow. "Darling, what's the matter? Are you all right?"

Darling. It was the first time he'd ever called her by that endearment.

Christine shook her head. It wasn't yes and it wasn't no. It wasn't even a maybe.

James moved closer to her. "Are you having regrets already?"

She knitted her brows. "Regrets?"

"About last night," he said gently.

Her eyes opened wider in comprehension. "You—you don't understand. That wasn't why I was crying," she stammered.

"Then why were you crying?" he whispered at her shoulder.

"Because I love you—" she inhaled a deep, trembling breath "—and because I saw what you did to your hands."

He gathered her to him. "It's all right. My hands will heal in time."

"I know they will, but I love you all the more for what you tried to do."

Then she raised his hand to her lips and one by one pressed a kiss to each fingertip.

His eyes darkened with emotion. He caught her chin in his free hand and brought her face to his. He kissed her. There was more than desire in his kiss. There was more than need. There was the love that came from deep down inside of him.

"You have no regrets about last night," he murmured against her mouth.

"Not a one." She sighed contentedly. "And you?"

"It was the most wonderful night of my life," James stated in that husky baritone of his.

"I don't think I will ever be the same." There was a kind of wonder in her voice. "You have opened a whole new world to me, James, a world where only the two of us may go."

"It will always be our special place."

"Yes, our special place."

He gazed intently into her eyes. "Whatever else happens, my love, we will always have Paris."

"WE WILL always have Paris."

The words echoed in Christine's mind in the days and weeks to come.

She had done it for James's sake, she told herself. But she knew she had done it for her own sake, as well. She had not only given her love to James, she had received his love in return. He was the missing half of herself. For the first time in her life she was whole.

Their goodbyes had been bittersweet. Yet he left taking her heart with him. And she remained with his locked securely within her. Neither would ever be entirely alone again.

Chapter Fourteen

A Time of Peace

The American Expeditionary Force
in France and Belgium 1918

June 9-15: 27,500 U.S. troops are engaged in repulsing the German advance and retaking Belleau Wood.

July 18-August 6: 270,000 U.S. troops play a major role in the advance on Château-Thierry.

September 12-16: 550,000 U.S. troops advance near St. Mihiel. 16,000 Germans are captured.

September 26-November 11: 1,200,000 U.S. troops are involved in a major advance near the Meuse River region.

"LIEUTENANT WARREN, the CO would like to see you right away, sir!" snapped the young recruit.

James rubbed the sleep out of his eyes and muttered, "Right away, huh?"

"Yessir!"

Five minutes later James was dressed in full uniform and out the door of his dugout.

Five minutes after that he was bending over a map along with a dozen other men, listening to their commanding officer give them their orders.

"We've been instructed to make a clean sweep of the area between our encampment and the river to make sure it's clear of enemy troops. Advance scouts have reported that the Germans have pulled back beyond the Meuse. It's our job to make sure. Poor devils have been surrendering by the thousands. They're exhausted and half starved. From all accounts those who are retreating are moving too quickly to stop and set mines or booby traps. Still, keep a sharp eye."

The CO gave each of his men their instructions. Then he turned to James. "Lieutenant Warren, I want you and your men to clear these woods—" he pointed to a specific area on the map "—and meet up with Lieutenant Jenkins and his men at a village. Here." He stabbed at a small black dot with his finger.

"Yessir!"

Half an hour later James and his platoon sergeant had roused their men.

Sergeant McKee growled with his customary good humor, "Okay, soldiers, get off your duffs! We're going for a walk in the woods on this lovely autumn morning. So get your gear together and look sharp! There could be enemy troops in the area, buried mines or booby traps. So let's not make a muck of it and maybe we can all come out the other side in one piece and enjoy a smoke."

James issued his orders like the seasoned professional he had become in the past year. "Once we reach the woods we walk abreast, twenty paces apart. It could be a little foggy this morning, so keep doubly sharp."

With that, James and Sergeant McKee led their men toward the thick woods the map indicated were two miles down the road from the Americans' temporary headquarters. They were moving deep into what had been enemy territory only a few days before.

One of the fresh-faced recruits caught up with James and marched along beside him for a while. He could see the eagerness and the excitement in the boy's expression.

"Think we'll meet up with any of the Boche, sir?"

"Not if we're lucky, son."

James shook his head imperceptibly. He wasn't even twenty-four years old yet and he was already calling younger men "son."

The thought niggled at him. It was because he was an old man in a young man's body. Sometimes he felt so old that he wondered why his hair hadn't turned pure white by now....

By first light they were approaching the woods. As James had predicted, the morning fog was still thick enough to slice with a knife. They couldn't see more than twenty yards in any direction. The trees had an eerie, ghostlike look about them.

James called his men into a huddle. He spoke in a quiet voice. Yet each of them could distinctly hear him. "Remember, no heroics. Keep alert at all times. Don't touch anything that looks suspicious. Even an old metal helmet lying on the ground could be a booby trap. If you think you've come across something, pass the word down the line. The sergeant or I will come have a look at it. Does everybody understand?"

"Yessir."

"Yessir, Lieutenant."

"Let's go."

They marched into the thick fog.

James took in a deep breath and let it out again. He knew his men were afraid. He could taste their fear in the air. This might be a routine cleanup to Sergeant McKee and him, but to many of these raw recruits it was their first time in battle.

He heard a twig snap and the man to his left swore under his breath. Then a quiet "Sorry, Lieutenant."

An hour later the word was passed down that one of his men had found something. James went to see what it was. It turned out to be an empty oil drum, but he commended the soldier for using his head and following orders.

The fog began to burn off and visibility gradually improved to the point that they could clearly see each other. The platoon reached the other side of the woods by early afternoon without incident.

"Jenkins." James nodded to the officer who had been ordered to rendezvous with him at the village. "Nothing to report on our end. The woods are clear."

Lieutenant Jenkins leaned back against a tree at the edge of the village—or what was left of the village, anyway. "Nothing to report on our end, either. I'd say the Boche have pulled out. It looks like they've been gone for several days, too. We found a few filthy trenches and that was about it." He pulled a pack of cigarettes from his pocket. "Care for a smoke?"

James declined. "How about the village?"

Jenkins took a look around. "Not much of it left, is there? Everything's been reduced to rubble."

James squinted. "Part of the church is still standing."

The other officer grunted and said, "I'll report to the CO that we've made a clean sweep of the area. I suppose he'll order the rest of the troops to move up by nightfall."

The two men took off in opposite directions. James found himself headed toward the empty churchyard. Except for a hearty weed or two that dared to poke its head above ground, it was barren land.

It reminded him of another afternoon and another churchyard. The one where he and Coop used to toss a makeshift football around. He often thought of the last day they'd had together and he was saddened. But he was no longer angry. Somehow he'd let his anger go. Perhaps it had been during those few precious days he'd spent with Christine in Paris.

His dear, sweet, loving Christine. She had given herself so utterly and completely to him. She had held back nothing. The gift of love from a woman like Christine was the rarest gift a man could receive. If he had the sense to appreciate it—which, James reminded himself, he did.

He wondered how she was faring since they had last been together at the end of the summer. Much to his regret, and her anguish, there had been no more leaves and mo more trips to Paris for him. Not even for her birthday in September. He wondered if she had received the box of chocolates he'd sent.

James glanced up and found himself standing in front of what had once undoubtedly been a charming country church. He took his helmet off and held it in his hands as he entered the bombed-out sanctuary.

There was no roof overhead, only blue sky. The altar had been crushed beneath a huge beam that had fallen from the ceiling. James found a pew partially intact and knelt down. Bowing his head for a moment, he said a short prayer for Coop. It only seemed right. He added one for Christine, asking the Almighty to look after her since he could not.

Then he heard a faint noise off to his right, and the tiny hairs on the back of his neck came to attention. Silently, James rose to his feet and withdrew his revolver from its holster. More than likely it was a rat scurrying around in the debris. But he wasn't taking any chances.

He cocked his head to one side and listened. Nothing. Then, there it was again. A light metallic scratching. He crept along the pew. When the noise stopped, he stopped. When it began again, he moved forward. He finally pinpointed the direction it was coming from: a small room off the sanctuary that must have served as the village priest's private quarters.

Suddenly a sound came from overhead, not off to his right! He turned on the balls of his feet, aimed his revolver and watched as a bird flew down from its nest in the rotting timbers above.

James nearly laughed out loud at himself. He wasn't usually this jumpy.

He was about to relax from his stance when the scratching noise came again. He flattened himself against the wall. If this turned out to be a rat, he was going to feel pretty silly about all the precautions he was taking. But then he reminded himself that he was still alive because he was a cautious man, because he trusted his instincts.

He inched his way along and peered around the corner into the next room. Nothing. There was nothing there. Just as he was about to walk away he saw something move. Then the torn sleeve of a uniform and a blond head appeared in his peripheral vision.

James twirled, raised his revolver to shoulder height and took careful aim.

"Who goes there?" He barked out the command.

The man dropped whatever it was he held in his hands and jerked around. He was all eyes and they were filled with naked fear. The mouth was slightly agape. The muscles of his body were frozen and unable to move. James could see it in the young German soldier's face: he knew he was going to die.

James didn't know who was more surprised. Or for that matter, more frightened. His own heart was racing at breakneck speed. The last thing he had expected upon entering the ruined church was finding himself face-to-face with an enemy soldier.

He took stock of the situation. There was no weapon in evidence. No rifle. No pistol. Nothing. The man had no defense except his bare hands. And he could see that they were shaking so badly as to be utterly useless.

He looked closer. The soldier was thin and gaunt. There was a look of desperation, exhaustion and starvation on his face. He'd been searching for food.

James looked again and swore softly under his breath.

For he finally realized that the slender figure standing in front of him was a boy. A boy of maybe twelve or thirteen, at the most. He'd heard, of course—they all had— that the Germans had resorted to drafting the latest round of recruits from their schools. He had just never imagined they would be as young as the one standing in front of him.

A thought flitted through James's mind. The boy wouldn't even be ready to shave for a couple more years.

The youngster finally found his voice. It was high and slightly squeaky. *"Amerikaner?"*

James nodded. He wished he knew how to speak German. Even a few words would help. He would have liked to ask the boy how old he was. And what in the world he was doing here when the rest of the German army was miles and miles away.

The fear subsided only slightly in the boy's eyes. James knew what he was thinking: is the *Amerikaner* going to shoot me dead, after all?

James knew in his gut that he had no intentions of killing the boy. But he had no wish to take a prisoner of war who was barely out of short pants, either.

His mind was made up. He knew what he was going to do. He knew it was the right thing to do, maybe not as a soldier but as a man.

"Get out of here." He made a gesture, then pointed in the direction he'd heard the Germans had retreated. "Go on! Get out of here!" he said more emphatically.

For a moment the boy didn't seem to understand.

James tried again. "Go. *Allez!* Vamoose."

The young German took a tentative step toward the gaping hole in the back of the church, keeping one eye on James all the while.

"Go on home to your mother, boy. I'll not harm you." Maybe he couldn't comprehend the words but James knew the tone of voice was unmistakable.

"Mutter?"

"Yes, go home to your *mutter*."

The boy turned and began to quickly make his way toward the rear of the building. Just beyond the ruins of the church were more woods, then the river and freedom.

He stopped once and looked over his shoulder at James, still not certain whether he was going to receive a bullet in the back as he ran away.

Then he began to run as fast as his legs would carry him. The last glimpse James had of the boy was as he melted into the woods.

James stood there for a good while, then he made his way out of the church and back through the village toward his platoon.

As he rejoined his men, he murmured under his breath, "The war is over now for both of us, Coop."

"What'd ya say, Lieutenant?"

James turned to Sergeant McKee. "I said, sergeant, the war's about over for us. The Germans are on the run."

"Yessir." He shook his head thoughtfully. "Thank God, this is the war to end war."

CHRISTINE HEFTED THE BOWL of sliced onions in her arms and carefully emptied it into the huge pot of hot soup on the stove.

Irene Chandler was working at another counter in the canteen kitchen, peeling a mountain of potatoes in preparation for the four hundred men that Miss Lambert estimated they would be serving supper to later that day.

The Englishwoman looked up and chuckled under her breath. "I declare, Christine, that pot's as big as you are. Can you manage?"

Despite the chill of the November day outside, it was hot in the kitchen. Christine wiped the perspiration from her brow with the sleeve of her dress. "I can manage."

"Do you want to exchange jobs for a while?"

There was a smile on Christine's face as she teased, "Oh, I wouldn't want to do that when I know how much you enjoy peeling potatoes."

Irene mumbled under her breath, "When I volunteered for Red Cross work overseas I expected it to be glamorous like in the posters up all over London. I pictured myself wearing a nice neat uniform and holding the hand of a dashing lieutenant who was eternally grateful for my tender care."

Christine laughed. "Did you now?"

Irene picked up another spud from the pile. "I never thought I would end up slaving in a kitchen doing exactly the same chores I'd been doing at home for my mum. Only it's more work and harder work here," she grumbled. "At least my mum never asked me to cook supper for four hundred hungry men."

"No, I don't imagine she ever did."

The North Country woman looked over at her friend and roommate. "Of course I don't regret coming to France, mind you. I really don't. I've seen a sight more of the world than I would have if I'd stayed put in Northumbria."

"I'd never been more than thirty-five miles from home before I volunteered," Christine said as she stirred the pot of soup.

Irene stood and stretched her arms above her head, then rubbed her aching back with both hands. "Never thought I'd see Paris, and I've done that."

"Paris, the City of Light. I used to dream about it," said Christine wistfully.

She didn't see the look of genuine affection with which the other woman regarded her.

"Never thought I'd actually meet a Yank," Irene blurted out. She glanced down at her hands. "I've never had a friend I liked as much as I like you, Christine. And here you being an American and a Quaker and all."

"And I never imagined I would find a dear friend like you, Irene."

They went about their business without speaking of it again.

During a brief respite several hours later, Christine called her friend over. From her apron pocket she produced a small package wrapped up in white paper. She placed it in Irene's hand.

"What is it?" she asked, trying to keep the excitement out of her voice.

"Just a little treat for you to enjoy," said Christine.

She undid the paper and stood staring at the delectable pieces of chocolate inside—six in all. "Chocolate candy—" the woman hardly dared to breathe "—my favorite."

Christine smiled. "I know."

She began to shake her head. "But I can't take your chocolates, Christine. I just can't. They were a birthday present from that handsome young lieutenant of yours. And they're so hard to come by—"

"Hush, now. I want to share them with you."

Irene swallowed hard. "I don't know what to say."

"You don't have to say anything." Then Christine pointed out, "Didn't you share your licorice with me on the voyage across the Channel?"

"That hardly seems the same."

"It is to me. You offered your friendship when I was all alone and I didn't know a soul. I will never forget that, Irene Chandler. Now, I insist that you keep the chocolates."

"Well, if you insist..."

They both went back to their chores with lighter hearts.

AS THE AFTERNOON WORE ON Christine peeled carrots and turnips for the soup, and listened with only one ear to the conversations of the other Red Cross workers in the kitchen.

They were all laughing about a story Irene was telling when Christine thought she heard something in the distance. She couldn't quite make out what it was. It sounded a little like a church bell and then the roar of a crowd.

The knife in Irene's hand stopped in midair. She cocked her head to one side. "Did you hear that, Christine?"

"Yes. I wonder what it is."

One of the other women paled and whispered, "You don't suppose it's bombs, do you?"

"Of course, it isn't bombs," scoffed Irene.

Christine tried to reassure the woman. "There hasn't been the threat of bombs or shelling over Paris in weeks, in months."

"What do you think it is, then?"

In her usual practical fashion, Christine wiped her hands on the front of her apron and adjusted the fire under the pot of soup before she suggested, "It would be best if we simply went outside and saw what it was for ourselves. That way we'll know there's no cause for alarm."

Irene obviously agreed with her. She set her knife on the counter, dried her hands and followed Christine to the kitchen door.

They walked through the canteen to where the building fronted on the street. A number of other Red Cross workers were intent on doing the same as Christine and Irene. They could hear them voicing some of the identical questions the women in the kitchen had been asking.

"Do you think it's bombs?"

"I don't hear any aeroplanes."

"It's church bells," one woman finally declared as she opened the front door. "Can't you hear them? It's church bells."

Irene turned to her friend. "It *is* church bells."

"But why?" was Christine's response.

Then from every doorway and byway people began to pour into the streets of Paris.

Viviane came up behind them and demanded in excited French, *"Qu'est-ce que c'est?"*

"In English, Viviane. Please speak in English," Christine reminded the girl.

She quickly translated. "What is it?"

"We don't know. There seems to be a great deal of excitement, but we can't understand what the people are shouting," Christine explained to her. "Can you find out for us, Viviane?"

The girl nodded her head. She dashed into the street and stopped the first passerby. *"Qu'est-ce que c'est?"*

The man shrugged his shoulders and continued on his way. Viviane ran to the corner, where their street intersected with a major thoroughfare. She immediately disappeared from sight.

"If she ever does find out what's going on, she'll probably forget to come back and tell us, anyway," Irene muttered.

But Irene was wrong.

A few minutes later Viviane came running back down the street toward the canteen. Her cheeks were flushed. Her hair was flying wildly behind her. She'd lost the white cap that was always pinned to the top of her head.

She was gasping for air by the time she reached the canteen door. For the moment speech was beyond her.

"What is it?" Irene prompted, desperate to know. "Tell us, Viviane. What is happening?"

"C'est fini!—" she had to pause to catch her breath *"—la guerre est fini!"*

"Speak English."

Viviane tried again. "It's over! The war is over!" she told them, and promptly burst into tears.

The women stood in the doorway, dumbfounded. They watched as more and more people began to pour into the streets and avenues of the French capital. Bells were ringing everywhere now. Horns were beeping from autobuses and automobiles alike. The din was deafening.

Then, in the distance, they could hear the familiar strains of *La Marseillaise* being sung. They joyously raised their voices and joined in, although the words were awkward on their tongues.

Christine and Irene Chandler ran into the street. They could hear it being shouted from windows high above the street and doorways below.

"C'est fini!"

"La guerre est fini!"

The two women turned and threw their arms around each other. They jumped up and down. They shouted with the rest of Paris: *"C'est fini! C'est fini!"* The tears were streaming down their faces.

"The war is over, Christine! It's really over!" Irene cried out as they danced with one another.

"Thank God," intoned Christine. She added silently, *Wherever you are, my dearest James, the war is over!*

Later that evening—while Paris still celebrated, indeed, while the whole world celebrated—Christine sat down and wrote to her mother. They were the same words of joy and comfort that Mary Long had once penned to her mother, Elizabeth Banks: "I'm coming home, Mama. I'm coming home!"

ON NOVEMBER 11, 1918, the word officially went out—an armistice had finally been signed.

On the eleventh hour of the eleventh day of the eleventh month of that year, the fighting stopped. The war was, indeed, over.

Then there was only silence. . . .

Chapter Fifteen

The Golden Raintree

James looked out over the crowd of officials and dignitaries, and concluded his speech with "That is why we must make certain that the Great War was truly the 'war to end all war.' "

The audience burst into applause as it rose to its feet. The band began to play a stirring rendition of "The Stars and Stripes Forever." Women and children in the balcony of the statehouse waved the small American flags clasped in their hands.

It was a colorful and moving sight from behind the podium, acknowledged James as he reminded himself for what seemed like the hundredth time that day to smile and wave to the crowd.

Several top government officials came up to him and shook his hand in congratulations.

"A wonderful speech, Lieutenant Warren!" one of the men shouted near his ear in order to be heard over the celebratory din of the crowd.

"Stirring. Patriotic," the other declared as he, too, turned and waved to the audience. Every elected official in the capital was interested, it seemed, in being associated with a returning war hero.

Especially if he were an all-American boy, James thought sardonically. Then he corrected himself—especially if he were an all-American *man*. For his youth had surely been left behind him somewhere on the battlefields of the Western Front.

Lord, he was tired. He was tired and he wanted to go home. And he wanted to be left alone: no more newspaper interviews, no more luncheons or dinners, no more speeches and heroic honors heaped upon him. He wanted to be allowed simply to pick up the pieces of his life and go on.

Assuming he still had a life to call his own, James reminded himself.

He'd heard from Louise that Christine was finally arriving home this week from France. She'd stayed on to work with the Red Cross for several months after the armistice. The devastation of war always lingered on long after the last shot had been fired.

Christine was coming home.

Just the words alone created a strange feeling in the pit of his stomach: it was excitement mixed with a certain amount of dread. For he wondered if she would find home as foreign as he had upon his return several weeks earlier. The real adjustment, he had discovered, wasn't in going away from home, but coming back to it.

Christine. Was she still his lovely and loving Christine? James did not know the answer to that question. But he would soon enough.

He looked up one last time and waved to the crowd. Then he walked off the platform and made his way through the throng of waiting officials.

For Lieutenant James Wilson Warren had decided it was finally time to go home.

"YOU SIT YOURSELF right down, Charlie Brick. If you need something I'll get it for you," Hannah fussed as she jumped to her feet for the tenth time that afternoon and fluttered about her brother.

"I'm sitting. I'm sitting."

"What do you need? A handkerchief? Your pillow fluffed? Your medicine? A bite to eat?" She ticked the items off on her fingers. "Of course, Louise and James are due to arrive anytime now. Christine and I have a nice tea prepared. If you can wait."

Charlie sighed and sat back in his chair. "I was just going to help myself to a glass of water, sister."

"Well, you stay put. I'll get it for you," she said in a voice that would brook no argument, and bustled from the room.

He looked over to where Christine was sitting on the sofa, reading a book. "Sometimes Hannah reminds me of the matron at the hospital in London."

It was their private joke, and never failed to bring a smile to her face. "Some people will try to run your life for you, Charlie, unless you put your foot down. Hannah is one of them, I'm afraid."

"She means well."

Christine sighed. "Yes, I know."

Charlie admitted a bit sheepishly, "I never could stand up to her the way you do. You always knew how to handle her, from the time you were a little girl."

There was no sense in trying to explain it to her brother. The only way to "handle" Hannah was simply not to let her boss him around. He was almost twenty-seven years old and he hadn't managed it yet. Christine didn't think he was about to begin anytime soon.

He cleared his throat, and she looked up from her reading again.

"There's something I've been wanting to say to you for the past couple of days, Christine."

He sounded so serious. She gave him her complete attention. "What is it?"

A muscle in his face started to twitch. He fingered the lap robe that Hannah had insisted he cover his legs and feet with to keep the chill away.

"I never had an opportunity to tell you how much I appreciated what you did for me in London."

She was perplexed and said so.

"I found out just before I was sent home that you'd left the extra money with the matron for the cakes and flowers and slippers and things. They made all the difference in those last few weeks, I'll tell you."

"I'm glad, Charlie. It was a small enough thing to do."

"I wanted to say thank you, all the same." But he wasn't finished. He gave her a long, measuring look. "You've been kind of quiet since you got home."

She began to explain. "It was a busy morning with all we had to do in the kitchen, and then I had to run over to the general store for Hannah at the last minute when she discovered we were nearly out of fresh cream."

He furrowed his brows. "That's not what I meant. And I think you know it."

Christine nodded her head. "I guess I'm just—" Just what? She didn't know the answer to that question herself.

Charlie was sympathetic. "I do understand. You're at loose ends. I know the feeling. I've been home since last summer and I'm just getting used to it again myself. All I can tell you is give yourself some time."

"I will." She agreed. "I'll give myself some time."

"Here's your water," announced Hannah as she returned to the parlor. She inspected the room one last time to make sure it was ready to receive their company. "Here are the Warrens now." She glanced at the clock on the mantel. "Punctual as usual. You can always count on Louise Warren being on time."

It was one of the higher compliments Hannah gave anyone, as her brother and sister well knew.

They all watched as the large black automobile pulled up in front of the farmhouse.

It was Hannah who remarked, "Can you believe the five of us together again? Why, it seems like only yesterday that we were waiting for Louise and James to come by and drive us out in the country for our picnic." She shook her head. "It's been close to twenty months. Imagine that."

Christine nearly blurted out that it seemed like a lifetime ago to her. But she bit her tongue and held her peace.

"There's Louise," Hannah remarked before she headed toward the front hallway, "but I don't see James. I wonder where he can be."

As the elder sister, Hannah Brick assumed the role of hostess. She opened the door and cheerfully greeted their guest. Louise Warren was dressed in a beautiful dress and cape of red wool. She was wearing fashionably low-cut shoes.

"Please join us," said Hannah, after the red cape was removed and hung up in the closet. "Christine and Charlie are already in the parlor."

Louise Warren made her entrance and placed a buss on Christine's cheek. She fussed a bit over Charlie, excusing him with "Don't bother getting up, my dear man. We all know you must save your strength," before she lighted in the chair next to his.

Christine didn't think even Charlie had quite figured out what he was supposed to be saving his strength for.

But he was too polite to make a point of it with their guest.

Once they'd all settled in, Louise made her brother's apologies. "James wasn't home yet from that speech he was giving today at the statehouse, so I came ahead without him. Perhaps he'll join us later."

"I understand he's been very busy," Christine remarked, trying to hide her disappointment at his absence. She'd waited so long to see him. Months had seemed like years—at least to her.

His sister chattered away. "It's been one thing after another since James got home from France. Parades and speeches, banquets and newspaper articles. Why, there was a call the other day from *The Saturday Evening Post*. Can you imagine that?"

Hannah piped up with "We saw the picture of James in the newspaper. He looked very handsome in his uniform."

"He did, didn't he? Mother was very pleased." Louise made an odd little sound. "It upset James for some reason, however. He said the editor only did it because it would sell more copies of his 'bloody paper if the hometown hero was on the front page.'" She blushed. "Those are James's words, of course. Not mine." She cleared her throat and inquired, "Are you planning a rose garden this year, Charles?"

Charlie took the hint. "As a matter of fact, Louise, I was sketching out a few plans just before you arrived. I've been thinking of trying something a little different this year. I may pattern my garden after the English rose gardens I so admired while I was overseas."

"I'm going to help him," Hannah spoke up.

"I shall be glad to be of any assistance I can, as well," Louise offered. "I won't be nearly as busy now that the

Liberty Bond drives are over. Although I understand we will still need to raise funds for the Red Cross since this terrible influenza has spread from one end of the country to the other. Why, only this morning I heard that old Mr. Popplewell has come down with it. He's quite indisposed.''

"I suppose it preys on his mind how his business will fare without him, too," speculated Hannah.

Christine made what minor contribution she could. "I was at the general store earlier today. Mr. Popplewell's son seemed to be handling things well enough."

"Maybe better than his father ever did," Charlie spoke up. "It might be time for the elder gentlemen to consider retiring and letting a younger man take over."

"I was under the impression that Mr. Popplewell's son was at least forty, himself," said Louise.

"Oh, he is," said Hannah, obviously pleased by the direction their conversation had taken. "He's nearer to fifty, according to Mama."

Their chitchat continued in a similarly inoffensive vein until well after the tea was served and the bread and cakes were eaten.

Christine insisted on doing the cleaning up, and left Hannah and Charlie with their guest. She put the cream in the icebox and covered the bread. Once she was certain the kitchen was tidied to meet even Hannah's rigid standards, she stood at the back door and gazed out.

It was a gray February day. The skies were overcast, and there was a brisk wind out of the northwest. An inch or two of snow covered the ground and the temperature hovered near the freezing point. But she didn't care. The last thing she wanted to do was return to the stuffy parlor and make small talk. What she wanted, Christine realized, was some fresh air.

She slipped her feet out of the shoes she was wearing and donned a pair of boots. Taking a woolen cape from a hook by the back door, she wrapped it securely around her and pulled the hood up over her hair. Then she opened the door and walked out of the farmhouse.

She paused on the back stoop, considering where she might go, then decided to climb the hill to the old family cemetery, to the Golden Raintree. The great tree stood silhouetted against the winter sky, its limbs twisted and gnarled with age, it branches bare. Yet, even in the middle of winter, it beckoned to her.

Christine pulled the collar of the cloak more closely around her and began the trek across the barnyard and up the hill. She reached the summit and stood there, looking out over the Happy Valley. Winter lay upon the land. The earth was taking its respite; the rich, dark soil lay dormant, waiting for spring. The ground was cold and hard beneath her feet.

CHARLIE BRICK BENT OVER the sheet of sketching paper on his lap and pointed to an area marked by a box of small *x*s. "Now, I was thinking of putting a row of Hume's Blush here. What is your opinion, Louise?"

"Why, I think that would look lovely, Charles. And perhaps next to the gazebo, we could plant some of those small tea roses. Tea roses always add a nice touch to any garden."

Charlie considered her suggestion. "Maybe. Maybe we could." He glanced up and commented, "I wonder what's taking Hannah so long?"

Louise delicately furrowed her brow. "Wasn't she going to make another pot of tea?"

"Yes," he said, pushing the lap robe aside, "and I don't want her to miss any of our discussion. She seems so interested in helping with my garden this year."

Patting his arm, Louise Warren said sweetly, "I'll just go along to the kitchen and see what's keeping your dear sister, then."

Charlie watched the pretty young woman leave the parlor. Darned if he knew how he had ended up with *two* females at his beck and call.

Louise paused in the doorway between the hall and the large country kitchen. Hannah was standing at the window, staring out at the winter's day. She was outlined in profile. Her arms were wrapped around her as if she'd felt a sudden chill, and her cheeks were visibly damp.

The dark-haired girl rushed over to her friend. "Why, Hannah Marie Brick, whatever is the matter?"

Hannah rummaged in her apron pocket for a hankie and quickly wiped her face. "Nothing's the matter, Louise." But she knew the fullness in her voice gave her away.

"Something is, too, the matter. You were crying."

She sniffed and dabbed at her nose. "Maybe I'm coming down with a bit of cold."

Louise Warren marched over and told her with uncharacteristic frankness, "We've known one another too long and too well to start telling each other lies now." She soothed her own ruffled feathers. "Now, what is the matter?"

In a voice barely above a whisper, Hannah answered, "I'm worried about her."

"Who?"

She sighed. "Christine."

Louise came and stood beside her. They could both see the outline of the figure standing atop the snow-covered hill.

"It is a cold day to be out walking," observed Louise. "Are you worried that she isn't dressed warmly enough?"

"No, I'm not concerned about the way she's dressed."

"She's certainly been gone long enough. Do you think one of us should make sure she's all right?" Louise inquired in a slightly dismayed voice.

Hannah perked up. "That's an excellent idea, my dear Louise. Maybe I should."

An emphatic "no" came from behind them.

Both women turned and found Charlie standing in the kitchen doorway. He slowly walked toward them.

"No?" echoed Hannah.

"No," he said adamantly. In fact, Hannah couldn't remember the last time she'd seen her brother quite so adamant about anything. "Neither of you is going to take one step outside this house. Christine does not need us checking up on her."

"But we're worried about her," claimed Louise.

Hannah got her brother's attention by repeating the words with even greater emphasis. "We are worried about her, Charlie. She hasn't been herself since she got home."

"Neither has James," piped up Louise.

He ran his fingers through his hair in a nervous gesture. "I know they haven't been themselves. I must confess that I've spent some nights worrying about it, myself. But it's not for us to fix. James has only been home a couple of weeks and Christine but a few days. They'll get together and work it out in their own good time."

She had to point out, "But what if they don't?"

"They will," he stated firmly. "They were meant for each other if ever two people were. Now, come away from the window, both of you." He made a shooing motion with his hands. "And what about that fresh tea you promised us, Hannah?"

"It's coming right up, Charlie," she assured him before he returned to the parlor and his garden plans.

Louise turned to her as they finished making the tea. "The war was so hard on both Christine and James. None of us knows what they really suffered, do we?"

Hannah Marie Brick felt compelled to correct her friend. "Charlie knows."

"Yes, of course, he does," murmured Louise.

The two women stood at the window a moment longer.

"Charlie was right," acknowledged Hannah. "Christine didn't need us checking up on her. There's James now. I'm sure they'll find their own way home together."

A MAN CAME AROUND THE CORNER of the farmhouse and looked up at the hill where she stood. He must have spotted her footprints in the snow, for he started toward her, following the path she had taken across the yard and up the incline.

It was James.

How odd, Christine thought, for him to be out of uniform. It was the first time she had seen him dressed in civilian clothes since the summer of 1917.

She recalled in every detail that August afternoon when she had waited beneath the Golden Raintree and watched as a soldier climbed up her hill. How unfamiliar the khaki tunic and jodhpurs had seemed to her then, how chilling and deadly the black revolver in its holster.

How naive she had been! How young. How foolish. How very self-righteous. She had changed so much since those days that there were times when she didn't recognize herself. She was, indeed, a stranger in a strange land.

Only she hadn't expected to feel like a stranger in her own country, in her own town, in her own home, in her own body.

Where had the carefree, innocent young girl gone?

The answer was both simple and complex: she had gone off to war. She had seen death and disease and destruction. She had witnessed man's inhumanity to his fellow man. She had seen her worst nightmares while fully awake.

Yet she had also journeyed across a great ocean, traversed the English Channel and sailed along the Seine. She had made friends with a matron in an English hospital, with a Red Cross volunteer from the region of Hadrian's Wall and with a sweet, young mademoiselle. She had seen the wonders of Paris, the City of Light.

And she had become a woman.

She whispered into the wind, "We will always have Paris."

Christine had not allowed herself to say those words for many weeks now. Or even to think them. The pain was too great. The regret went too deep. For she and James had not seen each other since that time in Paris. She was sore afraid that she was losing him, that they both had lived but their love had died.

James made his way to her. She could see his breath in the cold air. He came and stood awkwardly beside her.

"You're finally home."

"Yes, I'm finally home," she said, wondering why it was so difficult to breathe all of a sudden.

He hunched his shoulders against the wind. "I'm sorry I missed the tea party. It took longer to drive back from Indianapolis that I expected."

Christine watched him out of the corner of her eye. He was so familiar and yet unfamiliar. So dear to her and yet so distant. Her heart clenched.

She must find a distraction or she would lose her composure, Christine warned herself. Then she noticed that James had failed to button his overcoat. She gave him a gentle scolding as she reached out and did up two or three buttons. "You'll catch your death of pneumonia if you go around with your coat hanging open on a day like this, Jamie Warren."

There was the oddest expression on his face when he said, "You haven't called me Jamie in years."

"I guess it just slipped out."

He began doubtfully, "We haven't seen each other since you got back."

She studied the ground, then the way the snow dusted the lower branches of the Raintree, and finally focused on the third button down on his overcoat. "I've been busy. I know you have, too, with all of the speeches and public appearances you've been making."

Something flickered behind his eyes. "Yes, I've been busy playing the hero home from the Great War. Whenever anyone needs a speaker at a meeting, or a guest of honor at a banquet, or a picture taken for reelection, they trot out the local war hero to do his act."

She began tentatively, "The people here at home don't seem to understand what it was really like over there."

His voice hardened. "Understand? They don't want to understand, Christine. They don't want to hear the truth about the war. They want to believe that it was a glorious victory for our side, that it was a nice, clean, honorable battle and we won because we were in the right. They don't want to hear about the millions of men who died and the millions more who were wounded and maimed."

Her heart reached out to him. "I know, James. I've only been home a couple of days and already I can see the way it will be. Wherever I go people bombard me with questions: What was it like being in London when the bombs were dropped? Weren't you afraid to sail across the Channel in a troop ship? How did you find Paris? Did you actually see any Germans?"

He murmured sympathetically. "Poor girl."

She wasn't finished. "But they don't really want to know. Most of them don't even bother to wait for an answer. They brush it aside and start telling me all about the local gossip." Her voice caught in her throat. "I never expected to feel like such a stranger in my own hometown."

He gazed off into the distance. "I know the feeling. I look in the mirror and the face appears to be mine, but I'm not the same on the inside. I'm an old man in a young man's body."

"Oh, James—" She bit her lip.

He put his hand on her shoulder with apparent casualness. "I've never forgotten something you once told me in Paris. You were trying to cheer me up, to let me know that you understood what I'd gone through. You said, 'I'm skinny and I'm tired and sometimes I feel like an old woman.'"

She nodded her head. Her emotions were dangerously close to the surface. "It was true in Paris. It's true now," she said in a hoarse whisper.

"Then you do understand how I feel?"

She'd been so cold on the inside; now she began to feel warm again. "I understand."

The words poured out of James. "I hated the war, Christine. I hated the senseless killing and the men who sacrificed their lives for a lousy few feet of shelled ground.

I hated the cold and the heat, the filth and the awful stench, even the food. I hated everything about it. But at least it seemed *real* to me. Now that I'm home—" he struggled to explain it "—home doesn't seem real to me. I almost wish I were back in France. At least there I could see the devastation and the towns in ruin and be among people who knew what it was like to be in the war."

They stood shoulder to shoulder and gazed out over the Happy Valley.

He gestured, encompassing everything in sight and so much more, she knew. "None of this seems real. Look at the land, all snow-covered and waiting for spring planting. The trees are whole. The buildings are standing and all in one piece. When I see all of this, it's as if the war never happened. But I know it did. I know it bloody well did because I'm not the same man I was before."

"I know, James," she said. "I'm not the same woman I was before, either."

He confessed, "I can't seem to sleep at night, Christine. It's so damned quiet."

"I know. I know, my love," she cried softly.

He sighed and went on. "If I do fall asleep the nightmares start. I wake up with my heart pounding and my body covered with sweat. I can't remember what they're about. I don't want to remember."

She held onto his arm. "Charlie said something to me this afternoon before you came. He said to give it time. Time to get used to life back home, time to let the war go, time to heal. The war didn't end just because the generals signed a treaty."

He seemed resigned instead of angry as he muttered, "The war will never end for some poor blokes."

Christine said it as much for her benefit as his. "The war is a nightmare from which we are both still trying to awaken."

He gazed down at her with unexpected tenderness. "Since you were a little girl you've known about nightmares, haven't you?"

She nodded. "They do fade in time, James. You'll suddenly realize that it's been weeks, perhaps even months, since the last one. You will be able to sleep again one day without fearing their return."

He sighed. "The people here at home will never understand."

Christine told him the truth. "Not many. Perhaps a few who were in the war, themselves. Or the rare person who can imagine what it was like."

His face was tired and drawn in lines of heavy concentration. "I've changed in ways even you may not like or understand."

"So have I, James. They say that time heals all wounds. I don't know if ours will heal, but perhaps in time they will become bearable."

He turned his head and stared searchingly at her. "Do you have any regrets about Paris?"

She wasn't going to be coy about it. Those days in Paris were the best days of her life. She intended to let him know that.

"I have absolutely no regrets. Our time together in Paris was the best thing to come out of the war." Christine's heart was slamming against her chest as she asked, "Do you have any regrets?"

In a husky baritone, "None. I loved you then. I love you now. I just don't know if I'm any good for you."

She put a hand to his face. "You could never be bad for me, James. You are so much a part of me that if I tried to remove you from my heart there would be nothing left. If you live, I live. If you should die, then I will cease to exist."

"It will take us some time, Christine, to feel like this is home again."

"We have time now, James. We have all the time in the world," she reminded him.

He drew her into his arms. "Coop said something about you once. He said that you were the bravest woman he had ever known because you chose to go to war, you chose to find out for yourself what it was like. Not many women—or men—would have the courage to do what you've done. You always were a brave little soul, Christine Brick."

She lifted her head and met his eyes. "It wasn't bravery, James. It was love. My love for you."

Then he bent his head and kissed her, and all the emptiness, all the loneliness inside gave way to a sense of rightness, of completeness. He kissed her and it was as if her lips, her very skin remembered how it had been, how it could be and would be.

"Lord, how I've missed you!" James declared before he kissed her again and again.

"Welcome home, my love!"

Christine silently said a prayer of thanksgiving. James was home. She was home—at last.

Clasping her to him, he nuzzled her face. "Your nose is cold."

She laughed. "It's cold outside, my darling man, in case you hadn't noticed."

He grasped her hands in his. "My poor girl, your fingers are half frozen." He quickly began to blow on them, warming her flesh with his own breath. Then he unbuttoned his coat and drew her into the heat of his body.

Later he inquired, "Is that better?"

Toasty warm and as content as a cat curled up by the fire, Christine murmured, "Much better."

A bird flew overhead. James looked up and then out over the Happy Valley. "Spring will soon be on its way."

"The farmers will plant their crops. The birds will sing. The leaves will bud on the trees. The earth will come to life again, and everything will be made new."

James said softly, "Perhaps we can begin anew, as well." He gazed deeply into her eyes. "Will you marry me in the spring?"

"Yes, I will marry you in the spring." With complete trust Christine placed her heart in his care.

He could not take his eyes from her. "I promised I would always come for you, my love."

Christine nodded. "And I promised to always be there waiting for you."

Then James smiled at her and declared, "Next summer we will climb this hill as we did as children and we will stand beneath the Golden Raintree."

She joined in. "We'll shake the branches until the yellow blossoms rain down on our faces."

"We'll catch them in our outstretched hands."

"Golden rain."

"You remember," James murmured.

Christine's love for him shone in her eyes. "I remember."

Then they joined hands and walked back down the hill.

Epilogue

What Happened to Them...

<u>Billy Bathgate</u> was the first soldier from New Castle to be killed in the line of duty during World War I. His name is engraved on a plaque in Memorial Park, just north of town. The inscription reads in part: "Patriotic Sacrifice, Forever Remembered, To honor the men and women of Henry County who bravely fought in the great wars and to the heroes who gave their lives on land, on the sea, and in the sky that mankind might live in freedom..."

<u>Marygold Huckelby</u> had six children by her husband before she decided to divorce him on the grounds that he was "no good and a drinker, to boot." She took back the Huckelby name, claiming she had no wish to be reminded of the man. Lord knows how she could expect to forget the drunkard when he had already given her a houseful of young'uns.

<u>Lily Huckelby</u> quit her job at the steel mill and hitched a ride to California, where she became a star in silent pictures. Several years later she created a scandal by showing up at her sister's with her hair bobbed and wearing an indecent dress that didn't reach below her knees. It was the talk of the town for the next year.

Louise Warren married an up-and-coming young businessman from Chicago and became the premiere hostess of her community for the next fifty years. It was often said that if a charity needed to raise funds, Louise Warren Applethorpe was the woman to get.

Charles Jordan Brick returned home to a hero's welcome. He picked up his life where he had left off. He attended meetings of the Henry County Historical Society and tended his roses. He took therapeutic walks through the woods and then presented his papers on "The Tulip Tree" and "The Titmouse" to the newly formed Nature Club.

Although he never chose to marry, it was certainly not for lack of female attention.

And when Charlie Brick passed away some fifteen years later, it was written of him in the newspapers of three counties, "It seems too bad that a man in the prime of life, as he was, should be taken from this world, but that is not for us to say. He will be greatly missed in his home, by his neighbors and by all who knew him."

Hannah Marie Brick was to travel far beyond the boundaries of Henry County in her long lifetime. One day she would see the world, become a famous suffragette and meet a man who was both willing and able to take on Hannah and her "ways."

Christine Elizabeth Brick and James Wilson Warren were married in the spring of 1919. Their first son was born a year later and they named him Robert Cooper Warren. Their firstborn daughter was named Irene and her godmother, it was rumored, lived in the North of England.

Eventually the Warrens had four children, who brought them great happiness. James Warren bought a large farm not far from Ann and Benjamin Brick, and many years later the two farms were combined into the largest in the county.

Folks always said there was something real different about Christine and James Warren—as if they had a special secret and weren't going to share it with anybody else. There was never a couple more in love. They were still like newlyweds, it was said, on their golden wedding anniversary.

Their children offered to buy them airplane tickets to Paris, France, in honor of the occasion. But Christine and James declined, saying that they always had Paris in their hearts.

HARLEQUIN
American Romance®

COMING NEXT MONTH

#357 THE SENSATION by Rebecca Flanders

Alice Fontaine is the cheekiest flapper at the Handley Hotel for Young Ladies. She's bobbed her hair, shortened her skirt and come to New York to become the Sensation of the Decade. Thanks to Nicholas Crawford, life is Alice's for the taking: sipping bootleg champagne, sneaking into darkened speakeasies and dancing the Charleston till dawn. Step back into the Roaring Twenties, when every day brought dazzling surprises and every night became a sensual delight. Don't miss this CENTURY OF AMERICAN ROMANCE title.

#358 A WILD IRIS by Muriel Jensen

Melanie Quinn was looking forward to a relaxing summer at her childhood home in Harvest Lake. But she should've realized that when she attended her aunt's charity luncheon and met Erik Channing, her days of reckless abandon were numbered. Erik was a man who lived on the edge of danger, and Melanie found herself involved in a situation that could be trouble. But that was nothing compared to falling in love....

#359 A CHANGE OF SEASONS by Carin Rafferty

Liana Stevens wouldn't speak of the past, though the horror lurked in her eyes. So Sam Dillon simply loved her, hoping that she'd feel safe in the warmth of his love. But they both knew the past had to be exposed before they could face the future.

#360 RISKS by Stella Cameron

Peter Kynaston had been Jennie's family's best friend. And when he reentered their lives, she didn't know what to do. For in the past, she had blamed him for her husband's death, but now found herself wanting him in a way that would change her life forever.

HARLEQUIN
American Romance®

ABOUT THE AUTHOR

For Suzanne Simmons Guntrum, the story of Christine Brick and James Warren was one that lived in her heart and mind long before she put pen to paper to write *The Golden Raintree*. As a young girl, she listened endlessly to her grandmother's stories. Like Christine, Suzanne's grandmother was born at the turn of the century and was just graduating from high school when World War I broke out. Suzanne's grandfather went off to battle and his health was never the same again; he died prematurely in 1937. The obituary for Charlie Brick in the epilogue of *The Golden Raintree* is paraphrased from the newspaper account of Suzanne's grandfather's death.

One of Suzanne's favorite chapters in *The Golden Raintree* is "A Brother and Sister Are Reunited." She explains: "Walking into a military hospital to visit a dear brother who was wounded in war came from my own experience. It may have been another time and another place and another war, but the feelings were the same for both Christine and me."

Suzanne became fascinated with the Quakers when she lived in New Castle, Indiana, for nearly eleven years. She even planted a Golden Raintree in her front yard.

Today, Suzanne lives in nearby Fort Wayne, Indiana, with her husband and son. Her successful writing career spans eleven years and twenty-one novels.

CARA-1A

Take 4 bestselling love stories FREE

Plus get a FREE surprise gift!

COMING SOON...

For years Harlequin and Silhouette novels have been taking readers places—but only in their imaginations.

This fall look for PASSPORT TO ROMANCE, a promotion that could take you around the corner or around the world!

Watch for it in September!

★